AS SHE GROWS

LESLEY ANNE COWAN

PENGUIN
CANADA

PENGUIN CANADA

Published by the Penguin Group

Penguin Books, a division of Pearson Canada, 10 Alcorn Avenue, Toronto,
Ontario, Canada M4V 3B2

Penguin Books Ltd, 80 Strand, London WC2R 0RL, England

Penguin Putnam Inc., 375 Hudson Street, New York, New York 10014, U.S.A.

Penguin Books Australia Ltd, 250 Camberwell Road, Camberwell, Victoria 3124, Australia

Penguin Books India (P) Ltd, 11, Community Centre, Panchsheel Park,
New Delhi – 110 017, India

Penguin Books (NZ) Ltd, cnr Rosedale and Airborne Roads, Albany, Auckland 1310, New Zealand

Penguin Books (South Africa) (Pty) Ltd, 24 Sturdee Avenue, Rosebank 2196, South Africa

Penguin Books Ltd, Registered Offices: 80 Strand, London WC2R 0RL, England

First published 2003

1 3 5 7 9 10 8 6 4 2

Copyright © Lesley Anne Cowan, 2003

*Publisher's note: This book is a work of fiction. Names, characters, places, and incidents either are
the product of the author's imagination or are used fictitiously, and any resemblance to actual
persons living or dead, events, or locales is entirely coincidental.*

Manufactured in Canada.

NATIONAL LIBRARY OF CANADA CATALOGUING IN PUBLICATION

Cowan, Lesley Anne
As she grows / Lesley Anne Cowan.

ISBN 0-14-301328-9

I. Title.

PS8555.O85763A78 2003   C813'.6   C2002-905855-4
PR9199.4.C683A78 2003

Visit Penguin Books' website at **www.penguin.ca**

for my parents

BELLYACHE

You can have your cake and throw it up
but when I spilled my guts you didn't clean it up.
I'm beginning to hate the sight of you,
I'm beginning to love the fight.

My own arms around me can only choke.
My own words can only hurt.
I don't want to love your faults anymore.
It's all pushed down so far that it blows up in my face.
Got so much shit in my mouth,
I begin to enjoy the taste.

—Melissa Psarros
1999

AS SHE GROWS

ONE

.

1

It starts with the sound of butterfly wings, flapping, hundreds of them around my head, thump, thumping; and my hair lashing against my cheeks like wisps of grass. My face sprouts from the back-seat window like a tender green shoot through concrete. I can't hear my grandmother Elsie shouting to put my head back into the car. I can't hear Jed swearing about this godforsaken place in the middle of nowhere.

Instead I hear butterfly wings and smell warm country until Elsie's strong hand pulls me back into the scent of vinyl and sweat and Old Spice. Her fleshy arm extends over the seat to deposit a heavy margarine tub in the centre of me, forcing my fluttering edges down. She tells me to be a good girl: "Be still because you don't want to spill your mother." Then she turns back around, flicks the map, and says something like, "Jesus Christ, where the hell is this place?" I look down, feel the cool plastic against my bare five-year-old thighs, and contemplate a miniature mother I had never met, trapped inside that container.

We are scattering my mother's ashes in a river, by a field, where she, Elsie, and Aunt Sharon used to go and have picnics a long time ago. This is what Elsie tells me.

"Five more minutes and I'm gonna scatter her over Highway 7," Jed says as Elsie's hand slips onto his reddened neck and gently squeezes. His shoulders tense, she quickly drops her hand and turns her face to the window. I sink down into the backseat, disappearing from the rear-view mirror. I slowly slip off the lid to peek inside and find, instead of a tiny lady, a bunch of fireplace ash. I poke my hand inside and swoosh through. Pinch my fingers into the dust and press a brittle piece against my skin. I cautiously pull my hand out, study the chip perched like a Chiclet on the tip of my finger. And for some reason I still can't explain, I raise my finger to my mouth and slip the tasteless grey flake in.

Then there are flashes. Elsie's horrified face, hollow windy words coming out of her mouth, dust filling my nose, and gravel crunching under tires. My body dragged out of the car and Elsie's strong hands pinning firm my squirming arms. A sharp-nailed finger down my throat, loss of breath, and then the contracted release of a bowl of Alphaghettis, some cherry Coke, and my mother.

·   ·   ·

I wake up sweating and breathless. I wake up alone. I can still hear the receding wings, distant and thick, as if under water.

Elsie shouts from the couch, blathering on to herself, drunk or high on whatever she could put her lips around. Carrying on some insane conversation with an invisible person called Martha or Marma, or maybe Mother.

Her slurred voice gets louder and uglier. "You selfish little bitch," she yells out to me. "Com' out here! Can't ev'n help your own fuckin' grandmother."

It isn't the first time she's carried on like that, so I drift in and out of sleep, waiting for her to shut up or to just pass out. But you can only ignore something for so long before the act of ignoring becomes all-consuming.

"Oh! Susanna, don't you cry for me, cuz I com' fr'm . . ."

When I can't take it any longer, I storm up from my bed and rip open my bedroom door. "What the fuck! Are you fuckin' crazy?" My eyes drop to Elsie's crumpled body, squatted on the floor by the couch, an empty bottle of vodka hanging loosely in her hands, the bottoms of her jeans stained wet with spilt alcohol. I shake my head in disgust. "I have school tomorrow."

"Oh, the princess, 'fraid to lose her beauty sleep." She takes a swig of her empty bottle and then wipes the imaginary liquid from her chin. "Since when do you give a shit about school? You think you're sooo great, think you're the only person who has a life, you and those guys you fuck, don't think I don't know it, you little whore . . ."

"What are you talking about? You're insane!"

"You little slut, think you're so much better than me, you don't know what I've been through, you don't know . . ." She keeps going on, making no sense, spitting as she speaks, her face squished up thick with hatred. And I think to myself, Why was I born her enemy? I stare at her body, heavy and toppled, like a fixed anchor at the end of me. Sinking me. It's too pathetic to even bother, so I turn, slam the door, and get back into my bed. And then I wait. My body tense. Fingers firmly holding the covers over my head.

Elsie follows her words into my room, flicks on my light, stands over my bed, and keeps shouting, "Beauty sleep, booty sleep, booty seep . . ." I clench my eyes shut, screaming *go away, go away,* in my head. But she keeps shaking my mattress until I finally burst out from under the covers, hands over my ears, pacing back and forth, shouting, "Stop it, stop it, stop it . . . !" I'm bawling and my face is wet and hot and I feel like I am going crazy, like I am this mental institution girl. "Stop it, stop it, stop it . . ." Pressing my hands tighter over my ears, trying to squeeze her entire existence out of my head. Things keep spinning and I can't breathe and all I hear is the blood racing in my own skull.

And then I rupture.

Everything goes quiet and blank and cold, until my grand-mother's controlled voice fades in from black to blinding white. "You're going to pay for that. You're going to fix that."

I stand there stunned, like a bird that hit glass. I have no idea what she's talking about. But then my hand starts to pulse and the flakes of white plaster on the carpet beside me come into focus and my eyes fall inside a hole in the wall the size of an open screaming mouth.

"Who's the fuckin' crazy one now, eh?" Elsie smirks, shaking her head. And just like that, she is calm. Her body relaxes like those heroin junkies who release the fist and then slip into sudden satisfaction. She turns, stumbles back out into the living room, and flicks on the TV.

In the washroom, I lean up against the sink, stick my throbbing hand under cold water, and blankly stare into white porcelain. My brain is numb with nothingness. I am too tired to think. I just want to go to bed and forget everything. And then I see myself opening the mirrored medicine cabinet. As if there is a camera on the bathroom ceiling. I see myself pulling out a razor blade. I see myself cutting deep, precisioned slices into the soft white under-side of my forearm; the blade sinking easily into skin like a cake knife into white icing. I feel a brilliant rush, a whoosh of noise and air, as drops of blood escape like startled bats from their darkness.

Then the camera goes blank and I return to myself, my fist is back under the water, and my arm is totally fine. There is no blood. There are no cuts. It was like a dream, only I was awake. Scared, I walk back toward my room, cradling my swollen purple hand. I still can't breathe right. I lie in bed the rest of the night, my hand holding firm a photograph of my mother, tucked flatly away under my pillow. My eyes staring at the plaster on the dirt-brown carpet, settled and silent, like newly fallen snow.

.   .   .

I was given two truths: my mother named me Snow, and she drowned in a neighbour's pool.

Elsie gave me only one photo of my mother. It is soft and wrinkled, from years of carrying it close to me. It's a wallet-sized school photo of a pretty blonde-haired girl wearing a bright yellow turtleneck. Fleshy round face, a few freckles, and pouty lips. She's not smiling at the camera. Her eyes are like mine, with the changing moods of an ocean. Sometimes they look a hostile grey and sometimes an inviting blue.

The day she gave me the photo I was sitting on the couch, a shoebox on Elsie's lap beside me. It was my eighth birthday. "This is a picture of your mother when she was about your age. She was a strong little girl. Like you, Snow," Elsie said, her anxious hand rubbing my back.

"Was she hollow?" I asked.

"What do you mean?" Elsie responded, puzzled.

"Strong things are hollow, like old logs and chicken bones and pipes in the ground," I replied, staring at the photo.

"You're a clever little girl, Snow," she said, not looking at me, but somewhere distant, over my head. "You remind me of her," she said, her thumb firmly stroking my mother's face, in a way

that made me unsure if it was a tender caress or an attempt to
rub her out.

.   .   .

The morning light shines through the old sheet hung at my
window, the piss-stained centre like an explosive, scattering sun. I
slowly pull my arm out from under the pillow, my limp hand
dangling from my wrist. I study my swollen knuckles and, with
my finger, poke white blotches into purple skin. A greenish
purple, really, the colour of those cabbages they plant in funeral
home gardens in the fall. I do all this with only one eye open, the
other still firmly shut, refusing to begin this day.

I'm too late to take a shower this morning, and instead put my
hair up into a ponytail, the dark roots of my blonde streaks
exposed. I look through my dirty laundry pile for a clean-smelling
T-shirt and put on the same baggy jeans I wore yesterday. I do
everything in slow motion, my body still asleep, my head woozy
and vacant. I leave my school binder spread out on my desk. My
teacher will send me to the office for not being prepared for class
and I'll get a zero for the math test I would have failed now
anyway, even though I studied all week.

Elsie is still sleeping on the couch, her mouth hanging open.
The elastic of her baggy blue underwear creeps up her left cheek,
and her Toronto Maple Leafs sweatshirt is hiked up over her
fleshy stomach. The look of her makes me sick: her stringy long
brown hair, her cutting cheekbones, her yellow teeth. You can tell
she was beautiful, once. A long time ago. At least, that's what Jed
used to tell me. He also told me that I had inherited the Cooke
women's strongest weapon: sharp beauty. *Careful with this,* he'd
say, or *without knowing it, you'll slice a man's balls right off.* I had
no idea what he was talking about, but I liked the sound of it.

I start to pick up the empty beer cans around her, sticking my fingers into opened holes, five cans on each hand. I do this without even thinking. Habit, I suppose. But then I stop myself and throw them back on the coffee table, one by one, crashing down close to Elsie's head.

"Do you have to be so gaad-damn noisy?" she groans, her eyes still closed, face pressed into the cushion. "What time is it?"

I ignore her and she just rolls onto her side, a penny stuck to her sweaty thigh like some sucking parasite. It'll be another three hours till she gets up, stretches the wine-and-beige polyester Dominion uniform over her stiff body, and drags herself across the street for her shift. Then it will be six hours before she comes home, microwaves pizza pockets, and sits in front of the TV with her twelve-pack of Blue.

I don't talk to Elsie anymore and it's amazing, despite living in this apartment together, how easy silence is. Of course, the practical exchange of words is necessary, but we rarely move beyond I'm putting a dark load in, or, the toilet won't flush.

When we used to speak, a couple years ago, we yelled. Elsie used to be on my case about every little thing. She used to give me a curfew that I'd always break and an allowance that I'd always waste on cigarettes the first day. She used to yell when I came home drunk and called friends' parents if I didn't come home at all. But now she says I can ruin my life if I want to, and she leaves me alone. And it's better that way. We stay out of each other's business. I used to be in her life. Now I'm just in her apartment.

"How can you not love your own grandmother?" a snobby girl asked me, when we were partnered up for a grade nine biography project. I imagined her grandmother, smelling of flowery perfume, sitting on her living-room couch at Thanksgiving, sipping sherry and crocheting doilies. I shrugged my shoulders, knowing that an explanation would be useless for this girl, with her Birkenstocks and clear lip gloss. She said it as if it were a blasphemy, as if automatic love for a parent or grandparent was a requirement in life. "You *have* to love your *grandmother*," she persisted. "It's your grandmother. Even if I didn't, I'd feel bad saying it aloud."

"Well, I don't," I replied. "She's a bitch."

But I should love Elsie. She has made sacrifices for me. She tells me this. At times when I'm not grateful for her giving a roof over my head. And food in my stomach. And shoes on my feet. At times when I point out to her how much my life sucks. "Your life?" she says. "Your life? What about *my* life? I'm an old woman, you know. I should be on tropical boat cruises playing blackjack, not raising a kid." She says this like she's eighty years old, but she's only fifty-three, which is just a little older than Carla's mom, and she gets seasick on the Toronto Island ferry. And no matter how well I do in school or how nicely I clean the bathroom or fold the laundry, it's never enough for her because there is always a mouldy corner or a missing sock. And no matter what I do she will always, for a split second, scowl at me when I first enter a room, as if since I was born I've been paying for a mistake I never knew I made.

• • •

I have two mothers: one, a body, the other, a spirit. Elsie is the hand that pushed my baby carriage, the protective arm that shot out in front of me when suddenly braking, the lips that told me dinner was ready. My birth mother is the tuneless lullaby I hear each night, the ghost I feel in each breath.

All my life they have been competing against each other inside me, resentful and jealous of the other's role like bickering sisters seeking attention. My grandmother's presence over my shoulder and my mother's unoccupied space within me. And it's a strange confession, but it is the absence that carries the most weight.

Ever since I can remember, I have been piecing together the image of a mother. It is this mother who opens her arms to me when Elsie's push me away. It is this mother whose song I hear at night, a promise of something better. In my mind my mother talks and breathes and walks down a street with a sexy sway of her hips. She wears glasses when she reads and blows her nose with a handkerchief. Her fingers are double-jointed, like mine. Her eyelashes are long and curved like those of the woman who walks her cat in the courtyard. Her hair is blonde and curls slightly outward at the shoulders, like my grade four teacher's.

"Was she a morning person?" I used to ask Elsie when I was younger. Or, "Did she eat meat?" Or, "Was she smart?" Questions posed to her while I was folding laundry or passing a doorway, always somewhere trivial, to counter any possible interpretation of my thoughts. I'd pretend they were fleeting ideas, just points of interest; not tell her that I had been thinking about them for days. I used to not want Elsie to think that I needed this, that her being my mother was not enough. She'd pause at my question, look up to the ceiling like she was deep in thought, then respond with short dismissive answers like "I'm not really sure," or "That's a tough one," or "I think so." And before I could ask more, she'd somehow always manage to change the subject or leave the room, not in a rude way, but in a way that made me feel like a nuisance, or childish, for needing more.

And once, when I was young, I asked, "What about my father?"

"The men in this family do not stay and they do not deserve the spoken word," she replied with such conviction and intensity that I accepted it as an indisputable truth.

. . .

I learned later, from Aunt Sharon, that my father was a fling. A one-night stand. Something fleeting. To know you weren't created out of love is a disappointing truth. But there are ways I can imagine this.

I can picture a naked motel room, a bed with no sheets, a window with no curtain. A man, perhaps married, who was out with the boys, drunk, and flattered by my young mother who laughed at his jokes and gently rubbed her hand up his thigh. Inside this room there are shadows and closed eyes and lustful fingers tracing skin in the dark.

I can imagine my mother on the subway the next morning, hair smelling of smoke and running her tongue over thick teeth. Hiding her stiletto heels under the seat while women in business suits flap the *Globe and Mail* newspapers around her. A number written on the back of a receipt in her purse, though she can't make out if that's a *t* or an *f* in his last name. But it doesn't matter, 'cause it's not his real name anyway.

Or I can imagine it like this. I can imagine a man with a foreign accent and a polished stone hanging from black leather around his neck. A stone that means strength or spirit, that he found himself, say, at the bottom of the ocean or on a mountainside. A man who spoke of karma and coincidence and of travels to India in a way that made her want to leave her life. A man who was to get on a plane the next day so they booked a room at an expensive hotel, overlooking a scene, say, a castle or a tropical river. And they spent hours by the window, drinking wine and playing inside this tiny fold of time. And of course, there were words that were spoken, like *I'll see you again,* but we all know something like that can't happen twice.

2

I walk the long way along the Donway to meet my best friend, Carla, on the way to school. School is at Don Mills Collegiate, just across the street from our apartment building. When I can drag myself out of bed, I go, but it's only on the important days, like when we have tests and assignments, that I make sure I'm in class. Still, I do all the homework and I always get C's, except in English, which I fail each year because I can't spell and my words don't come out right on the page.

We live in what Elsie calls "a good neighbourhood." There's a plaque somewhere in Don Mills saying it's North America's first planned suburb, which was apparently brilliant urban planning at the time. I know this because we had to do a project on it in grade eight geography last year. My apartment building is off The Donway, a big paved moat surrounding all life's necessities: a shopping mall, post office, medical offices, movie theatre, bingo hall, skating rink, and bowling alley. Only they tore down all the good stuff, like the movie theatre and bowling alley, years ago.

And then Eaton's closed and Club Monaco moved to the upscale Fairview Mall. And now senior citizens push their walkers by store windows, looking for deals in Bulk Barn and Payless Shoes. And it's like living in the stomach of someone's decaying suburban dream.

When I turn the corner, I can see Carla waiting in the distance. I laugh because she keeps giving a forceful finger to passing cars that beep at her, as if she were truly insulted at this. As if she didn't like the attention from the men in business suits, confident and horny behind tinted windows. She's wearing a miniskirt with white socks and black platform shoes, which makes her look like a centrefold schoolgirl or something. But that's her style, innocent and preppy, with a little dirty mixed in. Even though she may dress like a slut, she's not. She won't even go all the way with a guy, unless he says he loves her, really loves her, and that hasn't happened yet. She says she'll do anything else though, which in the end makes the boys like her even more. Carla is Portuguese and beautiful and has perfect, olive, Portuguese skin. She permed her already wavy hair and tweezed all her eyebrows so that now there's just a brown arch pencilled in so high it makes her look even more stupid than she is. But I don't say that to her.

"Hey, gorgeous," she says, with an irritating perkiness, "Can I bum a smoke?" I reach into my schoolbag and give her the pack. She pulls out three cigarettes, puts two in her coat pocket, and lights the third, inhaling deeply. Then she notices my hand. "What happened?"

"Elsie," I say, not needing to explain any further. "Can I sleep at your house tonight?" I would tell Carla everything, but I don't want to think about it anymore. I just want my mind to be blank.

"Sorry. It's not a good time," she says, not suspecting anything major is up with me. "My mom's being a drag." Staying at each other's house is a normal request when we get in fights at home.

Though usually Carla's fights are over stupid things, like her mom refusing to buy her a pair of jeans or shrinking her shirt in the dryer.

"What's on your face?" I ask, referring to the glitter eyeshadow she's wearing. Carla's girlie girl like that: pink nail polish, silver glitter on her cheeks, fuzzy miniature stuffed animals hanging off her backpack.

"Sparkles. You like 'em? My dad bought 'em for me. Cool, huh?"

"Ya," I reply sarcastically.

"I'll put some on you today, okay? They'll look great." Carla is always trying to make me look more girlie, she thinks I'm too much of a tomboy. She's always telling me to stand up straight, roll my slouching shoulders back, put on some lipstick. "You have such a pretty face," she says. "You should use it."

"Sure." I roll my eyes, but secretly smile. I'm used to her up there, floating above my head. And she is used to me down here, occasionally trying to stick a pin in her.

"Yo, wanna ditch first period and chill at the mall?"

"Sure," I say, "but won't you get in trouble?"

"Fuck it," she says, flicking her hand in the air, and we turn around and head toward the mall. Carla is on the line at school, and the principal has already pulled her in three times this year, saying that she can't miss any more days. She takes basic-level classes and she says she knows she's dumb and won't finish school anyway, so what's the point? Besides, she wants to be a makeup artist and she doesn't need high school for that. She thinks it's unfair that I'm so smart, that I can miss classes and I still get C's. She jokes about it, but I know she hates me for it. I know it, because she always points out my spelling mistakes on the birth-day cards I give her.

It's hard to explain it to Carla, so that she'd understand me. Inside my head, my world is full of colour and beautiful words. Outside, it's ugly and harsh. In grade three I sat in an orange-carpeted office, on the floor. A doctor lady in a long skirt and glasses that dangled from a string around her neck passed me toys and told me to draw squares. After going back to her office three times, the lady told my grandmother two things: I was really smart and I also had a learning disability. I remember looking for the wheelchair they were going to put me in, only Elsie told me they don't have wheelchairs for brains.

And so I have three voices: one in my head, one in my mouth, and one in my hands. Each speaks a different language, but it's the voice in my head that matters most; the one that understands things. It's in my head where I understand Elsie's belief that the easiest place to lose yourself is in a bottle. It's in my head where I find certain things depressing because I see myself in them, like a fountain in the rain or a running shoe on a highway. Only, my mouth doesn't understand this language. It tries, but it confuses the vocabulary and things end up sounding simple or angry or dull.

My hands are the worst of all. My hands want nothing to do with me, they make no attempt to understand my mind. It's as if they're angry to be slaves to my thoughts and are determined to do their own thing. In class I look down at my pen, clutched between fingers, and feel as connected to my body as to the chair I'm sitting on.

.   .   .

Carla and I smoke a blunt behind the Dumpster by Home Hardware and cut up each student we see walking to school. Ugly shirt. Lazy dog tits. Fat pig. I suck hard on the butt, and soon feel the inside of my skin start to disappear, slowly, starting with my fingertips and then my tongue. The jagged corners of buildings smooth out like peanut butter and the weight of me is lifted.

We head toward the mall because there's nowhere else to go and Carla has to pee. Thoroughly buzzed, we do dumb things like throw jelly beans down on unsuspecting heads from the staircase. We heat up quarters with our lighters, drop them on the ground, and wait for the squawks of old ladies who scorch their frugal fingers. We sit at the edge of the fountain and inconspicuously reach down behind us, into cold water, sweeping up handfuls of dimes and pennies.

"Listen," I say, shaking a fistful of change in Carla's ear. "The sound of a hundred wishes."

In the afternoon, we sit outside Pizza Pizza, up against the brick wall, legs outstretched on the sidewalk. Middle-aged women in flowered dresses pick up their pace as they pass us, their plastic cleaner bags limply fluttering in the wind behind them. In front of us is the parking lot and then behind that is the buzz of traffic on Lawrence Avenue. Behind Lawrence there are apartments and behind those are houses and behind that, another mall. Now that we've returned to our sober minds, there's nothing to talk about except how there's nothing to do and nowhere to go, and how life will remain like this until we're older and we can buy beer.

"Don Mills is such a shithole," Carla mutters. "I can't wait to leave."

"What'd you say?" I spin my head around to catch her mouth frozen, still open, as if she were trying to suck the words back in.

She doesn't look at me, but instead stares straight ahead. Her face reddens and she closes her eyes for a moment like she's mustering courage from within. Then Carla turns to face me. "I didn't want to say anything, 'cause of your fight with Elsie."

"Say what?"

"My dad's splitting," she says, which isn't surprising news because Carla's mom and dad fight all the time and he spends half the time sleeping on the couch at her uncle Max's. "He's going to Hamilton," she adds. "Well, really, Mom's kicking him out."

"Shit," I say, in condolence. Carla talks about her father slapping around her mother all the time. She says she knows it's not right, but she says her mom kind of deserves it because she's always nagging at him, just like she always nags at her. Sometimes, she wishes she could beat her too. Carla pulls out her compact from her purse and starts inspecting her makeup situation. "What are you going to do?" I ask carefully, already knowing what she'll say.

She pulls away the mirror and looks directly at me. "I'm gonna go with him, obviously. I'm not staying with that bitch."

"You're leaving?" I say, with an edge.

"He's got this great house," she says, getting excited, overly excited, as she talks, "with a pool and walk-in closets and satellite TV." Carla looks away and her voice becomes cold. "I'll probably go next week."

I am silent. Blood rushes to my head and swirls like thick smoke in my skull. Carla sits there with a sudden interest in her shoelace. I fixate on her twitching, prodding fingers. I get pissed that she's sitting there, all happy about her parents splitting up, talking about moving like it's a vacation. It bothers me because everything seems to roll off Carla, and nothing seems to penetrate her. It's as if the world could collapse, and she'd still be worried about the poppy seed wedged between her teeth.

I feel Carla's challenging eyes glare at me, turn away, and then glare again. "What's your problem?"

I don't answer her. Instead, I get up, throw my backpack over my shoulder, and start walking away.

"What's your problem?" she yells after me. I continue walking, break into a run as I feel my tears start to well in my eyes, and all I want to do is move so fast that I run straight out of my own face. I don't know what's making me more angry, Carla leaving me or the fact I can't leave with her. "Not everything's about you, Snow!" Carla yells behind me and I stop in my tracks. I wipe my hand over a slimy mix of snot and tears and black mascara. I turn back toward her, staring her down as I approach, and I can see that my face scares her. She throws both her hands to the ground, as if to brace herself, as if I'm going to kick her. As if she can read my mind because that's what I want to do.

I stop, towering in front of her, the tips of our shoes touching. "WHAT THE FUCK DO YOU CARE, ANYWAY?"

.   .   .

People never leave suddenly. If you look closely, real close, you see they have left you many times before that last time you see their face. Carla stopped calling me every day about a month ago. About two weeks ago she called Andrea to go to a movie and said my line was busy. And on Sunday she returned my red sweatshirt. I knew she was getting ready to go. I knew the signs. Jed left me and Elsie three times. He took it in steps; he was a methodical man. He was like Carla that way.

Jed was the closest I've had to a father, though he was really more a symbol of fatherhood. Like the ceramic saint in Carla's living room, his presence represented an idea of something more. He moved in after I was born and he moved out when I was six. I didn't have much choice in the matter. I had to settle for what I could get.

I don't remember doing much together. Mostly, I'd sit and watch TV while he read his favourite book, the *World Almanac,* in his favourite chair, eating peanuts out of a glass jar. He was the smartest man I had ever met. Sometimes he'd tell me amazing facts: "Did you know that the word 'leotard' came from Julius Leotard, a nineteenth-century French aerial gymnast?" Or, "In 1990, 'John' stopped being in the top ten first names of Americans since 1880?" Or, "The biggest saltwater fish ever caught was in 1977 in the Canary Islands at eighty-eight pounds, two ounces. Can you believe that?" And I'd memorize these facts, as if he were passing on God's truths.

Even though I was only six, I knew he was getting ready to leave. Despite Elsie's assurances that "he's got business on the road." I never did know what Jed's business was. And though Elsie pretended not to care he was gone so much, I knew she did. Jed would only come home every few weeks, sleeping on the couch and snoring in the flickering light of the TV screen. Elsie would trek around the apartment, rolling her eyes and kissing her teeth as she folded his laundry or cooked him fish sticks. As if it was a huge nuisance. As if she was being forced to do these things. She'd try her best to look like she was mad, but I'd catch her humming or smiling when she didn't think anyone could see her, when she was busy stirring a pot or stacking towels in the cupboard.

The next year after that he only came by once in a while, for a night or two. I'd see him slip out of her room late at night or I'd find his undershirt in the laundry. Finally, one day, I came home from school and he had his shaving kit and *World Almanac* boxed up on the kitchen table.

"I'll still be around, squirt," he said, as he tousled my hair and got up to leave. "I love ya, kiddo," he said, as we walked out the door. But I didn't believe him.

Sometimes I think it's good my real father was a fling. That way I can allow my mind to fill in his blanks. I can never hate him the way I hate my grandmother. I can never claim him as a bad father because I choose to believe that he was good, the way you choose to believe that Goldilocks was not a greedy little bitch who took advantage of an unlocked door.

Still, I miss him. I miss a father who'll yell at me when I come home late, dressed like a slut, because he remembers what boys my age are like. I miss a father who takes the newspaper into the washroom on Sunday mornings and who makes scrambled eggs for dinner. I miss a father who'll be embarrassed to buy me maxi-pads and who'll give me a firm line when I am found dangling from a loose, wobbly one.

.   .   .

The door to Mark's apartment is wide open, as if someone had just walked in and didn't think to close it behind him, just like that, forgetting to close a door. I find Mark and four other guys lying on old tweed couches and sprawled out on the ground, listening to Wu-Tang and watching a Britney Spears special on mute. The ratty brown curtains are drawn and it might as well be midnight instead of five in the afternoon.

Mark and I have been together for four months now, though we've known each other for over a year. He's older, eighteen, and so much more mature than the other boys I've been with. He's got his shit together: an apartment, a job, and a cool stereo. And he's the first guy I've met who thinks about more than just sex.

"We make love," I tell Carla, who keels over and fakes vomiting noises. But I just smile back, because I'd have laughed too, if I didn't know what a real relationship was like.

As I step over plates of dried ketchup, some familiar faces nod coolly at me or mumble a lazy *what's up?* The stink of weed in Mark's apartment is strong enough to give me a buzz. Mark's only official roommate is Josh, but his *boys,* as Mark calls them, are always crashing there. Mark's boys are always nice to me. They have names like Crakhed, Smokey, Killah, and Ash. They call me "Wifey" and tell me I'm not like the other girls. And I wonder to myself, *What other girls?* but I don't ask because we haven't been going out long enough. Mark's boys think I'm like their collective little sister, lending me money and telling me that if anyone gives me trouble, I should come to them.

"Hey," Mark says as I squeeze in between him and his rottweiler, Spliff. They both growl a little, reposition, and then Mark's hand returns to Spliff's neck. I stare at his fingers, slipped under the studded collar, stroking Spliff's shiny black fur. Jealous of a stupid dog.

"Hi," I say, and suddenly wish I'd never come. I suppose I had imagined it differently. I had pictured Mark noticing my puffy eyes and asking what's wrong. And then me crying and holding him until he told me things would be okay. But I can't bring myself to be that way so I just sit there, sighing and shifting my weight, hoping that he'll notice and ask what's wrong. But he doesn't ask. He never asks.

Finally, he puts his hand around my neck. "Let's go to my room," he says. We rise, Mark's inseparable black shadow trotting and snorting down the hall behind us.

Mark's room consists of a bedside milk crate and a mattress on the floor with no sheets. The walls are entirely covered with his ten-year collection of Sunshine Girls, arranged according to blondes, brunettes, redheads, and "favourites." Taped up around his bed are pictures from *Penthouse* magazine of women with their legs spread wide and nipples like pencil erasers. I think the photos are disgusting and I tell Mark every time I walk in the room. Usually he just laughs at me, but then one time he got all

serious, saying I'm prettier than all of them, paid for me to get my
belly button pierced, and then put three photos of me in my tube
top and jean shorts above his bed.

Mark closes the blinds and we lie in bed in our underwear,
listening to music. He shows me his latest pencil drawing that he
did at work at the factory today, on his lunch hour. I tell him it's
amazing. He's the most talented artist I know. One day, he says,
he'll study art in college and maybe do graphic design. This sketch
is different than his usual pencil drawings of serpent monsters
and video-game girls with tiny waists and enormous round
breasts. I hold the sketch up closer to my face. It's of a girl's face,
but not mine.

He says it's the face he sees in his dreams. "Like an angel," he
says.

I look closer. "It doesn't have any wings."

"Nah," Mark says, taking back the drawing. "Not all angels fly."

"I wanna leave Elsie's," I blurt out, just like that. I immediately
wish I could stuff the words back in. Mark will think I'm an idiot,
because we weren't even talking about that.

"Hmm," he mumbles, leaning out over the bed and dropping
his drawing to the floor.

"I know I can't stay here," I say, pausing a moment, hoping
he'll correct me. But I know his deal. He's been straight up from
the beginning and that's what I like about him. No games. He
told me when I first met him that he didn't want any more relationships. He said he couldn't deal with any more clingy, psycho
girls. He said he wanted things to be simple. "I'll probably go
to my aunt's, I don't know," I continue. "Can I just crash here
tonight?" I stretch out my arms and yawn, pretending it's not a
big deal. Pretending I'm just too lazy to get up out of bed and
walk home.

"Just tonight," he says, leaning over and opening the bedside table drawer to light a roach. " I'm going to Montreal tomorrow."

"Montreal? Why?"

"Got shit to do," he says, which is always all he says and I don't bother asking more, because I know it will just piss him off. I turn over on my side and face the wall, because I feel my chin trembling, getting tight, and I don't want him seeing me cry. He rolls over and I hear the rustling of his weed bag. Then I hear the *phhhht* of matches, smell sweet smoke, and focus on Mark's sucking inhales. "I'll be back in a couple days," he adds softly, and starts tickling my back. I squeeze my eyelids real tight, to stop any tears from spilling out.

He runs a finger up around the edge of my bra as if he were a kid fingering a cookie plate. My body rises to him like a cat's responsive back, pushing into him. For the next hour, his hands are like water, patiently rubbing me smooth. He says things like *your skin's so soft* and *how does this feel?* He insists on facing me after we have sex, pulls me tight to him, leaving our limbs to intertwine behind each other's bodies like insignificant afterthoughts. Our sweaty stomachs stick together and make sucking noises when we temporarily pull apart, to release cramped legs. He holds me tighter than I do him, and in a strange way I know the reason he can let himself go like this is because he is already detached, in some eternal free-fall state, firm ground long forgotten. He pulls my face into his chest, squeezes me firmly, my mouth pressed into his ribs. I feel suffocated in his skin. I take short, shallow breaths and count the minutes till I can turn to face the wall, protected by the jagged bones of my spine. I am terrified that Mark's depth will swallow me, like a child who drowns in a puddle.

· · ·

The water in the kiddy pool is warm. I feel as if I'm in a bath. Greg, my gorgeous twenty-six-year-old instructor with muscular shoulders and washboard stomach, says the heater will be fixed on Friday. No rush, I think, and press my back against the side, fingers behind my neck grasping the edge of the pool. Two little girls in water wings doggy-paddle past me, their mothers' safe hands trailing them, ready to keep them afloat. The ladies glance suspiciously at me, like I'm some pervert hanging out in the kiddy pool. They steer their splashing children away to the deep end and keep them there, stretching their arms out to their sides to act as impassable barriers. I suppose it's instinctive, this need to protect. But I feel like telling them I'm not the one they should worry about. It's the water their daughters are floating in that will hurt them, not me.

·   ·   ·

"I'm taking swimming lessons," I said to Elsie, after she picked up her keys from the counter and placed her hand on the door. It was a Wednesday night, three weeks ago, and she was late for bingo.

"Oh," she said, cold and aloof. "Good," and then she paused, like she didn't know if she should continue, but couldn't stop herself, "Why?"

"I thought I should learn, you know? It's dumb to have been avoiding it, really. I mean, if anything, I should learn. Right?" I could barely contain the smile, feel the edges of my mouth curve upward. Elsie doesn't want me to learn to swim. I know this, and it feels so good to hurt her. She has always liked this convenient expanse of water, this moat, keeping me from my mother. Elsie is afraid that I will cross and leave her stranded on the other side.

"Right," she said vacantly, and turned to leave.

. . .

I allow my legs to levitate up in front of me, float away and find their own position. My bum sinks slightly and I feel the safety of the tile bottom beneath me. Gripping the edge, I surface on my back and stare at the ceiling. My breathing surrounds me, then fingertips leave tile and I am released. We were all delivered from water.

This is how I see her. My mother's body, floating face down, her long hair and dress billowing out around her. White sandals gently strapped to manicured toes. Perhaps a necklace hanging down like a shiny lure. Cocktail party chatter and loud music from inside a suburban house vibrates the wineglasses on the aluminum poolside table. She had taken a stroll outside, maybe tipsy from too much champagne or maybe she needed a break from the excessive questions of her recent labour.

I have constructed scenes of how it happened. In my mind I have a list of *could haves,* and, like selecting music, play them according to my mood. She could have just been walking along the edge of the pool, an overconfident foot slipping out from under her. She could have reached out a little too far to save a flittering bee or a stray cocktail napkin. She could have been with someone, a secret lover say, who pushed her ever so slightly after she spoke of leaving him. These are the scenes I create, but I never see her face in any of these narratives. They are like scripts, unassigned actions open for faceless actors. I do not own any of them.

When I do see her face, it's when she is floating dead in the water, calm and defeated, almost even smiling. In my mind she is beautiful and silent. Her skin is pale and smooth. I search the scene for me, wonder where my new pink body is. In a crib dreaming of my own nostalgic buoyancy? Or perhaps safely strapped into a car seat just a few yards away, breathless and terrified, sensing my second severing of bloodline.

I feel my body become heavy, as if it were filling up with water, as if my mind has returned with its rational weight. I begin to consider the depth of water, the sting of chlorine in my eyes, the foggy fluorescent lights above my head. My body starts to sink in the middle, like a folding chair, bending straight and slow. Then I feel Greg's hand support the small of my back, and his face appears above me, brown curls dangling down into his green eyes.

"You all right?" I hear his words in the muffled distance. "See if you can raise your hands above your head," he shouts and my arms go up like a snow angel. "Looks good!" He makes a thumbs-up motion, removes his hand, and leaves my vision, my body folding once more, as if he had pulled a cord and collapsed me.

At the end of the half-hour we stand, thigh-high in water, as Greg explains the physics of buoyancy and basic water safety. I'm embarrassed of my ratty swimsuit. I cross my arms, self-conscious of my pointy nipples and my snotty nose.

"So that's it. You did great. Once we master the floating, then we'll go on to some basic strokes." He pats me on the shoulder. "How did you feel?"

"Heavy," I say.

3

Jed, Elsie, and I are standing at the edge of a field, our toes over the steep bank of a river. I am wearing my favourite blue Adidas running shoes with three white stripes. The sun is warm and the country air is light and sweet in my nose. Above our heads, hanging off the tree branch extended over the water from the opposite side, is a frayed rope that Elsie says used to hang all the way down to the water. Elsie holds her hand out, sways it back and forth, and explains how my mother would swing like a monkey all afternoon when she was my age. And how Aunt Sharon would push her, but never went on the swing herself, because she was too scared.

Jed takes the lid off the margarine tub and throws his arm out, releasing the ashes into the slight breeze and down into the water. Little drops lightly blow back on my skin, like weightless snowflakes. I close my eyes, push my face out into the dust, and imagine tiny kisses. "Jesus Christ, Jed!" Elsie yells and my eyes bolt open. "It's all over my jacket." And I look up to her large hands, frantically brushing her sleeves. "Jesus mother fuckin' Christ," she yells hysterically, and Jed moves in to help but his hands get tangled up in her jacket that's now dangling halfway off her arms. And she tells him he's a useless son of a bitch, and as they wrestle about, my eyes return to the water, watching the dust get carried away down the river. And it makes me happy to know that my mother's floating forever along like that, but then my eye catches a grey line forming around the side of a half-submerged branch. I toss a rock to sink it and miss. I toss another and the branch disappears into darkness, releasing my mother once more.

"What are you doing?" Elsie's eyes are red and glaring at me. She looks disgusted. "It's not a game," she says, turning away. "See, she shouldn't have come. She doesn't understand."

Jed takes my hand and leads me back toward the car, pulling me away from Elsie. His hand is rough and firm, yanking me along. He looks forward while I look behind, to see Elsie on her knees beside the river. At first I think she's fallen, but then I see she's staying that way and she's rocking back and forth and she's crying and all of a sudden I'm uncomfortable, as if I've just seen her naked. When Jed asks me what's wrong, sensing my break in stride, I tell him nothing.

. . .

The glowing red numbers on my alarm clock are so bright the whole room has a devilish tint of red: 3:07 a.m. I listen to the screeching of the kitchen fan and try to lull my mind to sleep. It's surprising how calming the scrape of metal against metal can be. I try to forget the dream that just woke me up. *A recurring dream is a message unheard,* I think to myself, but try to stop myself from considering its significance. Surrendering to the impossibility of sleep, I take some blankets and grab the pillow and head to the washroom. The room is cold, but the night-light casts an orange warmth over silver and white. I throw the pillow on the floor beside the bathtub, lie down on the blankets, and listen to the tinkling of the broken toilet. It's an unlikely lullaby, but one that has soothed me to sleep after bad dreams since I was young. I finally close my eyes, roll onto my side, feel hipbone trying to force its way into the stone mattress.

.   .   .

I knew Carla wouldn't understand but I needed to tell someone. I write her a note in math class. I write about my swimming lesson and floating and about how each time I submerge my mother surrounds me. When we meet in the washroom at 9:50, I give it to her to read in the stall because I'm too embarrassed for her to read it in front of me.

"Isn't that a little weird?" she asks, emerging from the stall.

"What do you mean?" I ask, feeling my face go red.

"Well, you know," she says, and makes a series of facial gestures as if I were supposed to know what she meant. I remain purposefully confused. She takes a deep breath, "Well, it's just that you don't ever want to talk about your birth mom or anything, and now you're talking about feeling her death in the water, and I don't know. Isn't that kind of, I don't know, morbid?"

"No," I say defensively, unable to follow up with anything else. My face gets hotter and I look toward the exit.

"I'm sorry," she says quickly. "I'm an idiot. I don't know what I'm saying. I obviously don't know what it's like." Then she gives me a playful push on the shoulder. And I smile weakly in response.

The idea of my mother has always been foreign to Carla. She cannot understand why I don't search for her past, grill Elsie, inspect hospital records, or call distant relatives. She doesn't get that people don't sit around like on "90210" repeats and get all the answers. Conflict to Carla is something pointy, something you need to file down or extract, but to me it's more like a dull, accustomed lump just under the skin.

"Aren't you ever curious?" Carla asks.

"I used to be. Not so much anymore."

"But don't you want to know more?" she persists.

"No. What's there to know?" I ask. "She feels real to me. You know, in here," I say, pointing to my temple. "You'll probably feel that way when your mom is dead."

Carla just stares blankly at me, unconvinced. "As far as I'm concerned, the sooner she keels over, the better," she says, though I know she doesn't mean it, really. And I know it's useless trying to explain it to her. If I had more energy, I would ask her if she believes in God, or hate or love, and all those other unseeable things. And when she said yes, I would ask her how she can have such faith in that which she sees, when that which she doesn't see guides her the most.

"Besides, there's always Elsie," I said instead, like an after-thought, giving her something real that she could understand.

.   .   .

When you live with a crazy person, you almost become crazy yourself. It's as if that line of normalcy becomes blurred and you're no longer sure which side you're on. Each time I come home it is a surprise. I'm unsure if I'll be greeted by a sober-faced woman watching "Biography" or someone who stinks of shit and who will ground me for talking on the phone for too long. Tonight I open the kitchen door only to find Elsie on the other side of it, dizzied static hair and housecoat hanging off her shoulder. Her hands are clutching weapons, a spatula and a rolled newspaper. Her knees are bent, body ready to defend. She extends a protective arm, holding me back.

"Do you see them? Do you see them?" she says intensely, pushing me toward the living room. I stare out into the stillness, the quiet flickering shadows of blue TV light on the walls. "Do you see them?" she repeats, trancelike. Her eyes are glassy and vacant. I stare hard around the room, then stop my eyes from blinking and bulge them wide until I think I see a shadow grinning, or hear a couch spring screaming.

"Yes, Grandma, there's one there," I whisper, pointing to the cobwebbed corner of the room, and she hoists a glass from the coffee table and hurls it at the taunting demon.

"Good girl," she says and pulls me closer into her chest. I know these moments are crazy, that her hallucinogenic dramas should scare me, and they did at first, but once I knew what to do, I liked them. It's just her and me against these horrid little demons and I kind of feel like part of a team.

She hands me a spray bottle that smells faintly of bleach and guides me around the room with the hollow strategic voice of a soldier, instructing what wall, piece of furniture, or floor area to spray. "Atta girl, they won't like that," she says, sighing deeply, and then, finally, lying down on the couch. Her eyes slowly close, and I drape the knit blanket over her body and sit on the La-Z-Boy watching her.

I used to defend my grandmother to the bone. In grade six, I punched out little kids in the playground for calling Elsie a nutter, then I'd go home and write *crazy bitch* all over the mirror, using her good, red lipstick. But now I just ignore the comments people say because I realize I like Elsie best like this. Curled up on the chair like a little child, vulnerable and needing me.

.   .   .

At school, I book an appointment with Mr. Hensley, the wild-haired guidance teacher who knows all students by name. We all go to him with our problems. We know he's all right because he plays a guitar at student assemblies and he talks about the collective consciousness and Pink Floyd, and the only people who like to talk about those things are people who do drugs. When you ask him if he smokes weed, he gets all funny, like he wants to tell the truth, but can't. So he gives this unconvincing "no" that leaves you disappointed because for once, just once, you'd like to meet a teacher who can come clean and be human. The real reason, though, I like him is because he is the first adult who actually treats me with any respect.

"I want to leave home," I blurt out. "On my own. Get an apartment."

Hensley has sat on his glasses and has a thick piece of tape on the corner of the right lens. This makes them slightly crooked and makes him look even more confused than he already is.

"I don't understand," Hensley says, leaning over a desk too small for his body, his hands clasped as if in prayer. I figured if God was alive today, he'd be like Hensley: a slightly dishevelled, brilliant genius who occasionally forgets to wear socks in the winter because his mind is preoccupied with something slightly more significant. Somebody you'd trust the fate of the world to, but you're not so sure you'd let him drive your car.

"My grandmother is making me crazy."

He closes the binder in front of him. "How's that?" he says, one brow skeptically raised, as if he were calling my bluff.

I pause a moment. He wants evidence. What do I say? Everything? Or just what's gone on in the past few weeks? Do I tell him that Elsie poured Windex in my cereal instead of milk, or that she was so drunk she left the oven mitt on the burner last week? Do I tell him that if it weren't for my skull holding my mind together, my thoughts would just disperse like water without the glass? I assumed Mr. Hensley would be different, I thought he'd be on my side, but now I'm not so sure. Now I'm beginning to think that Mr. Hensley has no clue about anything, and that he sees me as just a kid with an attitude. I begin to think that Elsie's games worked on him. He's met her, several times.

Elsie would take a shift off work and come in. I used to think she did it to punish me, but really she did it to look like a good mother. She'd buy a new scarf or slacks, something she said was classy and teacher-like. Still, she'd always get wrecked the night before, even though she promised she wouldn't. And then, in the morning, she'd have her friend Barb come over and curl her hair.

At the meeting, she'd laugh with Mr. Hensley, dangle her shoe from her toes, tilt her head flirtatiously. She would tell him how difficult I am but how she was going to keep trying. She'd tell him that she knows she has some personal problems, but she's doing the best she can, considering the circumstances, and she couldn't bear giving me up to the Children's Aid Society, because I deserve a real home. *I don't know what else to do with her,* she'd say, sighing deeply. And then both their accusing adult eyes would stare at me and words like *accountability* and *responsibility* and *lazy* would squeeze through their thin, tight lips. And I'd end up sitting there, glaring at Elsie, fixating all my hate onto a single flittering nose hair or a cigarette burn on her sleeve or yellow armpit stains.

Mr. Hensley must think I didn't hear him because he rephrases his question. "How's she making you crazy?"

"She just is," I say cautiously.

"I see," he says, with a disappointed look on his face. He thinks I'm doing this for attention. He thinks I'm making a rash adolescent decision. "It's hard getting along with parents at this age." He stands up, runs his finger along the spines of the binders on his shelf, and then pulls out a blue binder labelled "Life Skills." "That's why communication is really important," he continues while thumbing through the binder. "When you're older, you'll get along better with your grandmother." He passes me some sheets with titles like "Personal Budgeting" and "Rental Agreements." He says he'll work with me on these activities if I'm really serious about it. "Living on your own is a tough reality, but take a look at these sheets." Then he tells me about group homes and social agencies and gives me a list of emergency numbers and shelters, in case I need it.

I take his useless papers and get up to leave.

"You're not in danger, are you?" he asks just before I reach the door, as if this has just occurred to him.

I consider what he means by this. Am I in danger for my life? Am I starving? Is my grandmother threatening to kill me? Does a slow death by insanity count? I know the deal, they'll only respond if you've got skin hanging off your wrist or if you've got a bloody nose from your father's fist. I know there's no place for my story. There is no place for a story without extremes. "No," I say.

"I didn't think so," he smiles. "You seem like you can handle things." Then he winks at me. "See what you can do with those sheets."

I smile. "Thanks," I say, and shove the papers in the bottom of my knapsack.

. . .

"Don't fuckin' help or nothing," Elsie mutters when she gets home from work. Her body is wedged in the doorway, Dominion bags dangling from her hands. I'm too exhausted to get up from the couch to do anything about it, and by the time I pull my hands back to push myself up, she's already through the door. She bangs cans and cupboard doors and jars around in the kitchen, ensuring that I know she's spending her good money on feeding me. As if she wants a reward for it. As if it isn't me who usually has to fill the empty cupboards, even though she works in a goddamn grocery store. As if it isn't me who cleans the house every week, without her ever once saying thank you.

"Jesus Christ, Snow! This chicken's rotten!" she yells. I lean forward to look into the kitchen and see her head stuffed inside the fridge and the rest of her body bulging out. I think of the tempting view Gretel must have seen, that irresistible opportunity to just push and close the door.

"You're the one who put it in there," I say. "I don't even eat chicken anymore, remember?" I start picking at a blister on my foot with a safety pin. I don't have the energy to argue with her. I don't have any energy at all lately. I know she's waiting for me to say something, give her a reason to split open that "customer's always right" sweet smile she's had to paste on all day. Instead, I get up and drag myself into my room, close my door, lie down on my bed, and think of water and my mother.

The smell of onions from the kitchen makes my stomach turn. Just the thought of food lately makes me sick. Elsie is making hamburgers, which means Mitch is coming over for dinner, which means I'll leave for my swimming lesson early to avoid him. Mitch is Elsie's creepy boyfriend who has been around forever. Since Jed, and maybe even before. Almost everything about him disgusts me. The way he horks in the shower, the way he always rests his hand down the front of his jeans when he watches hockey. Elsie says she thinks he's sexy. She says he reminds her of a small Michael Bolton, with his shapely mullet and his broad jawline. But I just can't get over those baggy tank tops he wears, with gaping holes down to his elbows as if the world wants to see his stinky armpits and his hairy nipples. And then there's the slimy tattoo on his forearm of an arched-back woman with perky tits. The kind of silhouette pictures you see on the mud flaps of trucks. Still, he cleans up after himself and he leaves the toilet lid down and he makes a point of telling Elsie when I've vacuumed, so he's somewhat tolerable, if I keep my distance.

At six o'clock, I go to the washroom to get my swimsuit, hanging on the back of the door, but it's not there. I check the laundry bag and my schoolbag and under my bed.

"Where's my swimsuit?" I yell from my bedroom doorway.

"How should I know?" Elsie yells back.

"I left it on the back of the bathroom door." I wait for an answer. There is banging and clattering, so much commotion for bloody hamburgers.

I walk to the kitchen and plant my arm firmly on the door frame. "Where the hell is it?" I ask accusingly, "Where'd you put it?"

Elsie throws her fist down into the huge slab of ground beef. "I didn't put it nowhere." She glares at me. "Why would I touch your gaad-damn swimsuit?"

"Because you don't want me to swim!" I snap.

She squishes her face up, her mouth hanging open, as if my words are the most unbelievable thing she's ever heard. "Don't be an idiot," she says, shaking her head and returning to her meat pounding.

I storm back to my room, determined to go to my swim lesson even if it means going naked. I ransack my drawers and find my old swimsuit.

"You'll miss dinner," Elsie says as I stomp past her to leave. As if I'm supposed to stick around the one time she's cooked something, like I haven't been feeding myself for years. As if I don't realize she's cooking for Mitch, not me.

"Good," I reply and slam the door as hard as I can. I know the bitch took my swimsuit. I'd bet my life on it.

.   .   .

I sit on the edge of the big pool, extend my legs so that my feet are barely skimming the water. Behind me the Dolphin toddler class shrieks as the instructor pretends his elbow is a shark fin and chases their bubble-floating bodies.

Water has skin. A strong layer caused by surface tension. It explains how bugs skitter across water as if walking on stone. *The women in our family have thick skin,* Elsie's voice resonates in my head, as if we had these heroic pioneer ancestors who chopped firewood for their freezing children. And I remember thinking, *What family? What women?* I dip my big toe slightly into the water, watching it pierce the surface. That's the strange thing about skin. This thin layer can be stretched forever, holding all of you together, but it can be broken by just the smallest pinprick.

Greg leads me back toward the kiddy pool and I scan the deck to see if anyone is looking. I jokingly suggest the bigger pool. "We'll get there," he says, winking at me, "but you'll have to settle for being a big fish in a small pond first." His arms go above his head and he slips off his T-shirt. I stare at his chest and lose myself in the waves of his stomach.

I am officially the only person in the class now. He says that his supervisor wanted to cancel my spot because they are losing money, but Greg told him it wouldn't be fair to me. "It's not good business," he says. I should feel guilty, but I don't, because it's better this way.

First we spend time dunking down in the water. "Get a feel for the water. Feel it on your skin. Just let your arms float," Greg says. I squat waist-high in water, limbs angular and stiff, and feel the cold bite the back of my neck. After a while, Greg tells me to put my chin down and practice blowing bubbles, like we tried during our first lesson. He demonstrates, putting his face in the water and making a blubbering sound, the kind kids make in the bathtub. It amazes me how good-looking he is, even with fluttering lips.

"Can I face the other way?" I ask, embarrassed of my flapping mouth. He gestures that it's all right, and I turn, immerse my lips, and try to flubber without making noise. After that, we sit on the edge of the pool, and as he shows me the rotation of arms for the front crawl, I stare at the drops of water on his chest. I imagine this must be what he looks like when he steps out of the shower.

We get back in the water so Greg can show me the final step. "You need to know how to breathe properly, because when the lungs are full of air, it gives the body buoyancy. You'll need to learn how to take a deep breath. Now, it's not a fast deep breath, it's a slow, drawn-in breath through your mouth. I usually tell the kiddies it's like slowly breathing in the smell of freshly baked cookies, but you ever smoke weed?" I nod my head smiling. "It's like that, nice and slow. When you're blowing out, think of candles on a birthday cake."

I start laughing because I can't believe he's talking about weed like it's normal. And it shocks me because it's the first time an adult has ever talked to me like this.

"So breathe in weed, blow out candles?" I ask, just making sure I really did hear him right.

"Awesome. Perfect. Wonderful," he says, and I beam like a five-year-old.

I practice breathing deeply in, then out, in, then out, until I feel dizzy. Greg tells me to try it underwater, to hold my breath and count to five before blowing out. He tells me to put my whole face in, ears submerged. When he gestures to begin, I breathe deeply and seal my lips, feel my face break through the water's skin. I submerge into the peaceful quiet, thoughts of Elsie disappear as I press my face to my mother's liquid soul. Then, without warning, I am invaded. Water swallows my face, penetrating ears and nostrils and tiny pores. Thoughts of my mother's water-filled body flood through me. I hear her desperate fingers above me, scratching the thin, clear layer. A layer she couldn't break. And I suddenly realize the dual purpose of skin.

"You didn't exhale," Greg says, when I can breathe once more, after the coughing and gagging.

I wipe the chlorine tears from my eyes. "It didn't seem right," I answer. He gives me a few minutes to relax on the side of the pool before I submerge my face once more.

. . .

I go to Mark's house after swimming class. My hair is still wet, leaving a big round mark on his pillow. He licks my stomach and says I taste like chlorine. Then he tickles his tongue down my thigh till I can't take it any longer and I clamp my knees together to trap his head and stop him.

It is strange the places on a body that summon you. Mark has six scars: two on his hands, one on his forearm, one on his leg, one on his face, and the one we don't talk about, on his left wrist. I am drawn to these silent marks, rough edges of once-perforated skin, indications that there *is* a way inside. Evidence that there is something beneath Mark's surface.

I reach down, his head still at my knees, and brush the scar streaked across his cheek like a generous paint stroke. "Tell me about this one again," I say.

"You're crazy," he whispers, smiling.

"I like to hear it," I whine, until he brings his head up to my bare chest and tells me how he got into a fight when he caught some skinheads trying to beat up his little brother in a park. How after he pulled the pimply faced guy off his bloodied brother, a bunch of fourteen-year-old kids jumped Mark. How one smashed a beer bottle on the sidewalk and then sliced Mark's face. I think of new questions to ask each time he tells me: *Was it a cloudy day? What did you eat before that? Were you wearing running shoes?*

He laughs at my strange questions, but I persist. Then I listen to his answers, envious of the privileged facts. I need to know this, this detail; I need to know what it takes to break skin.

Mark holds up my hand above us and plays with my fingers. "So small," he says, "like a chicken bone. I could just snap it." Then he softly kisses the tip of each finger and I am suddenly compelled to mean more.

"Did you talk to your father?" I ask, knowing he was supposed to receive the collect phone call from jail today. He's in for assault with a weapon, for beating some guy up at a bar who took his beer.

"Yep," he says, holding my hand up to his, comparing size.

"And?"

"Was nothing." He puts down my hand and reaches over to the night table, grabs a spliff, and lights it. "Wants me to get some papers or something for him." He takes a deep drag and then extends it out for me.

"Will you?"

"Are you fuckin' kidding?" And that's the end of the conversation. Mark hates his father. Not the way I hate Elsie, but a complete flat-out hate that offers no tiny folds of forgiveness. He lays his head against my chest and I play with his hair, imagine I am touching moths' wings, hoping some of him will flake off and I'll ground him.

4

I'm in a kitchen, though it's not really a kitchen, it's more like all rooms in one. There's a bed in the corner and a couch by the fridge. Mustard wallpaper lines the walls and in the centre of the room is a fake-wood table with chrome legs. It stinks like the public washrooms in parks or hockey arenas. There's a dark-green shag carpet, and if you look close enough, you can see things like cigarette butts and pieces of food like chunks of dandruff in thick hair. I cling to Elsie's arm, my back pressed against her leg, averting my eyes from the woman in front of me who Elsie says is her sister.

"Come sit over here." The woman pushes out the chair beside her so hard it topples over and almost hits my leg. She scares me with her scratchy voice and her yellowed fingers. I freeze and look to Elsie's unresponsive face for permission. But then the woman starts to laugh like it's all so funny. "What'd you do to her? She's scared as a mouse!" She then turns to me. "That's all right, just a chair, won't bite you." In the absence of Elsie's objection, I move closer to the chair.

"Caw, caw!!" The woman sticks out her fingers like claws and startles me backward. She is laughing hysterically, her wide teeth like rotting corn.

"You're scaring her!"

"Oh, don't be an idiot," the woman spits at Elsie. "I'm fuckin' family." She holds a cigarette in her mouth and motions to the chair again. I cautiously walk toward her as she speaks through me to Elsie. "She's got my eyes," she says, her hot breath on me. Just as I'm about to sit, she starts to cough and splutter.

"You stink," I say, surprising myself, "like garbage."

And the woman stares at me, mouth opened wide, with no air coming out until I think she's dying, but then I realize she's actually laughing. "She's just like her mother," she finally breathes out and laughs hysterically.

"That's enough. I don't know what I was thinking. We're going." Elsie pulls my hand so hard I start to cry.

"What's wrong with that woman?" I asked in a dark and smelly hallway.

"She's dying." Then Elsie bends down to me and firmly presses her hands on my cheeks. She squeezes so tight my teeth hurt. "Don't worry—to us, she's already dead."

·   ·   ·

I wake in Mark's room with a pain in my gut. I have to pee. When I climb back into bed, I'm careful not to disturb Mark's sleeping body. He groans and rolls over, wraps his arm around me. I lie there, wide awake, staring at his arm draped over me like a limp fish. I want to turn and press my body into his, but I don't. Instead, I just lie there cursing myself for not being able to just do the things I feel. *A restless sleep is a restless mind,* Elsie used to taunt, often finding me reading in my bed at four a.m. And I'd glance back at her drowsy form standing in the doorway, her pale-blue cotton nightie clinging to her large, tired breasts, never bothering to ask her in return why she was awake.

•   •   •

Since it's our last Saturday night together, Carla and I decide to celebrate. She arrives at my apartment, throws her bag on the kitchen table, and pulls out two plastic Baggies with the shrivelled brown mushrooms her brother carefully weighed for each of us.

"It's not very much," I say, disappointed, holding the bag up in the air and moving my eyes in for a closer inspection.

"Believe me," Carla affirms, as if she knows what she's talking about. "It's enough."

We boil the water for the Lipton Cup-a-Soup and then fill our mugs. Carla carefully drops in the hardened dried-up pieces, crushing them between her fingers like spices. She concentrates hard, tongue slightly out, as if she were a scientist working with dangerous chemicals.

"Cheers," we say, clanging our mugs together, eager to start slurping disorder into our minds. "Here's to our friendship!"

We drink the watery soup, stopping every once in a while to chew the mushroom bits. When we are done, we slam our mugs down on the table and stare at each other. I can hardly hold back the excitement. But nothing happens. We wait another half hour and, still, nothing happens.

"We got ripped off," I announce angrily, pulling back my chair.

"No we didn't," Carla says. "My own fuckin' brother wouldn't rip me off."

"Whatever," I say, thoroughly pissed. "What a waste of cash."

We move into the living room and turn on the TV. We are not talking to each other. Every once in a while I mutter how much of a waste this was and Carla tells me to shut up. But then, after about two hours, I'm watching the TV and I see people's faces start drooping and bulging, and rainbows trail behind their moving bodies like rustling flags.

I look over to Carla, who is staring glaze-faced at the television. "You see that?" I ask, and though she doesn't respond, I think she must, because she starts laughing uncontrollably.

Time becomes liquid. I pick up my mug and stare down a hole a thousand feet deep. I want more. My upper lip detaches from my mouth, creeping over the rim like a wet slug. I watch it inch slowly to the bottom of the mug, sucking the last drops of cold liquid with its pulsating mouth. Butterfly wings miraculously sprout from its side and then my winged lip floats out into the room, my hands wildly trying to capture it in flight. I call for Carla to help, but she just sits there, laughing and pointing at my nose, trying to say something that only comes out as incomprehensible giggles. We move out to the apartment courtyard, where wet grass licks our bare feet with a thousand hungry tongues. Our sore stomachs ache from laughter as we take turns watching light drip like honey through a plastic water bottle balanced on our foreheads.

When things become ugly and real once more, we lie in the dark, back on the couch, eating chips and watching MuchMusic. I am in a bad mood, disappointed I can't stay in that magic world, pissed at Carla for not bringing more. I scan the room with disappointed eyes, no longer able to see the beauty in the ugliness around me. And then the phone rings. It's Mark. He's mad that I did 'shrooms, tells me he doesn't want me getting into that stuff. I tell him it was just this once and then I lie and say it was awful.

"It's that Carla bitch," he says. "She drags you into this crap."

"Shut up!" I want to say more, but I can't, because Carla is staring at me as I talk. "I can make my own decisions."

For some reason, Mark backs down. He tells me to come over, he wants to see me. When I tell him I'm staying with Carla, he gets all sweet and starts saying how much he misses me in his bed. His voice sounds so good, I consider going but I look to Carla, who knows what's going on, and she shoots me an evil look. She gestures for me to hang up.

"I can't come," I say firmly. But then Marks gets all mad, telling me I can't always be the one who gets to choose when I come over. That sometimes he should get a choice. He tells me Carla is jealous that I have a boyfriend and that I shouldn't let her tell me what to do. He keeps going on about it, getting more and more mad, until finally I tell him I'll be over in an hour and hang up the phone.

"It's just easier if I go," I explain to Carla, who's rolling her eyes and shaking her head at me. "You can stay in my room. Elsie won't care."

"As if," she says angrily. "Why's he such an asshole?"

"You don't know him," I say defensively. "He's not like that." And I can't explain because no one understands him the way I do.

Mark treats everyone like shit and people can't understand how we've lasted so long. No one crosses Mark because they know he doesn't care, doesn't care whether you're a friend or a stranger; he'll turn on you over a stolen cigarette. But I know he would never hurt me, he tells me himself how he wouldn't, ever. It's like I'm this little egg Mark can't bring himself to crush. Still, I'll pester him over something stupid like him not phoning me. I'll keep going on and on, calling him an asshole and prick, not letting it drop. Till I know I'm just testing him. Till his fist comes out in front of my face and he's got spit on the corners of his mouth and the veins on the side of his forehead are popping. And even though I know he'd never do it, there's that second of silence when I close my eyes and brace.

And I know what people would say to that, which is why I never mention it to Carla or anyone, because no one understands Mark the way I do. No one gets that he's trying with me, really trying to be a good person. And although people might think it, no one would admit that there's something admirable about a crazy dog who obeys the mere snap of his master's fingers, or a child who will stop frantically crying only in her mother's arms. No one would admit a certain jealousy for such selective loyalty.

.   .   .

The next morning I drag my tired body to Carla's house to say goodbye. I thought Carla would be angry that I'm late, but she's not. Instead, she's waving excitedly at me from in front of her house, jumping up and down on the curb, like she's going to summer camp or something. She has only packed one suitcase because she says she'll be coming back lots and can slowly move her things. She asks me to come to the bus station with her because her mom is refusing to drive.

"She's being a bitch," Carla says dismissively and shrugs her shoulders. She says that her mom had been all nice to her the past couple weeks, buying her clothes and ordering take-out food every night. She says she knew she was being like that just so that Carla would change her mind. She says she knew it wouldn't work, but she wasn't going to pass up the opportunity to get some new clothes.

We stand out in front of the house for a few minutes, waiting, but I don't know what for. Carla fiddles around in her purse as if she were stalling. I see her mom peeking out from behind the drapes and I quickly look away, but her sad expression lingers in my mind. It's a look I've never seen before, one that's never been directed toward me. It's the look of someone being left behind.

"Did you say goodbye to your mom?" I ask, trying to sound casual.

"Yep," she says happily and picks up her suitcase.

I look to the window and see that the drape is back to normal, but I know Mrs. Costa is still standing there; I can see the shadow outline of her body. I feel sorry for her and get mad at Carla for being so stupid. Because there's nothing wrong with Mrs. Costa. There's nothing wrong with a mother who nags at you only because she cares. I get so pissed at Carla for having a half-decent mother and not appreciating it that I can't keep my mouth shut.

"Don't you feel bad?" I ask.

"Whose side are you on?" she blurts out, dropping her case on the sidewalk. She stands there, fists clenched, glaring at me. Like she's going to take me on, right there, on her front lawn.

"Yours," I say, caught off guard by her intensity. "I was just wondering."

"Well, shut up, then."

We walk in silence until Carla starts breathing heavy, says she's tired of carrying the fucking case and that she needs a cigarette break. We sit on a bench and I ask her about this guy named Jason that she met last week and that's all it takes before, suddenly, she's in a great mood. Carla blathers on about his car and his hair and his Rolex. I watch her mouth move and wonder how she can be so vacant in her own life. And I wonder why I can't be the same.

When the bus pulls away from the station we wave at each other, like we're in a movie. Carla is frantically flapping her hands and yelling something through the window, but I'm just standing there, my arm held fixed in the air. I don't care what she's saying to me, something probably like *I'll call you*. It doesn't matter. In a few moments, she will sit back down, open her M&M's and eat them in priority order of favourite colour. And I will pass through the bus station, tell the homeless beggar to fuck off, and then enter the piss-stained washroom and kick in the cubicle door as hard as I can.

.   .   .

That night, I wake slowly. Mark's breath on my face, a mix of beer and toothpaste. His gentle fingers brushing the hair off my forehead. His skin close to mine, heated and rough. I nuzzle my face into his. My mind slowly rousing from sleep. But then suddenly my eyes rip open. Reality strikes me like a swift kick to the head. I'm at home in my room, it's dark, and that's Mitch's face, not Mark's, inches away from mine.

"What the fuck are you doing?" I yell, and at the same time I'm bounding out of bed, pulling the sheet off with me. Mitch is standing now, stunned, his mouth is hanging open like he's about to say something but doesn't. The smell of alcohol hits me hard.

"Get the hell out of my room, you disgusting bastard, you motherfucker!" I start throwing words at him, my strength increasing as I see him shrinking, helplessly, like some drunken bum. He turns to go, but I move in behind him, push him so hard he stumbles forward and hits his head on the door. It's then that I see Elsie at the entrance. I see her lips wildly moving but I don't hear anything because my head is pounding. I concentrate on her mouth until the sound becomes clear.

"What are you doing!" Elsie yells.

I look to Mitch, who's looking at me, and then I look back to Elsie. I realize that she's saying this to me, like I'm the one with the problem. "What?" I scream at her in disbelief. "He's a fuckin' pervert. He was in my room, kissing me. Fuckin' pervert!" I spit on the ground, my gob of saliva hitting Elsie's bare foot by mistake. "I'll fuckin' kill him," I shout, grabbing the scissors off the dresser and moving forward through the door. But Elsie moves in and blocks my way, grabbing my arm.

"Don't be a stupid fool," she says, her voice eerily calm. "He wasn't doing nothing. Just saying good night."

I am stunned. I can't believe she's saying that. Can't believe she's not believing me. All those times I stuck up for her, lied for her, and this one time that I need her to back me up, just this once, she doesn't. "Are you fuckin' crazy? You don't believe me?" I stare at Mitch, now leaning up against the far living-room wall, arms outstretched and fingers spread as if he were bracing himself. He looks like an animal caught in headlights. He lowers his eyes to the floor. "Deny it! Deny it! Try to, you fuckin' pig!" I yell, tears now coming down my face, my body starting to crumble. "A fuckin' pig!" Elsie keeps blocking the doorway, but my shaking body is hardly worth the effort. "If I see you again, I'll kill you! I swear to God!"

"It's okay, it's okay . . ." Elsie repeats, half holding me back, half hugging me. "He's going home. We'll deal with this in the morning," she assures me, and then gently but firmly pushes me back into the room. "Go to bed."

The door closes in my face, and I stand there stunned, unable to comprehend what exactly just happened. I fold my arms in front of my chest and start bawling and wheezing, dropping to the ground as my back scrapes along the wooden door. I expect Elsie to open the door any minute, expect her to come in after he's gone. But after a while she doesn't appear, so I go to the bathroom to wash my face, scrubbing it hard with soap. And when that doesn't seem like enough, I press my toothbrush against my skin, scraping my lips and cheeks and forehead till all of Mitch is off me.

Back in my room I prop a chair up against the door and crawl into bed. I put the scissors under my pillow and lie in the dark, thinking of all the heavy things in the room that could be used as weapons: a lamp, a stapler, one of the empty wine bottles that line my windowsill. I remain still and alert, listening to the darkness for anything, a footstep, the slight ping of a door-handle spring. And then I hear it, soft and steady at first, then louder and faster. It's a familiar noise, my grandmother having sex on the pullout couch. The frenzied squeaking springs, the deep-throated animal moaning. And finally, Mitch's rough grunt suspended in the black air in front of me like ejaculated terror.

My body thrusts forward on the bed, stomach muscles clamp, mouth opens, and I start convulsing, but nothing comes out. Just ugly noises, as if I were being strangled by a thick unforgiving rope. I hang my head over the side of the bed and stick my finger down my throat, only to heave unsatisfying air. Then I look down at my thighs and see the opened scissors in my determined hand, roughly scratching back and forth like a knife in hard wood. I scratch and scratch, harder and harder. And I don't stop until I see the tiny droplets of blood rise through the unexpected cracks in me. Until all of a sudden, I am calmed. And I can breathe once more. My skin broken.

5

There is another photo.

In the morning, when Elsie has gone to work and there is no sign of Mitch, I sneak out of my room. I take the photo from the shoebox at the bottom of the hall closet and carefully place it in the pages of my math textbook. Then I put the textbook in my duffle bag packed full of clothes and shoes.

It's the photo Elsie used to show me at Christmas. She'd let me hold it in my hands for a while, but then she always carefully put it away, back in the box, when she thought I wasn't looking. I'd watch her slide it neatly in an envelope, tsk-tsking and shaking an annoyed head at the tiny bent top-right corner.

The photo is of me as a baby. Maybe one week old, Elsie says. I'm round and pink and drooly. I'm in a little yellow jumper, my eyes all clear and innocent and pure. I love myself like that. But that's not why I love the picture. My mother's hands are in the photo. Her outspread fingers, firm and strong, on either side of me. No rings, bony white knuckles, chipped middle fingernail, a mark on her right hand, probably from the IV drip. She is holding me high and tight, proud to show me to the camera. And that's why I love the photo. Because she could have left me in my crib, or lying on her chest. But instead, she held me up high and took the weight of me in her hands.

. . .

Aunt Sharon's apartment is a tiny bachelor down at Wellesley and Yonge, in a three-story brown-brick building. She's been living there forever, since before I was born, though I only see her at our pathetic family gatherings at Christmas and Thanksgiving. And lately, the past few years, I haven't seen her at all. I throw down my heavy duffle bag and stand outside her door, in the hallway that smells of old people and mothballs. I have been in this apartment before. When I was ten I stayed for two weeks. My memories are shades of blue: blue carpet, curtains, bedspreads, turquoise towels with ducks on them. It was a strange place. Strange, but cozy. Aunt Sharon was a person who took care of things. All things. I knew this because stuff in her house, like kettles and spare toilet paper, would have little knitted coats on them.

. . .

It was five years ago and it was the third time that year it had happened, but this time was the worst. By the time the ambulance had arrived I had Elsie's purse, health card, and a change of clothes stuffed in a garbage bag, ready by the door. I had combed her hair, rubbed her arms and socks with a magazine perfume sampler, and squeezed toothpaste on my finger and put it in her mouth. There wasn't enough time to fix up the living room, so I just kicked the empty liquor bottles under the couch and sprayed some hairspray into the room. When the ambulance men came to the door, I calmly showed them in, told them not to mind the mess since we weren't expecting company.

I pointed to my grandmother's unmoving form on the couch. One man rushed up to her, knelt down, and started pulling things with cords out of his bag. Then it was like he just froze, picking up her pill bottle and holding it up in the air for the other guy to see. The guy then rolled his eyes, shook his head, and started to put the cords and things back into his bag. There was walkie-talkie static and numbers being called, like in a taxi. The younger one told me to come into the kitchen where he asked me questions, speaking to me like I was a baby, like I didn't understand what was going on. He didn't know that this wasn't the first time.

"How old are you, Snow?"

"Thirteen," I lied.

"How long has she been like this?"

"Just a few minutes," I lied again. It was actually more like hours. When I had come home from school she was passed out on the couch, which wasn't that unusual for four o'clock in the afternoon. Her nightgown hiked up around her waist, her yellowed cotton underwear with the elastic cascading like Christmas tree trim. I had pulled her nightgown down and tucked it in around the edges of her as if making a bed. Then I went about my usual routine, moved around the lump on the couch, brushing her outstretched arm each time I passed between her and the coffee table. After I finished my homework I made some ravioli, pushed her heavy legs over, and sat squished on the side of the couch to watch TV. It wasn't until I was going to bed that I climbed up and peered down at her face pressed into the cushion. It looked strange, not her usual sleeping face, but pale and lifeless and there wasn't that snoring gurgle that she usually does. All of a sudden my blood drained from my face, my head went spinning, and I grabbed the phone.

I got to ride in the ambulance but it didn't have its siren on and it wasn't going as fast as an ambulance should. "Your mom will be okay," the young one said to me, trying to make conversation.

"She's not my mom," I said defensively. "She's my grandmother."

I patiently answered his questions, one eye on Elsie's foggy breath in the plastic cup over her mouth. I told him about my school, my favourite subject, and that if I could be any animal I wanted, it would be an elephant. I said it all to be nice to him, even though I couldn't understand why he'd ask such dumb questions when Elsie was lying there with tubes up her nose. "You'll probably need this," I finally interrupted him and passed him her health card. "She's allergic to peanuts, and she takes a lot of pills. She has a drug and alcohol history and her blood type is AB negative. Mine's the same."

At the hospital, nurses stood in threes, whispering about me as my grandmother's stomach was pumped behind the curtain. I scowled at them, knowing they were saying bad things by the way their tight faces forced smiles in my direction. One of them called my aunt Sharon, whose arrival at the hospital brought obvious relief to the nurses' faces.

I could see they were surprised, surprised that she was Elsie's daughter. Aunt Sharon looked responsible in her ironed clothes and her shiny shoes. Unlike my grandmother, she wore makeup and brushed her hair and always wore a silky scarf around her neck. Elsie said Aunt Sharon didn't have more money than we did, but it always seemed to me that she was rich in comparison.

Aunt Sharon took me home that night to her apartment. She told me we'd have a sleepover, *just us girls,* and when I got out of the bathroom I found her lying in the pullout bed in the centre of the living room.

"Hope you don't snore. I don't have much room for company," she explained and then smiled brightly. "Which one should sleep with me tonight?" she asked, pointing to the stuffed animals piled at the foot of the bed. They weren't my stuffed animals, and besides, I was too old for that, but I was too confused to speak, so I just picked up the zebra, gave it to her outstretched hand, and silently crawled into bed. I don't think I slept at all that night. Instead, I lay there, fixated on my aunt's steady breathing. The warmth of her body like itchy crumbs in the bed.

The next day I didn't have to go to school. We went to visit Elsie in the hospital, though I didn't get to see her. I had to wait by the pop machine while Aunt Sharon disappeared and then reappeared ten minutes later from around the corner, her heels clicking down the hall in quick measured beats.

"Is she sick?" I asked, worried that it was my fault.

"Kind of," she replied. "I'd say more sad than sick." Then she got all serious and patted her lap, motioning for me to come over. She was always like that, wanting to touch or hug. Always mushy. I went and leaned up against her solid leg, but kept my hands in my pockets. "What do you think of your grandma?" she asked.

"I don't know." A stupid answer for a stupid question.

"I mean, you think she's a good mom?"

"She's my grandma," I said and pulled away from her. Then I got angry because even though I didn't totally know what she was asking, I had a feeling. And all these bad thoughts about her came into my head, like her sharp pointed nails, her fat arms, and her powdery smell that itches my nose. "She calls you a cow," I said, not knowing where the words came from, unsure whether I said them aloud or just thought them. I watched her to see the answer but I still wasn't sure.

"You must be thirsty," she said, standing up and motioning to the machine. "Would you like a pop?"

.   .   .

An old lady stumbles out of her apartment and quickly passes by me. I see her body tense, her beady eyes panic, as if I'm going to attack her or something. I reach forward and knock on Aunt Sharon's door, lightly at first and then harder. After a few moments I press my ear to the wood, to listen for signs of life, and the door opens.

"Snow?" Aunt Sharon's round nose pokes out from the small opening in the door. I see her eyes peering behind me to see who else I'm with.

"I'm alone," I say. "Can I come in?"

"Of course, hon," she says warmly, opening the door and giving me a big hug. "So good to see you. It's been ages." She holds me a while, squeezes tight, her pewter cat pin poking into my shoulder. "Come sit," she says, and I follow her through the maze of stacked magazines and newspapers and books. There is barely enough room for the couch and the large chair that is full of more news-papers and books. It's not like it's dirty, just cluttered. The only thing I recognize in the apartment are the blue walls and furniture.

"Winky!" she calls. "Winky! Puss, puss, puss . . . come see! We have a visitor!" My eyes frantically scan the floor, wary of the one-eyed black cat who will dart out at my feet and scratch my toes. I remember this horrible cat from when I was young. It's about a thousand years old, Aunt Sharon's one love ever since she rescued it from a hit and run. Other than Winky, I think she's always lived alone.

We sit together on the couch, squished, Aunt Sharon's thigh slightly pinching mine, but I'm unable to move. A pile of clothes are at my back, and to my right is Winky's purring, arched body. It's an awkward position, and I strain my neck backward in order to gain a few more inches of space between Aunt Sharon's face and mine. I begin to tell her that I've left home, but as each word drops off my tongue, I feel my chin quivering and my face losing the strength it needs to hold itself together. Finally I start crying and wheezing, like I'm this little girl, and Aunt Sharon pulls me toward her and starts rocking me, which only makes me lose it even more. My face pressed to her armpit, I smell perfume and sweat. And part of me wants to stop, but part of me just wants to keep holding onto her like that. I tell her how I had to get away from Elsie and how I punched the wall and how I saw myself cutting my arm and how I don't know where that thought came from because I wasn't even thinking about hurting myself and how I think I'm going crazy, the way Elsie is crazy, and what if I'm becoming nuts like her? I don't tell her about my thighs, about the real cuts. And I don't tell her about Mitch. Instead, I tell her I just need to calm my head and make things quiet for a while. When my breath returns, Aunt Sharon passes me a Kleenex and gets a glass of water from the kitchen. Even though I'm not thirsty, I take it and suddenly I'm embarrassed, wishing I could lose my face in the bottom of that glass.

"You're not crazy," Aunt Sharon finally says, watching me drink. "And neither is Elsie." I lower my glass and dart a look at her. I'm surprised she's sticking up for her.

"I hate her," I say.

She smiles. "Hate's a strong word. She's not nuts. Well, maybe a little bit. But anyways, you're not going to be crazy. It's not in your blood."

"I feel bad for you."

"Why's that?"

"To have a mother like Elsie."

We sit quietly for a moment. And I feel bad for saying that, because it's not like Aunt Sharon had a choice in the matter. And besides, she is so different, with an apartment and a car and a cat.

I take a deep breath. "You never talk about my mom."

Aunt Sharon's face remains blank, but then she smiles slightly. "I didn't know you wanted me to."

"Did you get along?" I ask, nestling my body into the couch.

"Sort of. When we were young, just kids. We'd play, right? We'd dress up our dog Scratchy—"

"The black one?"

"Yep. In our clothes and things like that. We were different, though. You know, I was neat, your mom was messy. I hated reading, she did well at school. She got along with our dad, I didn't. When I became a teenager, we grew apart. I moved out when I was eighteen. So I didn't see her much after that. I didn't see anyone, really."

"Did she get along with Elsie?"

"Nobody gets along with Elsie." Aunt Sharon pulls a purring Winky onto her lap and starts firmly patting her head.

"So all of us left her." I reach out to stroke Winky's curling tail but it slides through my fingers.

"I guess so."

I think of all the things I want to ask Aunt Sharon about when she was a kid, but before I can she tosses Winky from her lap, springs from the couch, and claps her hands together, announcing, "I'm starved! Want some KD à la Sharon?"

"Mmmm." I smile widely, pretending I'm not bothered by the sudden change in subject. Aunt Sharon makes the best gourmet Kraft Dinner. It's what she always brought to family gatherings. Always something different. Indian curry KD, or spicy sausage KD. She's considered writing a cookbook, but someone told her that had already been done.

Without another word, Aunt Sharon places the TV converter in my hand and then disappears down the hallway and into the kitchen, leaving me sitting on the couch, all awkward and unfinished. Aunt Sharon is like Elsie that way, never around long enough to talk.

·   ·   ·

"Ta-dah!" Aunt Sharon returns to the living room with two plates heaped full of curried Kraft Dinner à la India. She motions for me to lay out a newspaper on top of the books piled on top of the coffee table. We watch her favourite show, "Judge Judy." She slaps her thighs and bobs her shoulders up and down, thoroughly entertained by Judy's insults unleashed at the man who trashed his fiancée's car. "This woman's brilliant!" she says. "Watch—she'll just pulverize the guy." She shoves another mouthful of curried macaroni into her mouth.

At the commercial, she takes her napkin and wipes the sweat from her forehead. "So where will you live?" she asks. I feel my face go hot and red, and then I pull one leg up between us and hug it to my chest. Truth is, I just assumed I'd crash here a bit, until I got a job and an apartment, but now I realize that it's just too small and Aunt Sharon probably wouldn't want a teenager in her way.

"I don't know." I shrug my shoulders. "I'm working that out."

"I'd ask you to stay but, you know—"

"Yeah," I say, not wanting her to finish the sentence.

"Well, we'll figure out something. You can stay here tonight," she says, slapping my knee. I feel like I should say something, but my mind is blank, so I get up and grab my schoolbag, reach down to the bottom, and pull out the crumpled papers that Mr. Hensley gave me.

"My guidance teacher gave me these," I say, extending the wrinkled sheets.

She scans the papers with a careful eye. "Hmmm"—she points midway down the paper—"I know a woman who works at Delcare Group Home. I'll give her a call tomorrow."

. . .

Aunt Sharon inflates an air mattress and puts it in the hallway, in between the living room and the kitchen. When I crawl into the bed, she leans down to check if my mattress is firm enough. "You used to love Elsie," she says, pulling the duvet up close to my chin and then tucking it in around my feet.

"I never loved her," I say. "I was just a kid. You think you love everything when you're a kid."

But she's right, I do remember thinking I loved Elsie. A long time ago. But it was a different kind of love. I had gerbils once, about ten of them. They just kept getting pregnant. And sometimes I'd find the mother in the cage, eating one of her own babies. It was disgusting. And the thing is, when she took the first few bites, you could tell the baby thought the mother was just nuzzling it. Even when I tried to move the baby away, it would just crawl back to its mother. And you could tell that, even when it was happening, the baby still held this crazy faith in its mother's gnawing teeth.

In the morning I hear my mother's voice. She's saying my name—*Snow*—soft, like whispered kisses in my ear. Snow. I roll my body onto its side, skin sticking to plastic as I float on the air mattress down a blue ocean carpet. I slide my hand down to my thighs, fingertips tracing the three rough-lined scabs. I carefully pick at the dried blood, flicking the scabby testimonies of craziness into the sheets. "Snow." I hear my name again. Only now I realize the voice is not my mother's, it's Aunt Sharon. She is talking to Brenda, her social worker friend. She is desperately trying to find a place to leave me, as if my very presence in her apartment makes her uneasy.

"Great," Aunt Sharon says enthusiastically. "Snow will be ready to go tomorrow."

．　．　．

In some cultures you are given a name only after you have lived long enough to earn it. In other cultures, you grow into your name the way a snail grows to the size of its shell.

"She called you Snow because it's beautiful and mysterious," Elsie said, compelled to explain because it's what everyone asked. But I could tell Elsie didn't approve and, in some small way, that made me happy. *Such an interesting name,* people would say in a way that was more like a question, and I'd proudly explain a poetic mother who dressed like a gypsy and had a passionate longing for the exotic.

I lie on my inflatable mattress and imagine my mother choosing this name. I imagine her at a library, with wood panelling and ceiling-high shelves, perhaps scanning a thick book on mythology or Celtic literature or modern science. I picture a woman with a round face and long fingernails and expensive socks. I imagine her arguments with Elsie, who couldn't possibly understand the breadth of a name.

My mother gave me a puzzle, a destiny I'm to figure out. And I'm determined to find my meaning. My high school science projects are on things like the James Bay Project, flash floods, and avalanches. At university I'm going to study Earth sciences. I'll study hydrothermal systems, glaciers and glaciation, oceans, hot springs, and geysers in New Zealand. One day, the epiphany will strike me: something someone says, a line I read in a book, a text-book photo. Suddenly, in one small moment, I'll understand my purpose. At least I have a choice of matters: solid, liquid, or gas.

TWO

6

I saw you for the first time today. A tiny, thin blue line. Just millimetres long, yet the biggest thing I could ever imagine.

Positive.

I think how strange a word to first associate you with: *positive*. I rip open another package and dip the plastic dispenser in the urine cup. Again, a thin blue line and again and again. I frantically search for the second line, the negative. I wonder, hope, the Tylenol I had last night may have affected the results. I try four more times with the packages I stole from the drugstore, slipping them in my knapsack while all the time smiling at the stock boy who was staring up my skirt.

A fist pounds on the bathroom door; metal bangles grate my ears. "Hurry up!"

I ignore the command. Jasmyn can wait this morning. I whip the last empty package against the wall; its weightless flight is unsatisfying. Sitting down on the toilet seat cover, I feel pain in my stomach and wonder if that's you. Then, I think, *That's my second word to associate with you:* pain.

The fist pounds again, so hard this time the mirror vibrates.

"Fuck off!" I hurl the words at the door.

"Snow?" Jasmyn's response is one more of surprise than anger.

"Fuck off, I said!" And there is silence. Jasmyn knows I never swear, except when it's absolutely essential. When I need a word to bite; to actually *feel* sound as teeth scrape my lower lip.

I stare with disbelief at the small white stick and close my eyes, promise aloud that if the results change in the next five seconds, I will never have sex again. Then peeking through the slit of my right eye I add another promise: I will never smoke again. I try this a few more times, thinking of all the sinful things I do, but nothing changes. I collect the wrappers and boxes into a plastic bag and tuck it in under my towel, concluding that it's probably a mistake, because I used condoms almost every time. I open the door. Jasmyn's crossed-arm body blocks my way, her mouth squeezed tight and pushed to the side. Our eyes lock and I know she is registering the hairline crack that, if touched, will implode me. I brush by her. She doesn't move out of the way, or retaliate, but absorbs my shove instead. It will fuel her. She will transfer it to someone else later on today.

I met my roommate, Jasmyn, on my first day at the Delcare group home three weeks ago. She was assigned to show me around the house, something she did begrudgingly, ensuring I knew it was the last thing in the world she wanted to do. I followed her toned body squeezed into a black dress, the impatient click-click of her fake red nails tapping on walls when I paused too long. She barely mustered the energy to flick a finger in the direction of closed doors. "There's a bathroom down there, but it don't have no shower, only a toilet, and that room got air conditioning, but you only get it if you have asthma." After showing me only the top floor, we skipped the second and the main levels, down the back stairs, and ended up in the gravel backyard spotted with weeds and overgrown bushes. Jasmyn lit a smoke and leaned against the rotting picnic table.

"Your name's Snow," she questioned, flicking her ashes in my direction, "as in Snow White?"

"No. Snow, as in Snow," I said firmly, my arms fumbling around for somewhere to be. I was unsure if she was messing with my mind, trying to make some black-and-white point. Even though she looked mostly white, her coarse black hair and dark eyes told me she wasn't. And the Jamaican flag tattoo on her right shoulder blade told me she didn't want to be.

"Eh, Snow White," she said. "It's tradition to give your tour guide payment, like a pack of smokes, good ones. If you don't, I'll stash weed in your bag and get you kicked out by tomorrow." She firmly exhaled smoke in my face.

"It's Snow," I said, my blood boiling. "Call me that again and I'll kick your ass." I regretted the words the second they came flying out of my mouth, because I could tell that Jasmyn was one of those girls who wanted to start something for the pure pleasure of it.

"Bitch," she spat back, bolting up from the table and pushing me back into the brick wall. Before I could say or do anything, Jasmyn stormed into the house. I watched her through the glass, talking to a youth worker, fingers ferociously pointing and zigzagging in the air, as if she were spelling out each letter. A couple of minutes later, Pat, the house supervisor, poked her smiling face out the back door. "You must make a good first impression. Jasmyn asked for you to be in her room. Is that okay?"

I shrugged my shoulders unconvincingly, as if it didn't matter, which seemed to satisfy her and she went back inside. And I sat on the picnic table, finishing my smoke. Thinking maybe I was mistaken to believe that leaving my home was the same thing as leaving my life.

.   .   .

I return to my room, hide the plastic bag in with my dirty clothes, and climb into bed. I can't handle school today. I curl up in a fetal position, realize what I'm doing, and then unfold into a straight line. I get all hot and sweaty and I start to see fuzziness out of the corners of my eyes. My heart feels like a basketball thrown up against the walls of my hollow chest. A few minutes later Jasmyn comes back into our room, hair dripping, wet feet slap-slapping the wood floor. She looks my way and kisses her teeth. I switch to face the wall. I feel her eyes on my back and hear the *psshh* of my expensive L'Oréal hairspray. There's a pause and then the *psshh* again and I picture Jasmyn spraying the can into the room like it was air freshener. My hairspray, the cause of many past arguments, seems stupid to me today. Everything seems stupid to me today. She turns the radio on, loud bass vibrates my bed. She tries her hardest to get a reaction out of me, but I retreat under the covers like an unimpressed animal at the zoo.

When Jasmyn leaves there is silence for only a few moments before, next door, Nicole begins her morning routine of refusing to get out of bed. She has composed it well: the rattle-bang of clock radio hitting the wall, the hollow-thump of a pillow, a bass-thud of a foot hitting drywall by my head. And then there are words. Nicole has the foulest mouth of all the girls in the house and can combine swear words together in ways I never thought possible. The chaos is intercepted with Staff's warning of grounding, which means Nicole won't be allowed to visit her boyfriend this weekend. Minutes later, I hear the shower running.

We are a family of women. We have no fathers. Only eight shift-work mothers who proclaim themselves rule-maker, lesbian, feminist, activist, college graduate, do-gooder, "I've been there," and rah-rah cheerleader. Together, they are a collective, featureless being named "Staff." It's unimportant to specifically name them. They are all the same. But no matter what I call them, they're still better than Elsie.

I hear a faint knock which is meaningless, because Staff are entitled to enter any time they want. I stay buried under my covers, closing my small air hole around my mouth.

"Snow, you okay? Feeling sick?" I feel the bottom corner of my bed sink, springs squeaking. It's Miranda, my "primary," the youth worker who has been assigned to me, which essentially means she's the one who is paid to annoy the hell out of me. I know it's her because I can hear the crazy collection of bangles lining both her wrists clang and jingle as she speaks. Fortunately for me, she's the coolest youth worker in the house. She gives us all henna tattoos on our birthdays and sometimes teaches us how to make the wire-and-stone jewellery she sells as a side job. Unlike the other youth workers who recite psychology textbook words from their mouths, Miranda will talk to us straight up. Tell it like it is. Which makes me wish it were Tina at the end of my bed today because if you feel sick, Tina is the one who'll make you tea and tuck you under cozy blankets in front of the TV. Miranda is more likely to just tell you to get the bug out of your ass and get on with it. And Staff lets her get away with this kind of talk because she's the first one to clean a girl's puke or unclog a toilet.

"Yeah, my stomach hurts," I groan, in my most sleepy, pathetic voice.

"Jasmyn mentioned something was up. Should I call the school and let them know you won't be in?" Her voice is warm and soft, unlike the annoyed, harsh tone I heard a few minutes ago outside of Nicole's door. It makes me believe she's up to something.

"Okay." I am taking advantage of this. Of being new. Of being good. Of being a resident who hasn't yet slipped sleeping pills in Staff's drinks in order to extend a curfew. There are benefits to being well behaved in a house of six troubled girls. I am spared the threat of consequences, loss of privileges, and time-outs in a locked room, for now. Staff calls it "honeymooning," because I've only been here three weeks. They are waiting for me to flip onto my damaged side like a helpless bug, legs flicking in the air, so they can reach out and turn me over. They are convinced that one day I will snap: throw a chair, stab a fork in an unsuspecting hand, take the van for a joyride. They can't imagine that any girl who leaves her home is a person in control of her life.

"You've been really tired lately," Miranda says. "A lot. Maybe you've got a bug. Do you want me to make a doctor's appointment for you?"

"No appointments," I murmur from under the covers.

"What about your appointment at four with Eric? Think you can go to that?"

"I'll try," I say, knowing that if I don't go, I'll be on "sick routine" and won't be allowed out of the house tonight. I poke my head out from under the covers, just halfway, my chin still hidden. Miranda is smiling at me. She raises her hand to move her dyed cherry-red hair, cut like a geisha girl's, out of her eyes.

Left alone in the silence of my room, my reality pulsates in my head. Tears start spilling out of me and I press my face to the pillow, muffling the ugly noises coming from the depth of me. For the first time since I've arrived at this house, I want to go home. I want my piss-stained curtain, my Billy Bee glass, my fraying pink towels and sixties flowered sheets. I want things that aren't bought in bulk or bleached white. I want that dull tint of colour: a yellowed mug, a yellowed pillowcase, the yellowed rim around the toilet bowl. I want stains.

"You idiot, you idiot, you idiot, you idiot," I repeat over and over and over again. I clamp my jaw down harder and harder each time, suffocating the words, until my teeth are clenched shut and my tongue spasms about my mouth like a trapped moth. I count backwards. I have missed at least three periods. My mind races through the options. Abortion. Adoption. Keep it. Live with Mark. Wish it away. This baby will ruin everything. I press my hands into my stomach, squeeze skin in my fists, and then push hard and deep into me. I squeeze out the thought of a baby. I squeeze out Elsie's laughter.

And it starts as a fleeting thought. Just like that. Whipping past my mind like a swooping bird. But then it returns, slower this time, lingering long enough for consideration. Till soon, all I'm thinking about is the paper clip on the table beside me. And I need it. I need it. I need the release of me. I reach for the curled wire and decisively open it up. Then I extend my arm and start scraping back and forth, line by line. Pain tingles up my arm, shooting through my numb legs. Thin white lines fade like streaks of dissipating smoke, and so I press harder and harder. And I feel like I'm going to burst if I don't split myself open, so I press a little harder and faster. Till finally skin spreads, parting like clouds, exposing a vast red expanse of me. And I recline back into my pillow, drop the paper clip to the floor, my mother's disappointment seeping from skin like warm red tears.

·   ·   ·

In the afternoon I drape a blanket around my body and head down the creaky stairs to make some toast. They call it a group home, but there is nothing homelike about a group of troubled girls other than the house where they eat and sleep. It stands neglected among other three-story Victorian houses on a shady treed street in the west end. Brown prickly bushes surround its bay windows, cigarette butts are scattered like dandelions, half the lawn is paved for parking, and a British flag lines the top window, even though no one in the house has ever been to Europe. My first day, I stood on the curb with Aunt Sharon and just stared at this house for a good long time before we took a step forward.

Inside it's like a hospital or a motel: a place that is not interested in making you so comfortable that you'll desire a longer stay. If someone was looking for beauty, say an abandoning parent or an optimistic social worker, they might find it—if the lights were low and it was the day after house-cleanup chores. They'd wander through the house and say something like oh, *it's so antique,* while running their fingers along the dark wood trim and hand-chiselled mantel. Or they'd crank their necks and look to the high ceilings and the little stained-glass window in the stairwell and comment on how lucky we are to have such a nice, big house. Perhaps, on a well-chosen day, this visitor wouldn't see that the photos on the Welcome to Our Home bulletin board are replaced so often it's hard to find cork thick enough to hold a thumbtack. Perhaps they wouldn't notice the names penned on food packages in the fridge, the locks on cupboards, the reused blackened birthday candles with dried cake on the bottoms in the kitchen drawer. Perhaps they'd think that jingling noise down the hall is a playful puppy and not the keys dangling from Staff's wrists.

And the girls here are the same. At first glance, they seem normal. But shine a bright light into their corners and you'll see the dirt caked high. They are incomplete, missing parts. Not like

people born without sight or limbs or even without a second
kidney. They are missing the stuff you get *after* you're born, the
stuff that makes you connect to people. It's like I'm talking to
them and they are only three-quarters there. It sometimes makes
me wonder if Elsie actually did something right with me, though
I'd never admit it aloud.

I mostly keep to myself, which seems to suit everyone fine.
There is no one here exactly pleading for my friendship. Because
I go to a regular school in Don Mills and not to classes in the
basements of churches or office buildings, the girls in the house
think I'm a suck-up. They make jokes about my schoolbag and
my pencil case and can't seem to get over the fact that I actually
use my locker. I just laugh off their comments, thankful for this
gap between us, this hour-long commute on bus and subway, a
distance that ensures I am nothing like them. And it's funny that
way: I only know who I am in terms of who I'm not. I am not the
girls in this house. I am no one at school. I am not Elsie.

. . .

At first Carla was envious I moved into a group home. She
thought it sounded cool having no parents around. She imagined
slumber parties and giggling girls giving each other manicures
and lip-syncing to old Spice Girls songs in their pyjamas.

"What are they like?" she asked my first week. I had called her
collect from the phone booth on the corner because at the house
the phone is in the hallway and Staff listens to every word you say,
even though they pretend they don't.

"They're idiots," I said. "Real fucked-up idiots. I don't like any
of them." And I described each one to her.

Jasmyn lived with her mother in Jamaica, but was sent to her
white father's house in Winnipeg when she was six. She ran away

from home eighteen times until she finally took a bus to Toronto when she was fourteen. She's tall, has a great body, and lots of tattoos, but the best one is of a teddy bear peaking up over the top of her nipple. She's a bit of a slut, but it's only Tracy who gets called that because once when Nicole called Jasmyn a slut, Jasmyn pushed her head through the front-door window. "Basically, Jasmyn is chickenshit, but she's got a lot of friends, so watch your back," Tammy warned me. "She also had sex with her dog," she adds.

Tammy is the fattest girl I've ever seen up close, but she has a pretty face. She came from Port-something up north. Apparently she and Jasmyn hate each other, but Tammy's too much of a freak for Jasmyn to care. Pretty much all of the girls say she's crazy. She wears dark-blue eyeliner and her eyes are crossed, though you can barely tell because her bangs cover them. She wears short miniskirts that barely cover her fat thighs and tops that make her breasts look like fleshy stomachs. "She goes out with guys who fuck her two at a time, waddles home with her legs spread wide, crying because it's too sore to close, and then Staff sends her to the clinic on the corner for a STD test," says Jasmyn. "She's a baby. Cries that her stepfather fucked her for three years and thinks that gives her rights to sleep with your boyfriend. Watch your back."

Nicole's downright ugly and there seems to be nothing that can help her looks. The girls have tried, told her what to wear, how to cut her hair. She calls herself Goth, but I think she's just trying to cover that ugly face as much as possible with all that white powder, black eyeliner, and lipstick. She writes things all over her knapsack like *Die, Die, Die* and *Fuck Jesus*. She keeps AWOLing, ending up in Brampton or Orangeville till the cops bring her home. "Nicole's just white trash," Tammy says. "She's a dyke. There are a lot of dykes around here. She hates men but she'll tell you she's bi." Apparently, she got charged last week for beating up some ex-girlfriend with a broken beer bottle at a party. "She and Mute Mary had a thing going," says Tammy, "till Mary started seeing this married guy."

Tracy is the real cocktease of the house. "The slut who will do anyone," says Nicole. "She thinks she's so much more mature than everyone, but just last month she held a fork to Staff's neck and got timed out from the house for two weeks." Everyone but Jasmyn pretty much leaves her alone. Apparently, she'll be moving back in with her parents soon, once she's successfully completed anger management and finishes family counselling. "Watch her though, she'll turn on you just like that," Nicole says, snapping her fingers.

Mary is the quiet one who just stares at me. Everyone calls her Mute Mary, and when she does speak, she raises her voice at the end as if it were a question. Mary has the kind of looks that you can't remember. Looks you can't really describe, just mousy hair and thin lips. "Like white trash," Tammy says. Other than that she seems to be totally normal, and I have no idea what she's here for. Apparently Nicole says when Mary was little her mom would make her use a kitty-litter box instead of a toilet and she ate out of cans until she was six. But no one else knew that. She's been in the suicide ward six times this year and now checks herself in regularly. "She's a nice girl," Staff said, suggesting I join her in the living room to watch TV one night.

"Sounds like a bunch of freaks," Carla said, slightly happier that she wasn't missing out on anything fun.

.   .   .

"How's everything going?" Eric playfully turns in his new swivel chair, pressed between the filing cabinet and the small desk. Each Tuesday at five o'clock the group home forces me to come to this office. It's a condition of staying at the group home. Each Tuesday, Eric sits staring at me like this, rolling a pencil in his fingers as if rubbing a genie lamp, wishing for significant words to come out of my mouth. He thinks he's being subtle, gently coaxing me to release. I sit there, unresponsive, focusing on my swirling stomach, my racing heart. My entire body worries about this pregnancy. All of it. Down to my toes. He clears his throat and my eyes frantically search the posters of rainbows and people climbing mountains for hints of what he wants to hear.

Eric is a long, skinny man, with a big Adam's apple that he tries to cover with a reddish beard. But I like his gentle eyes, poking through the harsh contours of bone, like small pools of water in rock. They tell me he's a good person and that is why I secretly don't mind coming here almost every week. I notice he's wearing the same socks as last week.

"Fine."

"I thought we'd talk about your mom this afternoon," he says carefully, lifting his pencil up to his lips. I look at him suspiciously. Until now we've talked about normal things, like school and friends. I think how ironic it is that he bring up the topic of Mother today. I wonder if he can tell I'm pregnant. I pull one knee up to my chest and pull my sweatshirt over it to cover my stomach.

"You mean my *grandmother?*"

"Oh, yes. I'm sorry. Your grandmother."

"Nothing to say," I reply.

"I think what you mean, Snow, is that you don't want to talk about it, not that there is nothing to say."

I start to get angry—it's the last thing I want to talk about today. "Whatever." I bite off pieces of my Styrofoam cup and then *thhpp* out tiny pieces like watermelon seeds.

"You don't like her?" he asks, leaning forward and moving the garbage pail closer to me.

I forcefully spit a large piece of cup into the bin. "No."

"Any idea why?"

"No." I spit another.

"You can't think of any reasons you'd have such strong feelings?"

"No." I start to squeeze the few remaining pieces of the cup tightly in my hand.

"I know this might be tough to talk about. It hasn't been that long since you left, but it might help you get through this better. You have any ideas on how you came to think this way?"

"No."

"No idea why?" His persistence bothers me. His mouth gaping open and shut like that. He reminds me of a baby bird, its stretched transparent neck frantically bobbing up and down until a juicy worm twice its size is shoved down its throat.

"Well, let's see." I crush the remains of my cup up into a little ball and chuck it across the room. "She's a crackhead alcoholic who lets her boyfriends fuck her, hit her, then leave her. I've had to clean up after her barfing all night, undress her when she's shit herself, and make up excuses when I call the ambulance. That's just part of it, but that may be why I don't like her." Of course, he already knows that. He's read my file. But it buys me some silence in our hour time slot.

Eric's tone changes. "Was she always like that?"

"No. Only during my lifetime."

"That's a lot to deal with."

"Yeah, well, I don't deal with it anymore, right?" I stare at the corner of the table, chew the inside of my cheek.

"You think that because you don't live with her anymore, it's in your past?"

"Yes."

His silence tells me he disagrees. He is funny like that, arguing with the absence of words. It paralyzes me.

"And what about your birth mom. Do you know much about her?"

"No."

"Do you think much about her?"

"No."

"We could talk about it more if you like," he says, getting all comfortable in his chair. And suddenly I hate him. I hate him with all the hate I have inside of me.

"Can I go now?" I ask, getting up and not waiting for his answer.

•   •   •

I thought after missing three lessons Greg would cancel my swimming class. But when I explained to him that I moved into a group home and that my life was pretty crazy for a while, he said he had a gap in his schedule and could squeeze me in on Tuesdays at seven.

It is the only part of my week I look forward to, though today I feel different about this liquid dialogue with my mother. I arrive at the pool deck early, arms folded in front of my stomach, exposed in my swimsuit. I sit on the side, hesitant toes in the water. The lights at the far end of the pool deck are not working and the water appears cold and deep and unforgiving. I look down to my stomach to inspect the slight swell disappearing almost entirely when I sit up straight and suck it in. My breasts, pressed flat against me, are sore and hard, marked with sunken streaks that bend and twist like woodworm paths. A few days ago I had considered these scars a tolerable exchange for late blooming. And now, a hostile infestation devours the person I want to be.

I smooth down the edges of the large patch Band-Aid that covers the scars on my forearm. I have prepared an elaborate excuse to tell Greg, something to do with a curling iron, a ringing telephone, and a slippery floor. This struggle is new to me, me against my body. This constant battle to bury the truths that keep surfacing from under my skin, rising from some unknown depth in me. But things like this happen. I've seen it on Discovery Channel. In England, an entire prehistoric village just surfaced one day in a farmer's best field, after a terrible storm. And the man didn't know what to do. He tried to keep it a secret, his cows munching around the crumbling stone walls. Until the neighbours started talking and the archeological protection people took it over.

There is another girl in my lesson today. An annoying eight-year-old who tells me her name is Kati and then points out her new Tommy Hilfiger swimsuit. She keeps trying to push Greg into the pool while he's explaining the lesson. I can tell he's irritated, holding firm her arms, but he pretends he's amused. Then she starts squealing, annoyingly high pitched, and I just know this little princess is some rich family's spoiled brat. Greg turns to me and in an apologizing tone explains it's just this one time, a favour for his friend who's been sick all week and can't come in to work.

"Just keep her away from me," I blurt out, regretting the words as soon as I hear them aloud. It's obvious from both their expressions that they're taken aback by this. Greg's brow creases with disapproval, and he takes a quick second look at me, as if checking to see that it's really me.

I slip into the shallow end. At first the water is cold and angry, but soon it's buoyant and weightless and forgiving. We practise floating on our backs and then on our stomachs. Kati's body skims the water like a leaf down a river. Greg and I silently stand in water and watch her flutter around like a pinwheel, her hands making little precise circles. I dismiss her natural buoyancy. At eight, you have nothing to weigh you down. Greg taps her on the head and she bolts up, embarrassed. Then she dunks under for a second to fix her hair, and gives Greg a wide smile. "Looks awesome," he says to her. "See if you can roll from back to front and front to back, like a rolling log." And she plunges back into the water like an excited puppy wanting to please.

I move off to the side to try a few reckless rolls on my stomach, until I inhale water and start choking. I burst up, coughing and spluttering, frantically reaching out and then clinging to the side of the pool.

Greg turns to me and his smile disappears. "Before you can learn to swim, you must float, Snow. You've gotta trust the water. If you fight against it, you are going to gasp and struggle," Greg explains patiently as I try to catch my breath. "You need to trust it. See—" he places his hand on the surface of water—"the water wants to hold you up, not pull you down."

I nod my head but I don't believe him. I don't have his faith, his simple trust in water. The cradling fluid we are born in, a cool drink on a hot summer's day, the shallow depth in a holy bowl. I know the danger of just a few drops in a gas tank, in a lung. I question Greg's trust in something that has the power both to give life and to take it away. I question why water is so easily forgiven.

But instead of saying all these things, I say, "The water's too fucking cold." Which makes Greg roll his eyes and leave me alone, clinging to the side.

7

As much as I want to be with Mark, I am afraid to call him. Afraid of what he'll say, that he'll blame me for getting pregnant. He thinks I'm mad at him, ever since a few days ago when he took off with his friends, leaving me waiting at his doorstep for three hours on a Saturday night. As if I didn't have anything better to do. So I try to make myself busy with Jasmyn, tagging along with her to parties I don't care about, just so I won't be home at night, if he calls, which he never does. Finally, he does phone, and even though I pretend I'm busy, he begs me to come over in his sweet baby voice, telling me he needs to see me and that he misses me. And hearing this, my stomach swirls and I can't wait to drop the phone and get over there. Jasmyn was right: ignore a guy for long enough and he'll come crawling back to you, all sweet and horny.

"Hey, babe," he says when I arrive, leading me to his room and then pressing me against the closed bedroom door, Spliff's paws scratching the wood on the other side. He kisses me hard. "Hmmm," he moans when he pulls away, as if he's just tasted a good meal. "Where've you been?"

"Out with Jasmyn," I say, still cold.

"And guys?"

"What do ya think, we're nuns?"

"Oooo, feisty. I like it." He playfully pushes me and I push back. He catches me in a headlock and I untangle through his legs, laughing. He flips me to the ground, my elbow slamming against hard wood and I give out an exaggerated scream as he rolls me over onto my back and pins my arms above my head.

"That hurt," I whine to his smiling face. He fakes like he's about to drop spit down on me and I start to laugh. "Don't! Don't! You better not!" I try to wriggle out of his grip but his hand is tight on my wrist, burns my skin, and when I think he's going to let go, he squeezes tighter.

"Ow!" I squeal.

"Come on, wimp," he growls and I escape his grasp. Mark's knee comes up and hoofs me in the stomach. I grunt and reflexively kick his chin.

"That fuckin' hurt!" I yell, clutching my abdomen.

He laughs uneasily. "Just tryin' to toughen you up, princess," he says, and cradles his jaw, moving it back and forth.

"Well, fuck off!" I yell, getting up. I walk to the bathroom, close the door, and look down into my underwear to see if there's baby on it.

When I come back out of the bathroom, Mark is waiting by the door. He pulls me close to him and gently rubs his hands up and down my back.

"You're different," he says.

"What?" I pull back.

He shrugs his shoulder. "Nothing. You're different than you used to be. I don't know. Harder." I push him away and squirm out of his arms to leave. I don't need this. But he pulls me back and then he whispers in a sweet voice, "Stay a while. I want you to." And I can't stand how he can always make me feel so good like that, especially when I'm most hating him: how just the tip of his finger can let the air out and deflate me into absolution.

"Okay. Till curfew," I say, still cold. He then releases me and walks past me into the bathroom. And I stand there, wondering what I'm doing. Because even though I'm not sure I want to stay, there's also no place I feel safer. It's as if his arms lock down on my sleeping body, freeing and trapping me all at the same time.

I lie down on his bed. I push aside his clothes and flick hash crumbs off the mattress. The little black specks that make me think of the cockroach shit on his kitchen cupboard shelf. Mark shouts over the running water as he shaves, laughs about his landlord's eviction notice that he and Josh are now using as filters for joints because the paper is nice and thick. Then he laughs about his buddy Jake who got busted tonight for B and E. "He walked right out the front door with the fucking TV. What a dick."

He comes out of the bathroom, towel wrapped around his waist. "Hey, beautiful," he says, and I get all warm even though I'm not sure if he's saying it to me or the mirror he's flexing in. He loves his muscular body as much as I do. It's not like the boys' my age, with their struggling chest hairs and pimply backs.

Even though he's had a shower, he still smells of alcohol and smoke. He nuzzles my neck I start thinking about the baby, and I cry as soundlessly as I can, but I know he can feel my wet face. Still, he doesn't say anything; pretends not to notice but moves his lips down to my shoulder. I tell him anyway.

"Well, what are you going to do?" he asks casually, not even pulling back.

"Me?" I question. He stares, oblivious to what I'm trying to say. "What are *you* going to do? What are *you* going to do?" I repeat his words until his face gets it.

"Well, it's in your body."

I look at him in disbelief and then curl away to face the wall.

"Babe." Mark lies back down and strokes my stomach. Then he pulls his hand away and strokes the back of my neck. "What I'm saying is, you're going to have an abortion, right?"

"Ya," I say, but don't tell him it's too late for that. *Stupid, stupid, stupid.* I grate my teeth together, biting hard, cursing myself for leaving it so long.

Mark's body relaxes and he slides his arm tight around me. "Even if you had kept it, I'd be here for you. One hundred percent."

He rolls me over and we have sex, real hard, like he's intentionally ramming the baby. And I let him, pretending I'm really into it, pulling him deeper, thinking the whole time, *It would just be an accident.*

.   .   .

Jasmyn and I are squatted behind the house, under the laundry vent that blows a cloud of clean above our heads. She is trying to convince me to go out tonight. I don't want to let on like anything is wrong so I pretend I'm up for it. Jasmyn isn't like Carla, in fact, she's almost opposite. She's hard and angry and says she'd be a good lawyer because she says she can get her way with anyone. I'm not sure I could ever call Jasmyn a friend, like Carla was, but it doesn't matter. That's what's nice about Jasmyn and me: this funny acceptance that we are each other's last choices.

"Come on. It'll take your mind off things," Jasmyn says, taking a deep drag of a joint. She can tell there's something wrong with me. Something probably about Mark, but she doesn't ask. High-pitched screams come from the kids playing in the backyard next door. "Brats," Jasmyn hisses dramatically. She extends the butt out in front of her for me to take hold. I inhale, watching the flutters of red and blue through the holes in cedars, flickering like the last few spotty frames of an old home movie.

It's a cold walk to the pool hall five long blocks away. The owner, Dan, will give us free drinks, "so long as the guys keep coming for you delicious young ladies." Jasmyn complains the entire way, toes squished in her cousin's high heels. She stops every few minutes to pull down the miniskirt that keeps creeping up into the warmth of her jacket. She asks me to fix her eyeliner smudge because her fake nails are too long—and as I'm doing it, she grumbles at my loose jeans and bulky sweatshirt, "Like my fucking grandmother," she moans. I tell her they're the tightest pants I have, which seems to be an acceptable response because she backs off.

When we arrive it's as if Jasmyn suddenly has cozy sponges on her feet. She bounces in the door, flipping her head back and laughing hysterically as if I just told her the funniest joke. Everyone in the bar turns to look at us and she pretends she's all embarrassed, puts her hand gracefully up to her mouth as if to cover her vulgarly exposed teeth. Her entrance is spectacular, and I don't tell her I see her practising in the mirror late at night. "I'm gonna be an actress," she says all the time, "a fuckin' star."

Dan gives us beers and a group of older regulars immediately call us over to the corner pool table. Most of the men are Italian, standing around smoking cigarettes, hairy stomachs popping through buttons sewed on again and again by dutiful fingers. Those same fingers that tap on the Virgin Mary's porcelain head in the front window, waiting for their husbands to come home. The way I've seen Carla's mom do. Jasmyn flirts, sticks her ass so high in the air you can see the edge of her underwear when she aims her cue. As she's waiting her turn, I see her rub her fingers up and down the cue all erotic-like, then press it tight up against her crotch. I laugh and pretend I'm having a good time, but really all I'm thinking about is my pregnancy. And all I want to do is go home, go to bed, and stop my mind from thinking.

The men can't take their eyes off Jasmyn. Within an hour, Jasmyn's drinks line the bar ledge like trophies. She offers me one of her Singapore Slings, all proud as if I'm the ugly duckling under her wing. I take it and drink it like it's a shot, slamming it down on the counter when I'm done, and the men around me cheer and buy me another. They start crowding around me, fat stomachs rubbing against me, thinking they're going to get some action, but I tell most of them straight up I think they're losers, so they back off. I feel sorry for one guy though, who seems pretty nice, so I don't mind when he sits beside me at the bar, telling me about how bad his marriage is and how I remind him of his daughter, his sweet daughter. He says he hasn't seen her in three years and tells me all the things he'd like to say to her. I start to pretend he really is my father, pretend the words are coming from my own dad's lips. But then, just when I'm feeling close to it being real, he tries to slide his hand up my top. And I get so mad at him for ruining a good moment that I grab his fingers and snap them back until he falls off the bar stool, squatting and squirming and pleading for me to let go. "Fuckin' pervert," I mumble and then flick him away like an annoying insect.

But I am luckier than most. I know this. While Jasmyn spends her life trying to forget her father, I can create mine out of the infinity of things I don't know. How he's the kind of man who plays football on Sunday afternoons with his buddies. Or that he's a great cook and can make chocolate cake from scratch. Or how every now and then, he stops in the middle of an ordinary moment and senses something missing, as if a part of him were walking around out there, somewhere.

Jasmyn waves from across the bar. "I'm going for a walk," she shouts, giggling and tripping over her stiletto heels. She trails behind the man who holds her hand as if she were a schoolgirl at the crosswalk. I wait about twenty minutes, till midnight, then Dan slips me five bucks and calls me a cab because I don't want to be late for curfew.

. . .

Back at the group home I lie in bed with my clothes on, my belt buckle digging into my stomach. The ceiling spins and I happily get lost in its dizziness. I think about how much I love this feeling, this inability to focus. Conclude that if we all lost our bearings every once in a while, we could bear life a little longer.

I fall asleep with the light on, only to be woken by banging and screaming and things breaking apart downstairs. Jasmyn's explosive words surface like air bubbles, popping when they reach my ears. I visualize the melting icebergs we saw in the documentary in class this week; the slow release of trapped air thousands of years old bubbling up through arctic waters. Something tells me Jasmyn's words originate from a depth none of us can perceive.

Staff will stand in the centre of the room tomorrow, hands on hips, shaking heads and whispering things like *what a waste*. Before them will be overturned chairs, scattered board-game pieces, broken mugs, inverted coffee table, and an unscathed TV that always miraculously avoids the fury. They will *tsk-tsk* their way around the room, picking up chicken bones and toast crusts.

They do this every time someone trashes a room, as if they just can't fathom such ingratitude for a home. They don't realize that's just it: we beat the walls to batter any lingering sense of home out of us. We all have this trapped urgency for release.

"Bitch!" Jasmyn yells downstairs and then slams the bedroom door behind her. Although I reached up to plug my ears before she even touched the doorknob, the noise still makes me jump. Jasmyn storms into the room, seemingly unconcerned that I am awake and fully clothed. "I hate this fuckin' place," she says as she rips off her jacket and whips it against the wall. "They think they're my fuckin' parents. They can't tell me nothing."

"What happened?"

"Fuckin' cop throws me in the car, says I'm a frickin' prostitute." She sits on the end of her bed and hurls her shoe across the room. It hits the dresser and knocks over the hairsprays.

"Why didn't you tell him you weren't?"

"I did! We both did. We said we were just fooling around, but he don't believe us. The prick gets up in my face and starts telling me how I'm gonna get killed. How just last week he had to spray down a sidewalk covered with the blood of some girl just like me."

"Who were you with?"

"This guy," she says dismissively.

"From the bar?"

"No, another guy." And we both know she didn't know him. It occurs to me in this moment that I know nothing about Jasmyn.

She throws some scrunched-up money from her pocket onto the dresser. "Not fuckin' worth it, man." And I can't figure out why she's so angry if everyone is right. And then I realize that's exactly why she's so angry.

· · ·

I used to call Carla every day. At the beginning, three times a day. But after a while we keep having the same conversation over and over again, talking about people neither of us knew or cared about. I find myself thinking of homework or my cleaning chore for the week while she is talking. Only her "are you there's" bring me back to her words. And it's depressing because our conversations used to be dizzy overlaps of listening and talking, but now we speak like old people, taking turns and pausing between sentences.

I tell Carla I'm pregnant. I tell her because I have no one else to tell, but part of me wants her to be the last person to know because of how she's always judging people, as if she were some perfect saint. For once, I have silenced her. "Well, say something."

"Oh my God. Holy shit. Oh my God," she finally says. And after another long pause, "What are you going to do?"

"Well, I don't have many options. I have to have it."

"Ya, right," she affirms, and I know she's interpreting my lack of options as a moral choice not to have an abortion because Carla is Catholic and I've seen the pro-life pamphlets her mother keeps in her kitchen drawer. "I'm so so sorry, Snow," she says in the most caring way, as if I just told her I had cancer or something. She is being so serious it starts to scare me and my eyes start to well. "What does Mark say?"

I don't answer. Feel my lip quivering and bite down hard.

"What did he say?" she repeats.

"He thinks I'm having an abortion."

"Figures," she says. "God, Snow. I don't know what to say. How pregnant are you?" I don't answer. My mouth pulls outward and I try to hold it closed. And then the tears come out, all messy and slobbery and I start to gasp for air, tugging at my knotted breath. "Snow?"

"I don't know, maybe three, maybe four months?" I say.

"And you didn't tell me?"

"I didn't know."

"I can't believe you wouldn't tell me."

"I said I didn't know!"

"How could you not know? It's called a period."

"Ya, well, I sort of bled. And I'm still not big. And my tits hurt, but they always hurt." Saying it aloud makes me realize how dumb I must sound. Saying it aloud doesn't even convince me anymore.

"Well, I suppose you're not the first. I know a ton of people who've had them. Even Mary had Jesus when she was just twelve."

"Jesus? What the hell are you talking about?" For someone who says she hates religion, Carla manages to slip it into a lot of conversations.

"I'm saying if Mary had a baby when she was twelve, then maybe it's not so bad."

"Twelve? That's young. But she was a virgin."

"Nuh-uh," Carla says and explains it all to me. She tells me that Mary probably wasn't a virgin. That people only interpret it that way, but really, the word *virgin* at the time meant feisty and independent woman. And it only got to mean no sex when monks hundreds of years later valued chastity. Carla says Mary was probably some young girl impregnated at some high religious ceremony.

"Feisty and independent. I like the sound of that. How do you know all this?"

"Dinner conversation. My mother is a religious freak, remember?" And it's funny that Carla hates her mom so much because the only time she actually sounds intelligent is when she talks about religion.

I imagine Mary as if she were alive today, claiming Immaculate Conception. I imagine her in a social worker's office, heads peeking through the doorway to get a good look at the twelve-year-old pregnant girl. Mary sits there, blue-hooded sweatshirt framing her pale face, brown stringy hair parted in the middle, eyes the colour of turquoise truth. Her hands are folded gracefully in her lap as the social worker with chipped nails passes her a juice and with a raw voice attempts to coax the truth out of her. "Come on now, sweetheart. Tell me who *really* is the father?"

And then there would be Joseph, with jittery eyes and nervous hands rolling into a fist. All worked up by his boys who slap their knees in hysterical laughter at their gullible friend. "Immaculate, my ass," he says to Mary. "Who'd you sleep with?" And Mary would just sit silently like this pillar of purity. Surrounded by unending yapping, while heaven brews in her belly like a swelling ocean.

"Don't tell anyone," I say to Carla before I hang up the phone.

"God, no," she says. "I'll call you tomorrow."

But Carla doesn't call me the next day. Or the next day. Or the next day after that. And at first I think it's just because she has forgotten, because she's like that, but then I get to thinking that maybe she's not calling on purpose. She is probably disgusted that I'm pregnant. Thinks I asked for it. And there's probably a part of her that just can't stand being friends with me now, as much as she won't want to admit it. It's all that Catholic stuff she constantly runs from but will never escape. It's as if she was poured into this religious mould that framed her as a kid, and now, she will never be able to truly move beyond its edges.

8

It starts slowly, like a cold. That slight feeling of being "off." And each day it gets worse. The world outside my body begins to fade farther and farther away till objects in my vision are closer than they appear. I bump into things. I forget things. I cry because I can't remember my locker combination. I feel like I'm wrapped in this thick misty cloud and I can't breathe right and I can't see clearly through the fog in front of me. And I feel so small.

I go to school almost every day, but only because I don't have the energy to make a decision to do anything else. In class, my head is all hazy and I can't focus on anything, and when I talk, words become like cold porridge stuck to the roof of my mouth. I rest my forehead on the desk, for just a second, and the teacher whips some chalk at me. She tells me to not waste her time and to go find a bed somewhere.

Mr. Hensley says I need to eat better. He gives me an apple out of his own brown-paper-bag lunch. He tells me sometimes our bodies just need a break. And then he adds, "Some bodies need more breaks than others." What I can't figure out is that it feels like my mind, not my body, that is breaking. I reach into my bag and apply some lip gloss to make me look more hydrated, so he won't worry so much, though I'm sure he's already seen the dried cracks on my hands.

"Are you menstrual?" Mr. Hensley asks, hopeful, as if this would explain my behaviour.

"No," I say. Normally I would die of embarrassment, but right now I just don't care. Don't care about my math test tomorrow, don't care if I brush my teeth, don't care if I see Mark on Friday or Sunday. It's all the same.

. . .

My swimming lesson is the only thing, beyond school, that I am able to bring myself to do. It's the only other thing that will get me out of bed. I am in the change room that smells of chlorine and disinfectants. An old lady is rambling on in front of me. She's wondering if I'm in the beginner's class. I've seen her before in the pool, in her bright-yellow bathing cap, pushing her flutterboard up and down the lanes. She puts one foot up on the wooden bench and starts smearing Vaseline on her fleshy, veiny legs because she says it makes her swim faster.

"Yes," I repeat, "I'm in the beginners' class."

"Isn't that something," she muses. "I thought everyone in Canada knew how to swim."

"Apparently not," I respond, shrugging my shoulders.

I'm used to this. Used to people looking at me like they don't believe me. As if I had a reason to lie about something so small. Although I don't say it, I agree with the old woman. It was always strange, not swimming, when all my friends did. But I had a reason, a good one, that put an immediate stop to questioning at community wading pools on hot summer days. *Her mother drowned,* friends' parents would explain to each other, as they stared at the odd little girl sitting cross-legged by the pool with her shorts on. *Poor thing,* they'd say and offer me panting dogs to walk around the playground or small children to jiggle plastic toys in front of. *Just try it. It's not hard,* my friends would say, squatted in the water, spraying water out at me from between teeth like deadly water guns. *Go on,* Elsie would encourage and dip her hand down into the water, laughing as I frantically dodged the wicked spray.

I wade waist-high in the shallow end, staring up at Greg who is telling me what we'll be doing. "Okay, Snow. Today we'll learn to open our eyes underwater."

"Doesn't that sting?" I ask, with this stupid nervous smile I can't help giving him when I talk.

"Might a little. But we won't do it for long. It's important to try because you won't always be wearing goggles. It helps you with balance and a sense of direction. Your eyes should always be open." I ignore his words and follow his hand that disappears under his shirt to scratch his stomach. As if answering my prayers, he slips off his tank top and jumps into the water with me, splashless.

"Lie on your stomach and see if you can open your eyes to see my toes." I do what he says, open my eyes to the chlorine sting. It never occurred to me that there is sight underwater. I had always imagined submersion as black emptiness. I open my eyes and see Greg's red shorts rippling like windblown flags, puffing up around his muscular thighs.

Next Greg gives me ten-pound plastic barbells to hold at the bottom so that I don't float back up right away. He tells me to kneel or sit cross-legged and just take a look around. "Have a little tea party down there," he says. Then he gets out of the water, stands on the deck beside the dumb blonde lifeguard with the big tits, and motions for me to start practising. I consider the lifeguard's fat thighs and greasy hair before I turn, find my own space, and face the other way.

After a few dizzy breaths, I clench the weights in my hands and allow them to pull my reluctant body under. My legs fold beneath me, I hold myself at the bottom of the pool, cross-legged like Greg said, and I slowly open my eyes. Strands of hair float weightlessly about me and a Band-Aid flutters by like an indifferent minnow. I notice a high-pitched buzzing noise and am unsure if it's coming from the pool drainage system or the air being compressed in my head. I turn to find the source, and when I accidentally breathe out, a frenzy of air bubbles scramble to the surface like a thousand scattering butterflies. Panicked, I burst out of the water, my mouth wide, gasping for air, my mother's grave no longer a peaceful liquid blue. I cling to the side of the pool, breathless, elbows in the drain, thinking how terribly lonely it must be to be the sole witness of your last breath.

That night, Jasmyn's wheezing breath becomes the air being forced out of my mother's bones. I dream of my mother's half-submerged body. I imagine her eyes, wide and bulging, helplessly searching for something her small unresponsive hand could grab: a ladder, a floating leaf, a stray hair. I imagine the last few bubbles rising from her mouth like silent screams.

And then I wake and stare at the ceiling and wonder, Were my cries calling her to the surface? Did she think of me when that last bubble left her mouth, releasing my name in one explosive final thought?

.   .   .

The next morning my mind is heavy and clouded and I refuse to go to school or even leave the house. My skin itches and smells of chlorine. My mouth is dry, but I can't be bothered to get out of bed and get a drink of water. I can barely muster the stamina to go to the washroom, even though I have to pee every hour. And the thought of having a shower or walking all the way downstairs for some breakfast is overwhelming. I don't want to deal with anything or talk to anyone, even Mark who left me an "emergency" message this morning saying it's real important I call him, but I know it's only because he left his foil of hash in my coat pocket.

All day I hear the floorboards creak in the hall and Staff's whispery *s*'s sneak under the door like hissing snakes. They are "concerned" about me; they bring me ice cream and girlie magazines and offer to rent my favourite videos. They approach my bed all quiet and polite, as if paying respects at a funeral, unsure whether or not to acknowledge the grief.

Days pass like minutes. Each morning Miranda opens the blinds in my bedroom and each morning I crawl out of bed and snap them shut after she leaves. "You need some light in here," she persists, opening the blinds again when she enters the room. Her insistence on sun irritates me, as if this alone would make me feel better.

She draws a chart on Bristol board and tapes it on my closet door. I get a sticker if I get out of bed and more stickers if I shower and even more stickers if I come downstairs. Each day, she visits with me, extra friendly, trying to figure out what's wrong. She thinks she's tricking me into speaking. She believes that if the right button is pressed, I'll spill open. First she tells me she's here to talk, about anything. Nothing will surprise her. Then she tells me about the time when she was seventeen and got dumped by her boyfriend and didn't leave the house for days. She asks me if I would describe myself as feeling sad, or tired, or numb. I tell her all three, and her mouth shuts. I start to feel bad for her, each day returning to figure me out. Each day, looking less and less intrigued with the puzzle of me.

"You can't put your finger on me," I say. "I don't think I'm a pin-pointable problem."

At first Jasmyn is concerned too. She brings me dessert. She twists my hair into tiny braids and ties rainbow-coloured elastics around the tips. She stands by my bed and asks if I want to talk. "Is it about Mark? About your birth mom? About school?" And if it's not about all those things, then it must be about her. I tell her that it's about nothing and everything all at once and to forget it, just leave me alone. Which she does, for a few days, but after a while she gets pissed off that I'm in the room all the time, that it stinks like B.O. and piss in here and that she can't think straight because I just sit like a *retarded lump* and *what am I fuckin' staring at?*

"Stop feeling so sorry for yourself. Get off your ass and do something, for fuck sakes!" she replies to my heavy sighs.

I tell her I don't feel sorry for myself. I tell her I don't *feel* anything, and it's like I short-circuited a button on her body because her eyes start rolling backward, her lips curl up, and her hands start flinging about in the air. Standing there, yelling, she reminds me of Elsie. Only, now, I wish it *was* Elsie. I wish my life were as simple as it was a few months ago. Jasmyn's mouth wildly snaps open and shut, but the air seems so thick between us that her words are gurgled and watery in my ears.

When she leaves, my head is bursting. Ideas are swirling around in a tornado. I feel like there's an elephant sitting on my chest. I lift my T-shirt and glare at the swell of stomach, imagining the baby there, between the ovaries and fallopian tubes, in that vacuous space I never could label on tests. "The Uterus," I remember Ms. Martin saying in grade six, holding her valiant fist up above a class full of baffled eyes, "is the size of a pear."

. . .

The body is generous. The way is just keeps spilling forth liquid. How considerate it is to make tears an infinite resource. And to make blood such a brilliant, beautiful red. Under my covers I carve lines into skin, my mind clear with purpose, my urgent hand releasing the pain out of me. All my thoughts are forced to the tip of a pin. So simple. So focused. The wails in my head become whispers compared to the stifling screams of skin.

. . .

This morning my body wakes up, and for the first time in almost two weeks, my mind wakes with it. I have a shower, I get dressed, I blow-dry my hair. I look at the calendar. It's Sunday. I go down for breakfast where all the girls are. Nicole and Mary at the table, bowls of cereal in front of them. Jasmyn is sitting on the counter-top, her heels kicking the cupboard doors. Tammy is leaning up against the stove with a piece of toast shoved up to her face, gobs of jam oozing out of the corners of her mouth. And Tracy is just inside the back door, one arm stuck outside, no doubt with a cigarette attached to the other end of it. Jasmyn is in the middle of telling the girls a story of how she met this guy last night who's got a Lexus and who bounces at the Diamond so she can get in any time she wants. She pauses for a second when I walk in, disinterested heads turn my way and turn back again to hear the end of her story. And just like that, everything is back to normal. I am back to normal.

"He just wants in your pants," I say to Jasmyn, and then survey the table to see what's left to eat. She jumps off the counter, reaches in front of me, and grabs the last bagel. "If he wants some, he can have some," she says, rolling her hips and doing this sex dance for a few seconds. "He's swee-eet."

We all laugh and I slide up on the counter and listen to Tammy brag about the guy she knows who drives a Mercedes and owns a bar, though she doesn't know the name, but it doesn't matter because no one is really listening to her anyway.

9

It is amazing the secrets clothing can hide: a scar, a bruise, a baby. Pregnancy scares are more regular than periods in this house. The girls announce them as dinner conversation, gulping milk and then smacking their lips: *I'm late again.* And then we all seem to forget about it until the next public announcement served with chicken and potatoes. Only, no one announces it if they *really* think that it's true.

One day, my shirt will silently rise, my zipper will break, or my tits will overflow my bra, and a meeting will be called, a door will be closed, a soft voice will whisper, *Are you pregnant, Snow?* And finally, I will breathe out and let my belly bulge to its limitless shape. *Yes.*

• • •

"Holy shit, girl! Holy shit." We are sitting cross-legged on my bed, Jasmyn is looking at me, stunned. Her mouth hangs open and then she exhales, "Fuuuck."

"I know. I'm screwed." The tears pool in my eyes and blur my vision. I had to tell her, not only because she's my roommate, but she is also my only friend.

"Fuuuck," she gasps again, reaches out to hug me, and I am stunned, as if bumping into the unforeseen glass; it is the first time our bodies have ever touched like this. Jasmyn must feel strange as well. She quickly releases. "Whose is it?"

I shoot her an annoyed look: "Mark's."

"How pregnant are you?"

"Maybe four, five months, something like that."

"Holy shit!" Jasmyn's jaw drops. Her eyes fall to my stomach. She reaches out and pulls up my shirt to get a closer look. "Nah, you can barely tell! You sure?"

I nod my head.

"What are you going to do?"

"Nothing. It's too late for an abortion. Don't tell anyone," I warn.

Jasmyn raises her fingers to her mouth and gestures that her lips are sealed. "That's one thing about me—I'm true to my word. True to my word," she repeats with conviction. And I believe her. "So, what are you going to do?"

"I don't know. I'm just not thinking about it. Not yet, anyway."

"Fuuuck," she exhales and then hugs me again.

.   .   .

I stand outside the public library door for a long time, watch women with small children and old people walk out in friendly afternoon time, holding doors open and smiling at strangers. What is it about churches and libraries that makes people believe that if you frequent them you're automatically a good and trust-worthy person? I stand in the parking lot and bum a cigarette off this Latino guy with bloodshot eyes, who keeps calling me, "Yo, Charlene," and asks me to come with him to some park. I stand there with him until I'm done my smoke and I head into the library.

I casually drift up and down the stacks, picking out books on volcanoes and plumbing, leafing through them with great interest, should anyone be watching. When I finally find what I'm looking for, I stand just to the left of the section and out of the corner of my eye scan the spines of books on pregnancy. A middle-aged woman comes by and seems to purposefully place herself right in front of my vision. She gives me a cold look and I'm sure she knows what I'm up to, so I pull out *Nutrition for Cancer Patients* and move to a carrel where I wait until the coast is clear. The moment she's gone, I quickly grab four books, slide them in the middle of my pile, and go find a table in the kiddy section.

I scan the books, stopping on glossy pictures of smiling couples staring down at bare bellies, the men's large hands spread over the women's stomachs as if they were holding basketballs. I imagine my photograph, in the unwritten chapter at the back of the book, entitled "Teenage Moms." In my photo, I'd be sitting alone in a chair, my round stomach exposed. I'd wear tons of makeup and I'd spike my hair, and I might even be smoking a cigarette because that's what readers would expect.

In another book, there are charts and graphs, but mostly I look at the magnified pictures of glowing eggs: pink, red, green, and orange, like spongy coral reefs or exploding fireworks. The egg I like best is a blue-grey circle with outward-moving rings, as if a stone was just thrown into its centre. In the later chapters, there are lots of photos of fluorescent-orange babies floating in circles of black space, curled like shrimp. Black dots for eyes and pink-grapefruit veins. They remind me of fancy finger foods, served at a party, with a dark pumpernickel bread beneath.

I read that my baby is about eight inches, which I measure with my school-agenda plastic ruler. They say that at twelve weeks, the baby is bigger than an avocado. That it hiccups and has a heart, and had eyelids after only thirty-eight days, though I can't imagine why it needs them so soon.

After seeing all the fetus pictures, the diagrams of women with inflated stomachs and veiny breasts start to catch my eye. I realize that I never thought of how much my body would change between the time of conception and giving birth. This gets me all scared and I become all panicky, as if I was just diagnosed with some terminal disease. I get a pencil from my bag and write down strange words—*linea nigra, areola, fundus, varicose, edema, Braxton Hicks*—but then I start to feel sick, my stomach swirls, and my head gets all hot. I take off my jacket and cover the books, go to the toilet where I throw up, twice. Still lightheaded, I return to my table, rip the magnetic strips out of the bindings, and slip the books into my knapsack.

I leave the library occupying another body. Leave behind my simple hokey-pokey classifications of right foot, left foot, and think about fingernails and eyebrows and that uncertain line that separates the wet part of your lip from the dry part. I think about breasts, nipples, and parts between my legs that I thought were there for sex, parts I never thought of before. I never questioned, really questioned, the stuff that comes out between my legs or why Mark's tongue can command my nipples to grow hard. But now, I walk home thinking about all my muscles and bones rubbing together each time I step and I wonder why all this never occurred to me before.

. . .

They say first love lasts forever. What they don't mention is that it's not really your first love. There are things to prepare most people for this, like the love of a parent, a dog, a grade one teacher, or even a stuffed animal. Really, most people have been loving in multitudes by the time they even kiss someone. But it seems to me that since Mark truly is my first love, he will penetrate my bones.

Mark is not feeling well. He has a cold. He asks me to come take care of him. He doesn't even mention anything about not seeing him for a while. I fill a brown paper bag with treats like orange juice and vitamin C pills and Tylenol and a comic book for him to sketch from. When I get to his apartment, he pouts like a little boy from his bed as I hold his tea with honey up to his lips.

"How are *you?*" he asks me as I scramble around the room picking up balls of crumpled toilet paper.

From the way he says it, I know he's asking about the abortion he thinks I had. That he thinks I've been at home sick for these past couple weeks, recovering. "Fine," I say. "Don't worry about it." And I climb into his bed, ignoring the funny look he's giving me, like he doesn't believe me.

We sleep all afternoon, or rather, Mark does. I tell him I don't care what we do, I just want to be with him. I take off my clothes and cling to his body, my fingers firmly pressed against his chest.

It's one thing to love only one person your whole life. And it's another to have that one person not love you back, not the way you want him to. I'd give anything for him to want me. I stay awake for hours, listening to his soft breath, mouthing the words *I love you* into the back of his neck. And I pray to a God I borrow every once in a while. I pray for him to just give me this one thing, this one small thing I ask for. *Just give me this.*

I wrap my leg over his thighs and Mark squirms, half waking. "You need to shave your legs," he mumbles grumpily, brushing my leg off, pulling his sweaty body away, and returning to sleep. I'm careful to keep my legs on my side, hold my bare chest into him, my stomach pressing into his back.

Mark would be a good father. I know it from the way he moves his marijuana plants around the apartment for optimal sunlight. I know it from the way he falls to the ground to play with Spliff the moment he walks in the door. Or how he talks about his little brother, like he'd give his life for him. And even though I work so hard at proving to Mark that I will love him no matter what, it's only Spliff and his brother who he absolutely trusts. And I think it would be like that with the baby.

·   ·   ·

"So how's it going?" my counsellor Eric asks nonchalantly, as if everything were normal and he were going to just ignore the fact that I'd missed my past two appointments. I notice he's styled his hair differently, brushed it down over his forehead instead of off to the side. It's as if he was trying to look younger or cooler, only trying to look younger makes him only look older.

"Fine," I say. "Feeling better now. Went to school today." It's a small lie. One that I know will make him happy. I don't tell him I have no intention of going back to that school. That I've missed too many classes in the past few weeks. That I'm too afraid of teachers yelling at me, astonished at my nerve, to just walk back into class after so long. I don't tell him I can't take another day of walking down those halls surrounded by stupid people I can't stand. And that I'm sick of dress codes and dumb-ass teachers who have nothing better to do than give you detentions for having bloodshot eyes.

I tuck my chin down deep into my jacket collar and wait for Eric to say something, but he doesn't. Then I notice the little fishbowl on the table. Inside is a single orange goldfish swimming through a pink castle. "Cute fish," I say.

"Yeah? You like him?" Eric gets excited and leans his face up to the bowl. "Bought him today. His name is Freddy." He taps on the glass, the fish ignores him, but Eric sits there staring and smiling anyway, like it's his child or something. Sometimes it seems like I'm a thousand years older than he is. "You want to feed him? I bought these fish treats"—he offers me a little plastic Baggie full of flaky orange things. I shake my head, declining, but then feel bad right away because he seems disappointed. So I reach forward, pinch some flakes, and sprinkle them in.

"What do you think they taste like?" I ask as we watch Freddy frantically suck them off the surface.

"Don't know. You want to try?" He jokingly offers me the bag again.

"Okay," and I dip a finger in and put the thin flakes on my tongue. "Hmm. I think that was steak and broccoli flavour."

Eric laughs and leans back in his chair. I realize that I've sort of missed him. "So," he says, "what have you been doing? Haven't seen you for a while."

"Just sleeping mostly. Thinking. Listening to music."

"Thinking about what?"

"Stuff. School. The house. Mark. Stuff."

"Did you eat?"

"A little. Not very hungry." He writes something down and I feel the need to explain before he jumps to his therapy conclusions. "I get like that sometimes, just need some time off, you know? Away. Only, I can't go away, so I just go to sleep."

"Were you thinking about your mom?"

"No."

"Your grandmother?"

"No," I shoot him a look of surprise and then annoyance. "She's the last thing on my mind."

"Can we talk about her? Our conversation sort of stopped short last time."

"Whatever," I respond, pissed off that he's pulling out the psychobabble, just when we were having a normal conversation.

"Have you talked to her?"

"No."

"Do you want to talk to her? I mean, are you trying to avoid her?"

"No. I'd talk to her, like if I saw her in the street or something. I'm not mad at her. I just don't want to go over and have afternoon tea, you know?"

"Do you worry about her?"

"Sometimes." Eric stays silent and I can tell he is waiting for me to say more, because he moves his finger up to his lips and gently taps, as if signing for me to talk. I roll my eyes, realizing the truth is the shortest way out of this one. "Sometimes I wonder who's looking after her. I did pretty much everything for her, shopped, cleaned. For all I know she could be dead for a week, lying on the floor. It's not like I wonder that all the time, it just crosses my mind."

"Well, how would you feel if I said she's okay?" I look at him. "She called me. Said she wants to see you."

"She called you?" I ask, annoyed and shocked all at once.

"Yes."

"Why the fuck would she call *you?*" I can't stand the thought of Elsie talking to Eric. I think of how she used to talk to Mr. Hensley, convincing him that I'm the one with the problem.

"Maybe she misses you."

"Ha!"

"She wants you to go by the apartment."

"She probably needs me to do something for her. She probably wants me to clean."

"Do you want me to ask her to come in? All three of us?" His words send panic all over me.

"No," I blurt out like an idiot. I don't want him to know her. I don't want him to see her. I'd be too embarrassed. "I'll stop by. See what she wants."

·   ·   ·

I pick a time when Elsie would be out at work, figure I'll just leave a note. But as soon as my hand touches the doorknob to the apartment, I know she's there. I hear the TV and smell the Marlboros. And then, as I walk in, something strange. Floor cleaner?

I almost don't recognize the kitchen. At first I think she's painted it, but then I realize that the original colour when it's clean is white, not dull yellow. There aren't any dishes in the sink and the table is cleared of magazines and ashtrays and unopened bills. There's even a new rug by the fridge, blue and green, with yellow circles on it.

"Elsie?" I yell. I peer around the doorway and into the living room. Comforted with what I see: just like it always is, messy, worse than ever. The radio and the TV are on. "Elsie?" I head to my room and find Elsie's back emerging from the closet. My clothes are piled on the bed.

"Oh, hi," she says, as if she wasn't surprised to see me. "Just in time. You want some of your clothes? I'm cleaning out the closet and putting my stuff in. I need the space."

"I have what I want," I answer coldly, knowing that she just wants to get me angry. "Give it away to the less fortunate. Oh, no, sorry, that would be me." She doesn't respond, scratching the hangers along the metal bar. Only she's pulling them so fast, I know she's not really looking at the clothes. "I can't stay."

"Yeah, okay. I'm busy anyway."

"What happened to the kitchen?"

"Me and Barb cleaned it. It was her idea." Barb used to be our family social worker, years ago. But now she just works with Elsie. For some reason, she likes her. She tells me that my grandmother is a good person in a bad life. When she says this I'm tempted to tell her all the things that could change her mind, but I don't. Because if Barb looks out for her, that means I don't have to.

"How's that shelter you're at?"

"It's not a shelter, it's a group home."

"Well, whatever it is, how is it?"

"Fine." I glance around the room. She's been sleeping in here, but everything else looks pretty much the same.

"Good." She turns around, puts her hands on her hips, and looks me up and down. I look away. "Jesus Christ, what the hell have they been feeding you? You're fat."

"I am not." I look down at my body to confirm there is no sudden bulge.

"You pregnant?"

"What? You crazy?" I deny, wondering how she could possibly guess. And there's no way I'd tell her, not face to face, to see the satisfaction in her eyes knowing that she was right about me all along. I cross my arms and look around the room. "You haven't moved my stuff," I say, trying to distract her.

Elsie ignores my comment, her eyes fixed on me. "Don't be getting pregnant or you'll end up a no-good mother like me." She starts picking up clothes off the ground. I consider denying it once more, but let it drop.

"You're not a bad mother," I say, more out of obligation.

"Hah. One daughter's dead and my granddaughter's at a shelter. I'm a bad mother."

"It's a group home. And besides, there's always Aunt Sharon."

Elsie glares at me when I say this. "I didn't plan it this way." She fumbles in her shirt pocket for a cigarette.

"I know." And for a second there it almost gets nice. It's so pathetically nice, I feel like we're in a movie.

Elsie lights her smoke and then shoots an angry look at me. "I'm not gonna change, so don't get your little therapy people to call me."

"What are you talking about? I didn't get anyone to call you."

"That guy"—she waves her cigarette in the air—"that guy asked me to come in and talk, 'open up lines of communication, start the healing,'" she says in a mocking voice. "Fucking dick." She storms past me out into the living room.

"I didn't tell him to call." I pursue her into the room, enraged that Eric lied to me.

"I can just see you in that little office," Elsie says, now picking up newspapers from the coffee table, "acting like some little fucking princess who's got it so bad. Did you tell him how you fuck any guy who says boo to you? Did you tell him about beating the crap out of that girl last year? Or that your boyfriend is a drug dealer?"

"Shut up!"

"You didn't tell him about that, did ya?"

"Shut up! You don't know anything about Mark. You don't know anything about me, so don't go saying shit you don't know about."

"Tell your shrink not to call. I sure as hell don't need anyone tellin' me how awful I am."

Suddenly I get the urge to flee. My head rushes, my heart pounds, and I just need to get out of there, for good. "Don't worry, *Grandma*." I turn and look around me for something to pick up. Something to take with me. Anything. "I can tell you that myself." I pick up the clay pencil holder, the one I made in grade three. I pass her in the kitchen, now sitting at the table, staring straight ahead, deeply inhaling her cigarette as if she wanted her body to get sucked right into the filter.

I slam the door behind me. My head swirls and I have to hold onto the wall for balance. I look down and see my hand clenching the pencil holder and I wonder why I took it. I think of the lady in the building across the road, whose basement apartment burned down when I was a kid. All she saved was some old jacket she hadn't worn in years. She just knelt outside of her smoking apartment, clutching this ratty coat, and, in between wails, listed off all the things that were going up in smoke: *my photos, my wedding ring, my CD player.*

As I'm walking to the bus stop I begin to taste sour tears in my mouth. I feel like a moron when I pass by some guys chilling on a bench, liquid pissing from my eyes. I lift my hand to wipe my wet face and I'm suddenly engulfed with the smell of Elsie. In my sweater. On my skin. Like she's inside me, seeping out of my pores. I spit on my hands, rubbing them together, washing her off me. Then I frantically start wiping my face, hard and rough with my scratchy wool sweater, until my skin burns.

·   ·   ·

Eric's office door is closed but I push it open forcefully. "Don't talk to her," I command. Eric looks up from the client across from him, a small freckle-faced boy, only about ten.

"Excuse me, Snow. Not only are you being rude, you're inter-rupting my session." He quickly rises from his chair as he speaks. His face is red, and though he's trying to hide it, I've never seen him so angry. "I'll be done in ten minutes if you want, but you're going to have to cool down first." He shuts the door in my face and I am so mad my body burns. I kick the door and storm down the hall, past the washroom, and out to the back of the office building. I pace back and forth in the gravel parking lot, kicking at stones and car tires. I drag my hand along the top of the mesh-wire fence and stop in my tracks when skin rips on a sharp broken wire.

"Ouch!" I raise my finger to my mouth and the sweet blood and bitter dirt dissolve on my tongue. After a few seconds, I inspect the injury. The cut is deep and thin and clean. I pull the skin apart, hoping for a glimpse of bone. Disappointed, I tightly grip the base of my finger and press upward toward the tip, as if squeezing the last bit of toothpaste from the tube. A line of blood pools on my purple finger. And when there's enough, I walk over to the back door, take my red ink, and smudge the letters *f-u-c-k* on the cold metal.

About a half-hour later, I'm back standing in Eric's doorway. He is writing something at his desk and doesn't appear to notice me.

"Don't call her," I say.

"Come in." Eric motions me to sit down without even raising his head. Then, after a few seconds, he gets up and comes to sit at our table. "Now, what's all this about?"

"Just don't fuckin' call her."

"I didn't call Elsie. *She* called me, then I called her back, but then she didn't have anything to say so I asked her some questions."

"You didn't call her?"

"No. I only returned her call."

"Swear you didn't call her?"

"Yes. She said she wanted to see you."

"She told me you called her."

"What can I say?" He raises his open hands, like he's at a loss, like he's all innocent. "I'd tell you if I did, Snow. She called me first, left a message saying she wanted to see you, so I called her back."

Then it occurred to me. "Did she sound wasted on the message? All funny, like slurring?"

"I'm not sure, maybe. Sounded like she just woke up."

"Shit," I mutter, kicking the table leg. Eric starts shuffling papers, seemingly organizing, but I see the corners of his mouth upturned. He thinks this is a breaking point. He will bend me back and forth, till I heat and crack. "You don't know her," I say. "You don't know me. We're not some little stupid therapy people who don't get it. She gets it. She gets all of it. Just like me. I get it. How come we're the only people that can accept that?"

"I'm not following you."

"No, of course not. That's the point. You can't understand. Just leave her out of it."

"She's part of it. She's part of you."

"She has nothing to do with me." I lean forward, half out of my chair. "She's fucked up. And I made a choice. A *choice* to leave and not let her fuck me up. Don't you get that? What am I supposed to do? Stay? Dissect it? Make it better? I owe her nothing. She screwed up my mother's life, she screwed up mine." I sit back down, lean on the table, and rest my face into the crook of my arm. I can feel myself getting upset and I don't want Eric to see.

"Of course, I don't want you to be in an unsafe place. And you're right, I did want to patch things up because I feel it's important for people to get along. I think that if they do, there's less pain. Pain for you. And I don't mean pain the way you're thinking. I mean pain like anger, resentment—that stuff eats away at you."

"That's bullshit. I made a *choice* to leave," I yell into my arm.

"Yes, but you didn't get to choose for a long time. You didn't get to choose the mother you got." His words burst through to my centre like an atomic bomb, clearing out all that's inside, leaving my unsupported bone to crumble. And then I notice my hand is clutching my belly, like it's trying to hold it up, keep it from falling with the rest of me. And I pull it away, all pissed off, like it's betrayed me because I didn't even command my hand to do that.

10

Since I stopped going to my regular school a few weeks ago, the group home is making me go to the Delcare Day Program. Like seeing Eric, it's a condition. A barter for my stay. They give me a house, I give them a chance to change my life.

I never thought I'd ever go to church, but that's where school is, in the basement, so I walk through the doors of God every day and come out feeling none the better. It's creepy down there, pictures of Jesus hanging in the bathroom, organ songs filtering down through the vents in the ceiling. It's as if I've been placed in God's dungeon, my secret sin burning in my belly.

It's called a section nineteen classroom, which makes you feel like you're part of a mental institution or something. Apparently, some of the school's classrooms really are for the retarded and psycho, but they're located across the city. The Delcare classroom is for "youth in care," which means that we are all fucked up in some kind of way. Most of us are forced to be here by either a social worker, probation officer, group home, or desperate parent offering her kid a last chance. There are ten of us delinquents, one teacher, and a youth worker, Sheila, who talks to us about our problems and gives the girls maxi-pads when they have their periods. We're here because by law we must be *serviced*. Which makes me think I must be fixable, like a car or VCR.

I pull out my binder right away and pretend to start working. There are seven of us in class today. We sit in neat rows and stare dozily at the mural of blue fish, burning bushes, and other godly things on the adjacent wall painted by the Sunday school kids. Last week, Kevin drew a hard-on on one of the fish and turned a burning bush into a giant spliff, but the teacher hasn't noticed yet. We cherish this silent rebellion in our room. It's our only sense of belonging here.

Ms. Dally marches into the classroom, carrying her trendy metal coffee mug, eyeing our seven awkward bodies folded in metal chairs, elementary school desks crushing our legs. She is a middle-aged woman who you can tell was once pretty, but her features are now dull and somewhat flattened, like a worn carpet. She wears Gap clothes and wood-bead necklaces and claims she has a tattoo of a mermaid on her back, but none of us believes her. When Ms. Dally is in a good mood, she'll bring in photos of her trips to Africa. If she's in a bad mood, she'll lecture us about self-respect and accountability.

She scans the room, disappointed daily with her apathetic pupils. "Tracy, is your homework in? Barry, where's your binder? Kevin, feet off the desk, cell phone away. Does anyone have a pen to lend Michelle? Did it occur to you that you'll need something to write with? What do you people do in the morning? Don't you think, 'Hmm, I'm going to school, so I might need a pencil?' Truly, it's unbelievable."

Kevin's hand darts up, straight and purposeful, fingers wiggling.

"Yes, Kevin?"

"Can maggots crawl up your ass?" He reaches his hand back between his butt and his chair and starts rubbing his jeans.

Ms. Dally's face hardens. "Get to work."

"No, I'm serious," Kevin continues. "Last night I was taking out the garbage—"

"Stop it." Ms. Dally moves in close to his desk. Kevin ignores her command and turns to face the rest of us.

"And there were all these white maggots crawling around . . ." Everyone but Ms. Dally starts laughing because Kevin is making these stupid faces as he strokes his butt.

"You need to stop it. Now!"

"And I think some got on my shoes and they crawled up my leg and somehow made it to my ass 'cause it's really itchy today."

"Get out," Ms. Dally says, disgusted. She takes back his math book.

"What?" Kevin looks up at her, laughing as he speaks. "What did I do wrong?"

"Get out," Ms. Dally repeats, gesturing toward the door. Sheila, the youth worker, moves in as backup.

Kevin packs up his books, mumbling under his breath. "Can't even ask a question . . . can't even breathe in here . . ." He gets all mad and kicks a chair on his way out.

Once he's gone, Ms. Dally continues on with her routine, unaffected, and I open my math book. It's not an uncommon beginning to a day, considering the load of shit we drag behind us into this place, a room where we know it can be dumped and not thrown back in our faces. Still, it always looks ridiculous when you see someone else flip out.

The school's a joke, and everyone knows it. We are given textbooks with corresponding fill-in-the-blank sheets. Our tests aren't even typed. They're handwritten bits of paper pieced together from other "real" schools. In the afternoons we talk about anger management, sex, drugs, homosexuality, racism, body image, and conflict resolution. We are given time-outs, time back, and privileges for doing our homework. Some students, like me, attempt to take things seriously, put in the effort to actually earn a worthwhile credit. And Ms. Dally likes us best, actually making up good assignments and writing comments on our work.

Ms. Dally writes today's date on the board and then stands at the front of the small room and passes out photocopied math sheets that are far too easy and don't require explanation. The students take them without complaining because it's better than any real work. But I insist on having real math, and so I get my own individual assignments. Ms. Dally comes over to check my homework and then writes the textbook pages on the blackboard. "Just let me know if you're really stuck," she says nicely, and walks back up to her desk to finish her coffee. I watch her flutter papers and stare down Kamar, who is refusing to open his math book. On good days, she tells us she loves her job, though I can't imagine why.

"It's a class for retards," Tyler, a grade nine student who wears a bike chain around his neck, said on my first day in class.

Ms. Dally corrected him: "We are all here for our specific reasons. You're all working on getting back into the regular system, and what's keeping you out has nothing to do with how smart you are."

"Well, I'm a retard—that's what's keeping me out," Tyler turned and said to me.

"Rubbish." Ms. Dally's consolation was well intentioned, but unconvincing.

Later I peeked into Tyler's open file on the table and read that his mother has a brain tumour, that he's been to fourteen different schools and was expelled for threatening to cut off his last teacher's breasts. And then I got a feeling I knew why he wore that chain around his neck.

.   .   .

Carla and I barely talk anymore. In the past month she's called twice and it's only because she has something to brag about. Sometimes I feel like calling her, but when I do, I usually can't wait to hang up. And afterward, it just leaves me feeling empty, like I'm witness to a long slow death of something that was once so alive. It's painful to see, right before my eyes. I just want to take a knife and put it out of its misery. And so I do.

I start to tell Carla about my swirling stomach and my sore boobs, but she cuts me off and launches into her weekend with her new boyfriend Brian and how he's going to buy her a guitar. The thing about Brian is that he's thirty-six years old and I think it's totally disgusting.

"He doesn't seem that old," she explains. "You gotta meet him. You'd think he's just in his twenties." She tells me he's really, really nice and that he doesn't pressure her to have sex at all and that his stomach is a little flabby but it's kind of sexy that way. She says her father doesn't mind, because he'd rather Carla date an older guy than some seventeen-year-old punk. Carla is working for Brian's trucking company and says it's way better money than a part-time job at the mall. She's not going back to school. I think it all sounds gross.

"I think you should be careful," I say.

"Why?"

"Well, he's so old, you know? He could be some pervert."

"What the hell? Did you just hear anything I just said?" she asks, instantly turning on me.

"I—"

"How could *you* possibly judge *me*?"

"I—"

"Fuck you," she blurts into the phone and the line goes dead. Normally, I would call her back and we'd fight for a while but then we'd be okay. This time, though, I call Mark instead, and he tells me she's not worth the effort.

.   .   .

At my last official swimming class I do my best to swim the width of the shallow end, only it seems as if my body's direction is up instead of along the water. My arms are like concrete, I heave them out of the water and then slap them down hard. My legs trail, half sinking behind me, until I remember every once in a while to kick. I see Greg out of the corner of my eye, a haze of red, as he walks along the deck. I can sense his eyes on my open, sucking mouth. I try to hide my face in the water, only I end up inhaling a mouthful of liquid. My feet drop to the bottom, and I gag and cough until the air comes back into my lungs. Then I feel a gentle tap on my head and look up to find Greg kneeling before me. "You're not breathing out," he asserts.

"Yes, I am," I say, like a denying child.

"I don't see the bubbles."

"I *am* breathing out," I say stubbornly, then push my feet off the bottom to continue plowing through the water, a forceful, splashing kick behind me. I try to breathe on my right side, away from Greg's watchful eye. I hold my mouth firm in the water, breathing in and out quick gasps of air only when my face surfaces. The notion of expelling needed air into water seems crazy to me. At school I learned that the Inuit word for breath and soul are the same. This makes perfect sense to me.

I stop after a few strokes to see if Greg is still looking and I'm relieved to see he's over by the office, talking to the blonde life-guard, who hugs her flutterboard to her chest. I try one more length, but before I reach the end, I inhale another mouthful of water. Panicking, I dart above the surface, gasping for air. When my eyes clear, I see Greg, cross-armed on the deck above me, shaking his head with disapproval. "Fuck it," I yell, slapping my hand against the water, its sting satisfying. I haul my heavy body up over the side and onto the deck. Then I grab my towel, wrap it around me, and storm over to the bench. I sit there a while, staring out to the water, sulking like some five-year-old temper-tantrum freak. For some reason, I don't care if I flip out at school or at the house, but here, in front of Greg, I'm embarrassed. Despite my wishing him away, he comes to sit beside me on the bench.

"You feeling okay?" Greg asks.

The way he says it makes me suspicious. "What do you mean?"

"Well, I don't really know how to say this, other than just saying it." He pauses a moment. "Are you pregnant?"

"What?" I turn and glare at him. "What did you just say?" The shock is real. I can't believe he's just come out and asked. I get up to leave. "No," I affirm, standing above him. "God, no."

"Okay," he says apologetically, patting the bench. "Sit down. I'm sorry. I shouldn't have said anything."

I don't want to sit, but if I leave, it will look like he was right, so I plunk back down. We both silently stare out to the water. I clench my jaw and get all shaky. It's as if my body wants to take off and run.

"My sister did that," he says, nodding in the direction of my bandaged arm.

"Now what?" I ask, whipping my arm behind my back, pretending I have no idea what he is talking about.

"She covered it with Band-Aids too," he continues. "I just couldn't figure it out. She got lots of counselling and one day she just stopped. Just like that. And now, she's totally fine."

I am mortified. My private, bodily act exposed. As if a door were flung open and I were caught, pants to my ankles, wide-legged on a toilet. I cower away from him, trying to cover as much skin as possible with my towel. I feel like an idiot. He thinks I'm a little kid. He thinks I'm crazy. He has thought this all along about me. That's why he's been so nice. I feel compelled to explain myself. Give him a reason he can understand.

"My mother drowned," I announce, figuring this will explain my actions. Maybe silence him.

"Whoa," he exhales. "I'm sorry . . . I mean . . . that's awful . . . I didn't know . . . I don't know what to say."

"It was a long time ago." I shrug my shoulders. We both sit there, silent. I extend my foot out into the small puddles on the deck and draw swirly shapes with my big toe. Greg just leans down, his hands clasped around either side his head, hair dangling around his face.

Finally he rises and turns to me, his eyes bright with enthusiasm. "You know, I can still teach you swimming. You don't have to pay. We could meet when you want to, at the pool. It could just be casual. On a Saturday afternoon or something."

"You don't have to . . ."

"No." He pats my towel-wrapped leg, though his hand isn't flat, it's in a fist, as if he doesn't want me to get the wrong idea. "No, really, I'd like to."

"Okay," I agree, more to get rid of this moment than anything else. And he goes to the office to write down his phone number. When he turns his back, I jump to my feet, run to the change room, and throw my clothes on over my wet swimsuit. As I rush away from the building, I keep looking over my shoulder, worried that truth will catch up to me, and slip his number in my pocket.

11

Thoughts of you come to me, in quiet moments, in class or lying in bed. Moments when I feel you move inside me, like popping bubbles under my skin. Moments when I think, *I can actually do this*.

I imagine myself pushing a stroller through a park. Bright-coloured leaves are crumpling under baby-carriage wheels. It's a sunny Saturday morning and there are kids and dogs and squirrels raising curious heads. I point over to the big crows the size of cats and say, "That's a crow, *caw, caw*," and you smile up at me and gurgle-laugh. Other new mothers are chatting on the bench and older moms are in the playground extending safety-net arms for toddlers climbing plastic trees. When they see me, they come to peek into my carriage, oohing and ahhing at my little baby. People who used to scowl at my inflated belly now smile and compliment me, actually envious of something *I* have.

They look up at me and ask me your name, and I'm about to respond, only then I realize that the face they look into is not mine but that of a woman in her late twenties. And I realize I am nowhere in this scene. This scene is not mine.

It belongs to this blonde woman with styled hair and perfect teeth and expensive skin. She's wearing a nice suede jacket with a brown scarf and leather boots. I've seen her before, in Pampers commercials or formula ads in parenting magazines. She's the kind of woman who never burps, and who prefers to use a condom because it's least messy that way. She's the kind of woman who is a good mother.

• • •

Jasmyn tells me she knows tons of girls who've had babies, even as young as fourteen, and they're fine. She says you miss out on a lot, but once you have a little kid, it doesn't seem to matter much. On a Sunday afternoon we shut our bedroom door, put the chair up against it, and I bring out my library books to show Jasmyn. We sit facing each other, cross-legged on her bed, and I turn the book upside down so she can see the pictures while she files her nails.

Jasmyn lowers her hands when I show her the diagrams of the growing baby. "I can't believe that's inside of you!"

"I know," I say and point to more photographs of a fetus at one month, then two, then three.

"Look, it's got little fingers," she says, all excited, pointing to a drawing of a fetus supposedly in the womb. "How old is yours now?"

"I don't know. About five months?"

She puts down her nail file and starts turning the pages, stopping at the picture of a four-month-old fetus in its amniotic sac. "Oh my God," she says, stunned, "it's like a little person already," and she passes me the book. "Look!"

"I know," I laugh, uncomfortable with her amazement, my smile fading fast. She puts the book down and lies back on her bed. I lie down beside her, flat out on my back, kicking the pile of books off with my feet.

"Show me it," Jasmyn says, motioning to my stomach. I raise my bulky sweatshirt and reveal a bulging tummy, my belly button stretching wide. Jasmyn reaches out and places her hand on my skin. "That's the weirdest thing," she says.

"Do you think Mark'll marry you?" she asks, stretching her leg out and up against the wall. She reaches out for the classified section of the newspaper I have beside my bed and peruses the marks I've been making on one-bedroom-apartment ads.

"What, are you from the fifties? Marry me, 'cause I'm knocked up?"

"Well, whatever," she says, mildly annoyed. "You know what I'm talking about—living together."

"I don't know. I was just looking to see what was out there," I say, referring to the circled classifieds. "Maybe someday." I pick at my nails and attempt to bite off a jagged edge. "After the baby is born. We're still young, you know."

"That'd be so cool. Fuck, I envy you. Your own place. We'd have some wicked parties, man, wicked."

"Ya." I smile. And even though we're just talking, it feels good to say it. Even though we probably both know, deep down, that it's not going to be like that.

.   .   .

Girls hate Jasmyn, call her a slut and cocksucker, but really, they're just jealous. She plays to their envious eyes, giving scornful girls the finger as they scowl at her stepping into the passenger seat of *his* tinted-window car, a child's shoes dangling from the rear-view mirror. She comes home with new earrings, clothes, plastic nails; things that are given to her as if they are presents, not payments. She adds up her profits and replenishes her purse with condoms from the jar in the front hall. She prefers to be given things she can sell, keeping the money in a sock to save up for acting classes. The girls who call her a slut say she'll suck cock for anything, and they're probably right, but Jasmyn claims she won't do it with just anyone.

"They've gotta be decent, you know what I mean?" she'd say and I'd nod my head, while definitions of *decent* would run through my mind. Clean fingernails? Kind to his mother? Someone who drops her off afterward?

Jasmyn's world is large. She seems to know everyone. We hang out almost every day now, around the Dufferin Mall, chilling with whoever is around. And we can't walk more than ten feet in our own neighbourhood without some man hissing or mumbling something perverted to her as we pass. Jasmyn walks down the street in her tight miniskirts and low-cut shirts like she's a star, never tired of the attention, turning and smiling at all the right moments. Sometimes young women with little babies on their hips storm up to us, shake their fingers in Jasmyn's face, and warn her to stay away from their men. And then all of a sudden Jasmyn will turn into this stranger I barely even recognize, get right up in the ladies' faces and spew foul words.

"What would your man want with *that* if he could have this, bitch?" she says one day, shaking her ass in the air, just making the lady flip her lid. There is cursing back and forth and at some point the woman walks away, mostly because the kid on her hip is bawling and Jasmyn is acting so psychotic it's obvious she won't let it go. Still, Jasmyn's voice trails behind the diminishing woman like a persistent thread, unravelling her confidence.

When she's finally out of sight, Jasmyn starts laughing, like it's all one big joke. She keeps going on about herself—"What would he want with that if he can have this"—over and over like she's idling down. We stand in front of a store while she walks in circles, spitting on the ground, still staring in the direction of the disappeared woman. I'm embarrassed by her. Also annoyed, because I don't think it's right she gets together with other girls' guys. I ignore her and stare into the window, unsure what to do because part of me thinks she'll turn on me right there if I say anything. She starts going on a rant about those baby moms, those stupid bitches, thinking just because they get pregnant means they have some right over their men, pretending they don't know their men are humping like stray dogs in back alleys. Whispering to small hands around their dicks: *Don't you want my baby?*

"I can't help it if they're stupid bitches. It's not my problem they can't control their men."

I half listen to her and consider what excuse I can make up to leave since she's rousing me all up and I can't handle this now. Just when I'm about to go she turns to me and speaks in a soft voice, like she's just now noticed I'm there.

"But your situation's totally different. I mean, Mark loves you," she says.

"What?" I dart an evil look at her. "I wasn't even thinking that," I say defensively, because I really wasn't. I'm pissed that she would even think I'd associate myself with that world. And then I start to wonder that maybe this is what Jasmyn really does think of me. That I got pregnant on purpose to keep Mark. That here I was thinking how pathetic her life was when all along she's probably thinking the same thing about me. And somehow, this realization, this mutual sense of superiority, changes everything between us. Because, really, the only way I could handle her was in knowing that I was so much better. It just never occurred to me that she believed the same about me.

.   .   .

I manage to avoid Jasmyn for the next few days, which is surprisingly easy to do, considering we share a room. I turn out the light when I hear her coming up the stairs, I get up extra early, and after school I go to the mall. But I can't avoid seeing her tonight. Every Wednesday night the group home has the creatively named Wednesday Night Group. Participation is compulsory and it's one of the few times a week all the residents are sitting in a room together. Sometimes we just have house meetings, sometimes we discuss issues like homophobia or body image, and sometimes we have guest speakers. Whatever it is, at seven o'clock we gather in the TV room, sprawl out on couches and chairs and the floor. Since none of us will be going out tonight, we have our hair pulled back, track pants on, and we have zit-cream-dappled skin.

Tonight Pat, the house supervisor, starts off the meeting, making some announcements about the broken washing machine and the problem of rotting vegetables in the fridge. Then she turns, smiling to the college student youth worker: "Michelle is going to lead the group tonight. She'll be talking about date rape and healthy relationships." Michelle is a third-year college student and has been working at the house for about two months. She tries to act mature and tell us what to do, but she looks no older than us, and I can see the piercing holes that line her ears, so I don't know who she thinks she's kidding, pretending she's all mature. None of us really listen to her because she doesn't tell us off when we say something rude and at moments of tension she'll crack a joke.

Our eyes turn to Michelle who is in the corner, poring over her notes. She motions to Pat that she just needs a second and so Pat opens up the floor to concerns. We decide to change the bath-room air-freshener spray from flowery to citron spray, Tammy will be after Nicole on the morning shower schedule, and Thursday nights will now have TV sign-up.

"Okay, guys!" Michelle claps her hands together, indicating she's ready to start. "I've been really looking forward to this." She sits positioned in her straight-backed chair, notebook on her lap. We listen attentively because we are all just grateful that it's not one of the regular boring Staff leading the group. "I thought we'd start with a little game, just to get things going!" She speaks slowly and simply, as if we were in kindergarten. She explains that we'll go around in a circle and we each have to contribute one word to an ongoing chain story. It sounds stupid, but once we start it becomes fun, even though Michelle's fading perma-smile suggests it's not what she had in mind.

"You . . ."

"Make . . ."

"Me . . ."

"Shit . . ."

"My . . ."

"Pants . . ."

"And . . ."

"Piss . . ."

"On . . ."

"My . . ."

"Cat."

"Okay!" Michelle interrupts us. "That was really great. I can see we don't really need an icebreaker, things seem to be flowing just fine." She opens her file folder and, despite our groans, starts passing out copies of a magazine article on date rape. Her tone completely changes and she starts listing off facts and numbers about relationship violence from the clipboard in front of her. We glance over to Pat to see if she'll release us from this guinea pig experiment, but she keeps her head down, furiously writing in her notebook. I watch Michelle's mouth, words loosely falling from her lips like soft fragrant petals: *violation, dishonoured, betrayal, assault, genitalia*. She makes it all sound like poetry from another century.

It's not difficult for us to discuss this topic. Michelle's body pulls back one jagged crank at a time with each harsh word the girls hurl back at her: *pussy-fuck, cunt, cock*. Everyone has a story of a mother's boyfriend or uncle. About guys' houses they should not have gone to and cars they shouldn't have gotten into. Or about having sex when they don't really want to, just to get it over with, because the guy won't let up. Tracy talks about going into a room at a party to make out with a guy she didn't know only to have him put a gun to her head. And even Mute Mary talks about a neighbour taking naked photos of her when she was six, which makes us all quiet for a few seconds until Pat pipes up and says that she'd like to talk about that later, privately, with Mary. It makes my story of Mitch seem so insignificant, not even worth mentioning, really.

Only Tammy denies absolutely anything happening to her. She keeps saying after each story what she would have done instead, how it wouldn't have happened to her. She keeps on at it, as if she's on some moral high horse, like anyone had a choice. "I wouldn't have gotten into the car with five strange guys . . . I wouldn't have let my uncle get away with it . . . I would have bitten his dick off."

We all ignore her, turn our heads to Michelle who corrects Tammy and tells her that it's sometimes more complicated than that and we're not here to make judgements. With only five minutes left, Michelle attempts to summarize our points, with diminishing enthusiasm. Then she turns back to her notes and discusses how we could have made better choices. Finally, she puts down the papers and for the first time her voice sounds normal. She asks us why we didn't lay charges. Why we didn't tell our friends. Why we didn't leave the next party when we saw the same guy again.

Nicole answers for us all: "We know what we should say, we know what to do, now. Only, it's different when you're actually in it. You don't want to rat on the guy because you all hang out together. And if you get the guy in trouble, he'll get you worse."

"I would charge any guy who raped me," Tammy persists. "I don't care who he is." She throws her feet up on the table and picks at the rubber soles with a pen.

"Shut the fuck up," Jasmyn snaps at her. "It never happened to you 'cause you spread your legs and invite them in."

"Fuck you." Tammy's feet come slamming back down to the ground.

"You watch your mouth, you little fuckin' cunt—"

"Sit on this, bitch!" Tammy sticks her middle finger up and thrusts it in Jasmyn's direction.

"Stick it up your girlfriend's pussy, you fuck—"

"Girls!" Pat yells for about the fifth time, though it's the first time Tammy and Jasmyn seem to hear it. Normally, they'd keep going, but we all want the discussion to go on so they both back down, keeping it to a subtle evil stare to be dealt with later. In a strange way, I think it's because Tammy is jealous. Jealous that she's not one of us.

After the session, we all go upstairs to the kitchen and make popcorn. Tammy makes up some excuse that she has a headache and needs to lie down. None of us convinces her to stay, not even Staff. The rest of us are all soft with each other. We say things like *excuse me* and *sorry* when pushing by, or compliment each other's hairstyle or clothes. Jasmyn offers to braid Mute Mary's hair and Tracy offers up her blue elastics. Michelle splurges for a pizza and for about three hours we act like real sisters.

· · ·

I stopped going to see Eric regularly. I haven't seen him for three weeks. Sometimes it's because I'm doing something else and I just forget about the appointment. Other times I just make excuses because it's pretty much useless now. There's no point in dwelling on the past, now that I'm going to have a baby. Now that I have to focus on my future. Stirring up all that history only makes it hard to breathe and I'd rather let the idea of Elsie hover deep inside me like a stagnant black smoke. When I do go, at times, I feel like just coming clean. Before the word *baby*, sitting poised on the tip of my tongue, leaps between words. Or my fingers that play dangerously close to the edge of sleeve cuffs make a quick dash to reveal my scarred arms.

"So you really hate her?" Eric asks. We are still on the endless subject of Elsie. And I have just finished one of my bitch sessions. It appears that Eric can't stand to mix his topics. I imagine him dining alone at home, chair pulled tightly up to the table, napkin on lap. I imagine him separating his food groups, eating the meat before the vegetable, carefully monitoring the gravy for break-away trails. That is, I assume he is alone. There's never another person across the table when I picture him.

"Yes, I hate her," I respond, sounding surprised at his question. Then I think a little more about it. "Well, wait. It used to be a *hate* hate, but now it's more like a *I-can't-stand-her* hate. You know?"

"Can you think of a time when you might see her differently? More positively?"

"Well, I suppose if she was walking down the street, I might think she's a good person," I say. I'll give her that. Strangers think she's charming, nice even. "She just never should have been a mother," I add thoughtfully.

Eric nods his head in understanding. "Sometimes distance can be good. You can see Elsie not just as a caregiver, but as a person. You might be able to understand her."

"Why the hell should I have to understand *her*?" I snap at him. "I'm the kid. She should be the one understanding me."

He holds his hands up, surrendering. "You don't have to understand her."

We sit quietly for a few minutes. We have long pauses like this. And I've come to like them, but only here. Most people like to fill them with useless words, panicked at the edge of the silent hole. As if they would fall to their deaths if they didn't quickly fill in the gap. But Eric likes these silences. He says they're like mortar in brick walls, the thought between words. He says they make discussions substantial.

"Did you like your parents when you were growing up?" I ask, skeptical.

"Yes," Eric answers, all serious, pulling a leg up to rest on his knee. He appears confident and ready to take on my challenge. "Yes, I did."

I shake my head and turn to look out the window.

"Is that a bad thing? Liking your parents? Seems like you disapprove."

"No. It just explains a lot, that's all," I say.

"Explains what?"

"What you say. How you make it all sound so easy."

"Can I not be helpful to you if I haven't gone through exactly what you've gone through?" Now I start to feel sorry for him, like he's going to go home and cry, believing he can't do his job. Because he is good at counselling, even though I don't know why he'd want to waste his time helping screwed-up kids who treat him like crap.

"Well, I suppose you can, a little. It depends."

"On what?"

I think a bit. "Did you do drugs when you were my age?"

"Yep."

"What kind?" I ask, sitting up in my chair. Now we are getting somewhere.

"Marijuana. Hash, maybe a few times. I was older than you, though. About eighteen. I had long hair, tight jeans, you know, a rocker. I didn't do it all the time, only the odd weekend. At parties, maybe." This makes me laugh. I can't imagine Eric all drugged up.

"Steal?"

"Yep. Once from Shoppers Drug Mart. I was thirteen. I took a pen and a Mars bar."

"Ooh!" I say. "Call the cops!"

"Felt guilty about it for years."

I think a few more seconds. "Ever hit a girl?"

Eric's face becomes serious now. "Never."

"Come on, never?" I am smiling a knowing smile, trying to coax him to the truth.

"Nope."

"No way. Not even if you're fighting and she hits you? Like you're hitting back. Not that hard, more like a punch in the arm or something?"

"No," he says. "I would never touch a girl like that."

I slam back into my chair, the fun over. I only half believe him.

Because every guy has a limit, a moment when he just can't put up with it anymore. I don't know one guy who doesn't. I don't know one girl who hasn't found it. And it's so hypocritical, Eric demanding I spill open each week, but him only willing to go so far. And maybe it's not intentional, but I know he's lying. How nice it must be to get paid to judge and not be judged.

"What happened? You're angry now," he says.

"No," I protest.

"You think that's normal? Hitting a girl? Has that happened to you?"

"Me and everyone I know."

"Whoa. I have to be clear about this, Snow. It's not normal. Even if it's a punch in the arm. Are you talking about Mark?"

I shoot him a quick sharp look. "No. We just play fight," I say. "Someone else." Then I follow it up with "a long time ago," just to make sure he drops it.

"Okay. Well, if it's ever anything more, I'm here to talk. Just talk."

"Yep." I am disappointed in Eric. Disappointed he won't make the effort to strip away his own layers of truth: the truth you tell, the truth you whisper, and then the truth that's buried so deep even your own ears don't hear it.

. . .

I get a message that Greg called. Miranda is interested, or rather, prying. She wants to know who this Greg guy is. She thinks he sounds old.

"I haven't heard you mention a Greg before," she asks suspiciously. As if she knew the name of every person I have ever talked to.

I immediately begin to worry. Greg knows too much. It's too risky that he speak to Miranda.

"He's my swimming instructor," I say, snatching the phone message out of her hand.

Greg is wondering if I'd like to meet. On Saturday. At the pool. One o'clock.

I call him back, Miranda is within earshot. "Ya, okay. One o'clock is good," I say. It feels strange to talk to him on the phone. I think how backwards that is. That I'm most comfortable seeing him wet and with his shirt off. "I'll see you there." Our conversation is short, much to Miranda's disappointment.

"Is he cute?" she asks me after I hang up the phone.

"You're gay," I say.

"I know, but is he cute?"

I can't stop the smile from spreading.

Miranda laughs, whipping a scrunched paper napkin at my head. I like this about Miranda. She's gay, but in a good way. She's not like the rest of Staff, who are convinced we're all closet lesbians anguished by our repressed sexuality. Sometimes I think the house is an underground recruitment centre for dykes. Miranda doesn't force us to sit through endless workshops on homophobia and she doesn't make every little thing in her life relate to being a lesbian. She lives with her partner, she doesn't wear a bra, and that's about as gay as she is.

.   .   .

Miranda is so determined that I go to my swim lesson she personally drops me off at the pool on Saturday. In the change room, screaming little girls in pink bikinis run barefoot up and down the aisles. Their tired mothers reach out to grab their squirming bodies, gripping them between their knees while they pull hair into high ponytails. I change slowly in the corner, covering my body with a towel. I feel sick to my stomach. I am dreading a pool full of splashes and waves. Dreading Greg's suspicious stare as his eyes trace the curve of my stomach. Dreading more questions about my cuts or my mother's death. Greg will expect things of me. He will make it his goal to see me swim. And I will disappoint him. I know this.

I convince myself I'm not feeling well. That I may throw up in the water, which isn't hygienic for little kids. And if I were responsible, really responsible, I'd put my clothes on and just walk out the door.

12

The thought of you doesn't make me feel sick anymore. Sometimes, the thought of you even makes me smile. You are not like other babies, the ones I can smell, the ones on the bus who screech in my ears. In my mind you are motionless, like a doll, permanently poised in an open-mouthed, drooling smile. Eyes wide, glassy, and blue, mechanically closing when I lay you down. I sing sweet lullabies to you, songs I imagined my mother singing to me, at night, alone and afraid of the dark.

The words that come out of my mouth will be good-mother words. I will understand you. I will tell you to go ahead and cry if it's over nothing because you don't have to be a big girl until you are one. And I won't throw the mashed potatoes against the wall if you don't like them. And I won't make you kneel on a cheese grater if you wet your bed, and I'll agree that maybe it *is* the end of the world if you don't find your purple crayon, because who's to say it's not?

. . .

It's the crazy bird at the library window that makes me snap out of my trance. I don't remember how long ago my eyes first lifted from the page of the math textbook in front of me. I can only guess it's been a while, because my neck hurts, cramped from looking up to the glass a few feet above my head. The little brown bird is fluttering up against the window, all panicked. It keeps flying into it and then rebounding, then flying into it again, wings frantic. And it's the strangest thing, because if it doesn't stop, I think it will kill itself. At first, I figure it must be sick, having some kind of trauma, like epilepsy, though I'm not sure a bird can have that. But then I recognize the anger, the focus, and I realize it's attacking its own reflection in the glass.

The window is too high for me to reach. I consider throwing a book up, so it can see that it's a window, that the reflection is not another bird. But then it gives one huge fluttering attack that lasts a good thirty seconds before it drops out of sight altogether. I jump up on my chair, on my tippytoes, but can't see where it's gone. Then I run outside, leaving all my things behind, even my jacket. Outside the building, I follow the window ledges until I see a brown lump in the grass.

I approach it cautiously. The little sparrow lies stunned on its back, its feet clenched in the air, eyes open, grey belly pounding. I gently scoop my hand under its back, making sure not to kink its neck. I plunk down onto the grass, watch the little thing cupped in my hand, its eyes all glossy, its chest heaving. And I'm staring there thinking how amazing this is, this little bird, its dirty feathers and tiny round head. That I'm actually holding flight in my hand.

Its breathing slowly becomes calmer and its black eyes peer around a little more. I think about how the boys in my building used to clip dead birds' feet and chase me with them, or how they'd blow up pigeons' heads using baking soda in bread. And I start wondering what I should do, if I should take it home or leave it. And if I do take it home, I start to worry about what I would feed it and what if its wing is broken?

As I'm thinking all this, its foot flinches and its body twitches and I extend my arm far out away from me. I close my eyes and push my face into my shoulder, not wanting to see squirming death in my hand. And I think, *Please, just die now, please.* Then all of a sudden, the sparrow jolts up, startled, and dizzily flies up to the branch of a tree. I stand there for the longest time, staring up at it, happy for it to be okay, but also disappointed I can't take it home.

I look at my watch. It's after six. I quickly head to the library door, but it's locked. I can see the librarian lady at the counter, her head down, glasses halfway down her nose. I rattle the door and knock.

"Hello! Hello!"

The lady lifts a stern bony finger and then points to the closed sign, then she holds up her wrist and points to her watch. It's only ten minutes after closing. I rattle the door. "Ya, I know!" I yell into the glass. "I need my stuff! I left my stuff!" And I gesture to my back to indicate a missing knapsack. She pretends she doesn't see me, purposely keeps her head down, her lips squeezed tight and wrinkly like a cat's bum. I pull at the door and knock even louder, anger rising in me. "I need my stuff, you fuckin' bitch! Fuck!" I punch the wood with my fist and she turns her back, completely ignoring my existence. As if it would be the end of the world for her to open the door. "You fucking ignorant bitch!" I yell, kicking harder and harder, my eyes fixated on the back of her head. When she starts to walk away, I just lose it. Thinking about my bag. And my math test tomorrow. And about people who can't bend a rule for just a second. I kick the glass window beside the door and sharp triangles of shattered glass scatter. I surprise myself, I didn't think it would break so easily. I pull my foot back out of a hole at the centre of the windowpane, cracks spreading like a spider's web. I look up and see the lady's head peeking horrified around the corner and then I see her rush to the counter and pick up the phone. I turn and run, through parks and railroad tracks, thinking every siren I hear is for me.

When I get to the group home I stand out back a minute to catch my breath, then I walk in, calm, like nothing happened. I grab an apple, say hi to Miranda, and go up to my room. It's only about an hour before the doorbell rings and I hear the static radio downstairs.

"Snow!" Pat yells. "Come down here, please!"

I slowly descend the stairs and turn the corner to the living room. The two cops look huge, feet firmly planted on the ground, their hats tucked under their arms.

"Hello, Snow," one of them says, firm but polite, a tone I know I'm given only because Staff is here. If I was on my own, it would be an entirely different story. "I'm Sergeant Blaine. I think we've found your schoolbag," he says, motioning to my backpack on the chair.

I look to Miranda who is standing with her arms crossed. Her cheeks are red and she's tapping her foot. "She wouldn't let me get my bag," I explain desperately, more to her than to the cops. "It would've taken a second to open the door."

The cop interrupts my plea. "You caused some serious damage to the library. The librarian was quite shaken."

"She wouldn't give me my stuff!" I blurt out.

"So you broke a window? That seems a little rash. Couldn't you knock?"

"I did," I say. "I did, but she ignored me."

The other cop pipes in and right away I can tell he's an asshole. "Why did you leave it in there?'

"What do you mean?"

"Why did you leave your stuff and go outside? What were you doing out there?"

"Nothing," I answer, folding my arms in front of me. There was no way I'd tell them about the bird. No way I'd let them ruin that.

"Sure you weren't outside smoking a joint? We found some butts by the entrance."

"No!" I say, even though I don't have to deny it, because there's no way they could have proven it, even if it was true.

"Why did you go out?"

"To have a cigarette," I say.

"You sure there wasn't anything else in that cigarette?"

Jasmyn comes in the door and stops dead in her tracks when she sees the cops and Staff and me in the living room. Miranda waves her along but Jasmyn ignores her.

I turn to the cop to answer his question. "I was just fuckin' studying and took a break. Jesus Christ, is studying against the law?" I say, feeling less outnumbered now.

"You watch your language, young lady. And studying isn't against the law, but vandalism is." He turns his head to Jasmyn who is standing in the hallway. "Hello, Jasmyn," he says. I'm surprised he knows her by name.

"What's going on?" she asks, one arm up on the door frame.

"This doesn't concern you." Pat moves over to her and leads her up the stairs.

The cops tell me that they won't be taking me in, but that they'll be releasing me to the custody of the group home. The big cop passes me a yellow paper.

"It's a notice to appear for a trial date."

I'm in disbelief. "She wouldn't give me my bag," I say, unable to comprehend how I'm the one who's so wrong here. "Don't you have something better to do?" I ask. "Like arrest a murderer or drug dealer or something?" Despite my comments, they are nice to me once they realize I'm not going to freak out on them or anything. They tell me that the lady wants them to follow through, but really, because my history indicates no priors, it'll just mean a few hours in court in about a year from now.

"To be quite truthful," the bigger guy says, "I wish more young people we picked up were studying at libraries."

By the next morning the whole house knows what happened. They all laugh and clap their hands when I walk into the kitchen. Jasmyn high-fives me and immediately starts telling the others about finding me in the living room with the two cops. They want to hear everything, about the librarian and the window. We have this whole discussion and it's as if I've passed a major test with them. It's as if this thin yellow court order in my back pocket is the secret pass to absolute acceptance.

13

Mark knows about the baby, knows I didn't have an abortion. He hasn't said anything, but my tits are huge, and even though I try to suck it in, my belly keeps getting in the way. We stopped having sex days ago and he won't even kiss me. He snaps at me over little things like spilling Coke on his already disgusting couch or for roughly pushing Spliff off the couch. He tells me I'm getting fat, and that I have dark roots and my fingernails are chipped. When I'm at his place, girls call all the time and he'll talk to them, all flirty and sweet, right in front of me. And even though I leave him five messages a night, he only calls me back once in a while. But still, it seems like the more annoyed he is with me, the more I need him to love me.

Jasmyn tells me I'm being desperate and that I shouldn't hang off him so much, but I don't care. I can't help it. It's like I'm stabbing a knife deeper and deeper into me each time I try, and though it hurts, I keep doing it. I hang out in places where Mark will be. I wait down the road from his building, watching for him to come home and then knock on his door, saying I left my school binder by mistake at his place. Or I'll walk ten times around his block, until I'm bound to run into one of his friends who'll tell me where he is. I find ways to throw him into my conversations with Jasmyn, just for the pure pleasure of possessing his name in my mouth. My mind becomes consumed with him and I can think of nothing else. Not even the baby.

"I'm leaving for Montreal tomorrow," Mark announces one night while we're just sitting on his couch having a smoke. "I'm going for a long time," he adds, and there is a sense of permanence to his words.

"Cool," I say, like it's nothing, like he's just told me he'll pick up some milk at the store. He leans over and gives me this little dry kiss, like he's saying goodbye, and I reflexively get up to leave.

"So, I'll call you when I get there," he says.

"Ya, okay." I feel stupid just standing there not knowing what to do, so I turn and leave. I stand a few moments in the hallway outside the closed door, trying to figure out what the hell just happened. And I know my body should break. I should be crying and blubbering, but it's as if I'm completely dry inside. Instead, I walk down the dingy hallway feeling this little satisfactory twinge of *I knew it*. As if in some weird way I am comforted knowing how things and people will always fail me. And that's when I realize I was waiting for Mark to leave me all along.

As the distance between me and Mark's apartment grows, it's as if I start to melt, from a block of ice to raging water. An ugly, taunting voice in my head hurls unanswerable questions at me. How can I get a child to love me when her own father can't? How can I raise a kid all by myself? What guy will ever want to be with a sixteen-year-old mother? I will be alone forever. I'm a fucked-up teenager. A horny little girl, too stupid to use a condom. It was

dumb to have thought this could have been any different, for
believing even for one second that this could work.

"You're such an idiot," I scold myself, digging my nails deep into
my palms. "You stupid little fucked-up idiot." I breathe heavily
through my nose like a bull. Like some panting, wild animal. My
jaw clenches. Blood blasts through me, shaking my body. It starts
to rain, but I don't care. I don't give a fuck about anything. I kick
the mailbox. I kick the parked car. And I yell, just yell, because I
need to let it out. Startled heads turn to me, terrified of this crazed
lunatic storming down the street. A circle of space opens around
me and I am unstoppable. I feel drunk. I dart in front of cars that
screech their brakes, drivers blasting their horns. I give them the
finger. Wishing they hadn't stopped. Wishing that man would just
stop swearing, open his car door, come over, and bash my head in.

I take the subway and then the bus to Don Mills. As I get closer
to my old area, I'm unable to remain still. I start pacing the back
of the bus, my legs shaking. I tightly grip a pole, imagining it to
be Elsie's skinny, cold neck. Time doesn't pass fast enough and
despite the rain I get off the bus two stops early so I can run the
rest of the way to Elsie's work.

As soon as I enter the grocery store, my eyes lock on Elsie.
She is at the far end of the store, behind her register, in her
wine-and-beige polyester uniform, pushing groceries along a
conveyer belt. I storm up to her, my purpose clear. I want to
throw it in her face. I want to throw my whole life in her face.
When she approaches, she opens her mouth to speak, but I hurl
my words down her throat.

"Thanks for ruining my life," I yell. "Thanks for fucking
ruining my life!"

"What the hell's got up yer ass?" Elsie asks, annoyed, continuing to check out the customer's groceries. "My granddaughter,"

she explains to a faceless customer, rolling her eyes. I don't lose my glare.

"I'm pregnant. You satisfied?" A smile breaks over Elsie's face and she shakes her head, like it's all a game. "Excuse me," she says politely to the customer in front of her and yells to the woman at the next cash to take over. Then she storms past me and out toward the exit. I trail at her heels, pursuing my kill.

We stand outside the Dominion, the automatic doors tirelessly opening and snapping shut as I pace back and forth.

"Now I get it. You're going to blame me for getting yourself knocked up, is that it?" Elsie pulls a cigarette pack out from her pocket and lights it.

"No. I blame you for everything before that. 'Cause being pregnant may be the only thing I ever did right." Even though it wasn't true, I had to say it. Elsie leans one arm up against the phone booth and starts laughing to herself, staring off into space. She sucks hard on her cigarette, cheeks caving in like deflating balloons. I want to hurt her. I want her to pay for everything. I pace frantically up and down, thinking of Mark and the baby and Mitch and the group home. "Ugggh . . . I could kill you right now," I yell, punching the wall.

"You need to relax!" Elsie orders, looking over my head, to see if there's anyone watching.

I ignore her command and just get louder and louder. "I wish my mother never died. I wish she didn't leave me with an alcoholic crazy fucked-up woman. You're crazy. Crazy! You *made* me crazy, see?" I push up my sleeve, showing her the red marks on my arm.

She stares at my skin, her mouth open and horrified. "What the hell is that?"

"It's how much I hate you!" I move out of the way of a woman pushing her cart, her head down, aware that she's intruding on something. "You probably made her drown! She probably jumped in! To get some peace from you!"

"What?" Elsie twitches her head as if she were trying to shake the words out of her ears. "*What?* Jesus Christ, what is going on in that stupid little head of yours?"

"If my mom were alive, I wouldn't be like this, you . . ." I spit out every possible swear word I know at her.

When I'm done I stand there, fixated on her. Her face is red, nostrils flared. I've never seen her so angry. She leans into me, her face so close I can smell her cigarette breath. "Ooh," she threatens, "you don't know how wrong you are." And then the truth oozes out of her like pus from a squeezed scab. "Your mother never drowned," she says. "She left you with me when you were a baby and then she died three years later. She was eighteen. Overdosed. Your so-called mother, who you think is your saving angel, was a junkie who was a waste of a life. How's that for truth? Your mother was a screwed-up pregnant fifteen-year-old girl. Sound familiar?"

And so it happens like that. The truth of my life, told to me outside a grocery store, among the clattering of carts, the price checks, the automatic glass doors opening and shutting like snapping jaws.

For a few seconds I stand there, unable to move. The rain pounds on the metal awning above our heads. I feel as if I've had the wind knocked out of me. My soul knocked out of me. It's as if everything that I thought was real isn't. I reach out to touch the wall, to see if it's truly there. Finally, I remember to breathe. Without saying anything, I walk past Elsie, across the road, and down the street. My legs just keep going like that, one after the other. My mind a tight fist of nothing and everything all at once.

I walk aimlessly in the rain, my jeans wet and heavy. I look for a place to stand, because there's something about absolute despair that requires being still in small spaces. I think of the places normal people go to cry: in stairwells, bathroom cubicles, inside their cars. Finally, I find an empty bus-stop shelter, pace around inside the glass perimeter, opening and shutting my mouth, gasping for air. I look up and see my reflection and think of Freddy in his fishbowl, only the water's on the outside.

Then I get this flash. This memory pops in my head, from out of the blue. I see this stupid clown's face, from some party I went to as a kid. I'm in a backyard with balloons and plastic tablecloths and this clown keeps pulling a quarter out from behind my ear. I remember him well because I made him repeat it over and over; each time thinking, *I'm watching for it;* each time angry to see his painted fingers twiddle a shiny coin.

Then it's like my mind jumps to this realization that Elsie and my mother at one point probably thought the same way I do. That no one really thinks they're going to turn out like this. That it's not like one day you stop fighting and resign yourself to what life keeps pushing you into. No, it's not that obvious. It's as if you keep fighting. Your fists are up and going crazy, but somehow you've missed the battle entirely, as if you mixed up the dates or room number. And then one day, probably years later, you pause for just a split second, fists hanging in the air. And you stand there, like I am right now, recognizing yourself for the first time, and wonder how it was you become a failure when you were watching for it so hard.

And then what do you do?

"How long have you been waiting?" an old lady with a clear plastic kerchief on her head asks me. She frantically shakes her umbrella, huffing and sighing like she's just come out of a tornado.

"I don't know," I say blankly and just stand there for a bit. Then the rain subsides and I figure I should go to the group home and put my wet clothes in the dryer.

·   ·   ·

There are truths I can no longer create. The mother's arms I felt all these years, the ones that used to wrap around me at night and comfort me, are no longer there. Instead, the mother's arms I feel now are bony and weak and resentful.

I find my small space. In the cupboard under the stairs in the house, behind the mops and brooms and broken vacuum cleaner. I squat on the sticky floor, my back up against rotting wood, the faint smell of lemon cleaner and oil. Heavy soles mount and descend hardwood stairs above my head.

My hand is resolute in its silent act. The safety pin firmly clenched between fingers. Lines surface from the depth of me, angular shapes connected by sharp corners travelling up my arm. I lose myself in the act of breaking skin, until my hand releases the wire and it falls to the floor and I can think clearly once more. I hold my arm up to the thin slant of hallway light slicing the darkness. I am surprised and pleased with what I see. I spit on my arm to wipe away the remaining blood, the red swell of letters from wrist to elbow: *M-O-T-H-E-R*.

·   ·   ·

The next day I appear at Elsie's kitchen doorway. She is sitting facing the door, as if she were waiting for me. There are cigarette packages and coffee mugs scattered out on the table before her. It looks like she's been there all night.

"Why didn't you tell me sooner?" I ask from the doorway, not sure if I will enter. We are strangely calm. This is uncertain ground for both of us.

"I was going to tell you, when you were older, when you finished growing up. I had you since you were a baby. Your mom couldn't keep you. You were young, little, only about two when you started calling me Mommy. I couldn't stand that. I needed you to understand *then* that I wasn't your mother." I come into the room and sit down at the table opposite her. "You were just a baby. You wouldn't have understood." She continues, her eyes pleading for understanding and kindness, but my face is blank. There is no expression for an emotion unrecognized by the body. "It was too complicated, too much explanation, so I said your mom was dead. That she drowned. And then later, she did die, only we waited a few more years to scatter her ashes. It was easier that way. For a while anyway. Till now."

I stare down at the table. In front of me is a ratty old placemat, one we've had for years. I start twisting and pulling at the fraying edges. "I dream about it, you know," I say. "I dream these strange dreams. Like when we went to scatter her ashes at that river. And that woman we saw, in that housing place, that was her, wasn't it? That was my mother. I thought they were just mixed-up dreams. You should have told me."

"How do you tell a kid that her own mother wants nothing to do with her? That she's a doped-up addict who doesn't give a shit about anything?" Elsie stares directly at me, waiting for an answer, for release.

"I don't know." I begin to pull out the tiny gold threads from the placemat and gather them in my hand. "You just do."

The silence is long. Finally, Elsie sighs deeply and puts her hands on the table and pushes herself up, as if that was the end.

"But that's not even the part that upsets me most," I say, my words breaking her calm.

"What's that?"

"That isn't the part I'm mad about."

"What?" she asks cautiously.

"She was fifteen. My mother was fifteen years old when she had me." My eyes rise to meet hers.

"Yes."

Elsie sits back down and reaches for her pack of Marlboros, lights a cigarette with shaky, brittle hands. She inhales deeply. Her body stiffens, then relaxes, the whites of her eyes fluttering somewhat. "It would have changed your life if you knew," she says in a defensive tone, flicking her cigarette into the ashtray.

"Yes," I reply.

"It would have changed who you are."

"Yes."

"For the worse." Elsie leans back and breathes out, the creases around her eyes and mouth relax, like loosened fishing lines. I think of how weightless she must feel. The burden now transferred from her to me by words, tiny combined vibrations. How heavy sound can be.

"Yes," I reply into the quiet.

.   .   .

It should be a shocking event. I should be shaking. I should be yelling and accusing, but instead I feel a numb overcast of grey. I imagine it will take time. That I will slowly start to distort, as if I'm dripping from the inside.

For the moment it's a simple sum of numbers.

I now have three mothers. This new one forcing its way between my two definitions. I line my birth mother up on my mind's shelf, in between Elsie and the image-mother I created all these years. I sense the others looking her up and down, jealous of her right to be there, angry that my birth mother can just step in like that, without doing the legwork, without putting in the time.

Look at her, so young. What does she know about being a mother?
I imagine Elsie and my image-mother saying to each other. They
worry that I will be swept away by the newness of her, that I'll
discard them like worn shoes. They straighten their backs, wave
arms to capture my attention, and remind me of all the times
they've been there for me.

I gave you a place to live and food to eat, Elsie says.

I was there every time you needed me. I never left you once, my
image-mother adds.

And then a small voice, from the corner of my mind, ghostly
and sour, *I'm not sure I want to be here.*

· · ·

Now that Mark's gone, I get all depressed. I don't care about my
body or what happens to me. Whatever was meant to happen will
happen. I can't change that. I never could.

On weekdays, I go to class, I return to the group home, I lie in
bed. I go to class, I return to the group home, I lie in bed. I live
inside my head, seek safety from my body and its crazy possession
over me. I can't shit, I can't sleep, I can't sit, I can't stand, I have
cravings for food but then can't bear to swallow. And it's like my
thoughts are scratching the walls of my skull, desperate for air.
Desperate for release.

I dart nasty looks at girls on the street, wishing someone would
just try it, try to piss me off. I stand close to the edge of the subway
platform, thinking it would just take a slight careless nudge to tip
me over. I want to kill something. I want to make something hurt.
I want someone to hurt me.

I fuck anyone who wants to. Mostly guys I already know, but
some are friends of friends, faces I recognize from the park or
from the mall. They get all sweet on me, say things they think I

want to hear. Tell me how great I am, or how beautiful I am, or that I've got *magic hands,* overlooking my swollen belly. And I just tell them to shut up 'cause I don't need it, that I'll do it anyway. And then I push their bodies down onto the bed and ride their skinny pale torsos, trying to ram feeling, any feeling, into me. And they lie there, dead weight, eyes closed, and gasp things like *you're wild, man, fuckin' great!* as I rock back and forth, underlining my self-fulfilling prophecy with my hips: I am a slut. I am what my mother made me.

When it hurts so bad that I can't keep going, I dismount as if from a horse, push off their stomachs, and plant feet firmly on the ground beside the bed. Some ask me to come lie back down, pat their hairless, sweaty chests as if tapping the shiny vinyl of a vacant chair.

"You got any smokes?" I say instead and extend an expecting hand, quickly slipping the pack into my bag where I'll hide them from Staff.

"I'll call you," they say as I leave. Then I walk home, their cum seeping out from between my legs like snot from a runny nose.

       •   •   •

I think of the bridge. The one people always jump off. I think of how I would get to it, by subway I guess. Then I consider if there'd be a ledge to stand on or would I have to sort of just vault right over? I wonder how long it would take to fall; would I have time to think or would my mind go blank? And what if while in midair I decided I didn't want to do this anymore? I think of hitting the ground and whether I would flatten like the Coyote cartoon or just kind of explode like a water balloon. And whether my legs would hit first, or my head, and if, while in the air, I could somersault or sort of fly. And then I think, *What if I land on something, kill it, like a squirrel or an unsuspecting pigeon?*

"Don't you dare tell anyone," I say to Jasmyn, who stands before me, eyes bulging from her head.

"I won't," she says, but then adds, "but you wouldn't do it, would you?" Without waiting for an answer she starts to say all the things people say when admissions like these are made. She explains how *everything will get better* and *in a year's time this will all seem like nothing* and then I feel sort of guilty because here Jasmyn is saying this to me, and look at her life.

The next day she comes back and sits on the edge of my bed and says, "Maybe you should tell Staff." She repeats this a few times, acting all concerned, but I know the real reason why she's returned. These thoughts of mine are a burden to her. They impede her stride, like a heavy head wind.

"No, it was just a thought. It sounds stupid now." And I smile, because it does sound stupid. And I think to myself that I'm not crazy, that I wouldn't really do this. I'm not like Mute Mary or the other girls I've seen in the house, who take a bottle of pills and then check themselves into psychiatric wards. Who return five days later with mixed recollections of shoeless lives filled with movie nights and crafts, and of corridors that smell of piss, and food seasoned with cellophane and cardboard. And besides, even if I were to do it, I would get it right the first time.

14

My own body disgusts me. My skin aches. I can feel the sides of my belly stretching, tired and tight. Some days are worse than others. I will not look in the mirror. I cover my reflection with my towel. I don't want to see my fat stomach. I don't want to see my bulging veiny breasts and stretch-marked skin. I don't want to see my ugly, puffy face or my oily hair. I don't want to see my mother.

I know she's there. She and Elsie. I feel them rising up within me, surfacing. I don't need to see my reflection to tell. I know it in the way I bend my fingers around a cigarette, the way I snap at Jasmyn when she just wants to talk, or the way my throat craves the burn of vodka.

"We either blame our mothers for who we've become or we blame them for who we haven't become. Heads or tails," says Eric.

"But I tried so hard not to be like her."

"Like who?"

"Elsie," I say, but as the word dangles awkwardly in the air in front of me, I realize it's not quite right. "My mother," I add hesitantly. "I don't know. I guess they're the same thing."

Eric's brow lifts thoughtfully, as if he'd just noticed a slight change in wind direction. He has never before heard me compare my mother to Elsie. He opens his mouth to speak, but then closes it quickly. He puts his hand up to his chin and strokes his straggly beard. Then he opens his mouth once more and words come out. "You know, I find many people end up replicating their parents' faults. Probably because they focus so much on avoiding them. It's like the difference between walking along a tightrope and saying, 'I will not fall,' or, 'I'll make it to the other end.'"

I put my hand above my head and motion that his idea just flew over it. "I'm tired of all this mother talk," I say.

. . .

"You need to sit properly," Ms. Dally says firmly, her nostrils flaring. She is telling me to take my feet off the desk. She has picked the wrong day to do this. I don't even acknowledge that she has spoken. I have learned this new skill in this class. I have learned the power of staring straight through a person.

"Get your feet off the desk and take out your homework." Her tone is harsher but I still I ignore her. Funny thing is, I'm not even comfortable. She moves in closer to me, silently fluttering her silly little lips before she formulates a sentence. In my mind I egg her on, her weakness feeding me. "You need to leave the room," she finally spits out. Backup arrives and I see Sheila appear at the front of the room, chest puffed out, hands clasped firmly in front of her as if she were a bouncer outside a nightclub.

"For what?" I stare both of them down.

Ms. Dally answers but I don't hear anything. Blood surges through my ears and I grit my teeth, squeeze so hard I feel like the roof of my mouth is splitting. An invisible drawstring pinches my brows tight. I imagine squeezing her tiny head and bursting it like a grape. Then I see myself calling her a fuckin' whore, see my mouth telling her these cocksucking rules are bullshit. I see myself hork two times on the door before I slam it behind me. I see myself doing these things, but I play no part. It's like another person I'm watching. It's like another body.

There is a meeting the next day, before I'm allowed back in class. I sit at the round table, shredding a paper into tiny strips while Ms. Dally recounts my outburst. She says how surprised she is that this inappropriate behaviour is coming from me, because I show so much promise and I could really get my high school education if I just stay committed to my goals. I fixate on her hands, soft and fleshy, with short efficient nails. I feel bad for this woman, in her brown skirt and thick flesh-coloured nylons with reinforced toes. I feel embarrassed for the words that came out of my foul mouth. I imagine her puttering around in her small apartment, expelling an explosive *fuck* after stubbing a toe; a reflexive apologetic hand immediately covering her mouth as if trying to push the blasphemy back in.

When she's done her lecture she waits for me to speak. Waits for an explanation or an apology or an acknowledgement that I was wrong. But I can't bring myself to speak because all I'm thinking about is how I wish I was anyone else but me. I wish I didn't exist. I wish my mother didn't exist. I wish Elsie didn't exist. I sit, lips pressed tight, strips of paper piled in front of me like curled pencil shavings. I lean down and blow them off the table and they drift like feathers down to the floor.

"What's your problem?" Ms. Dally asks, fed up. She is done with all the proper things she should say. "You walk around like you're owed something. Like the world owes you something."

"Ya, it does," I say firmly, fixating all my hate on her. "A life. It owes me a fuckin' decent chance to get a goddamn fuckin' life." My eyes start welling up, which pisses me off even more because I'm not sad, I'm angry.

We are both quiet for a while. I sit there, wiping my eyes, and Ms. Dally stares out the window, twirling her brown-bead necklace in her fingers. I want her to convince me that I have it all wrong. I want her to pull the answer out from behind my ear like a magic coin. After a while, she speaks in a calm and quiet voice. That's the thing about Ms. Dally, she yells in whispers. "I can't accept this behaviour in class, Snow. You are going to have to control your anger or you will not last in the program. This is a place for people who want to learn." She tells me she expects that I will meet with Sheila to talk about what's setting me off because it's not a habit of mine to do such a thing.

"Then I won't come back. I quit school. There's no point," I say, still angry.

Suddenly Ms. Dally gets all sympathetic, saying she knows it's hard and that she's here to help me, not fight me. She says an education is my best way out of a life I don't want. I used to agree with her.

Part of me just wants to blurt out something hurtful, squash her weak bones even more. Tell her that she has no idea, no idea whatsoever. The other part of me wants to say sorry. But instead I tell her I don't know how she can do this job, how she can tolerate messed-up students like me dumping on her like that all the time. I stand abruptly, take my binder from the classroom, and start cleaning out my locker, throwing each object forcefully into the large garbage pail. Ms. Dally watches over me, tells me not to act so rashly, to think things over. But the more she pleads and the more desperate her voice becomes, the more determined I am, pulling each object slowly out of my locker just so I can savour the concern in her voice.

. . .

Aunt Sharon comes to take me out for dinner. We go to the new Swiss Chalet that smells of industrial-dishwasher steam. She requests the spacious booth along the wall and an annoyed middle-aged waitress with sagging face and breasts slaps the plastic menus down on the table, stating it's not really her section. I order a rib dinner with fries and Aunt Sharon orders a salad, because she says she's watching her weight. She talks about her boring office job, Winky, and the trip she's planning to Cancun next winter. When she asks me about school and the group home, I am distant and bothered, answering her questions with short one-word answers.

"Elsie called me," she finally says, just after the waitress takes away our plates.

"Uh-huh?" I respond flatly.

Aunt Sharon's discomfort is painful to watch. "How are you doing then?"

"Fine," I answer, thinking she's talking about the pregnancy, but then I reconsider what she might be referring to. "Shouldn't I be?"

She raises her eyebrows. "Well, Elsie told me what she said about your mom. I'd think that's got to be hard to hear. I thought you'd want to talk about it."

The gaps of silence in our conversation require such an effort to leap over, I'm unsure if I will secure footing on the other side.

"I don't know," I say. "Kind of hard to fit it all in my head." I swirl my greasy fingers in the little bowl of warm water with the wedge of lemon floating. "I'm pissed at Elsie for not telling. I'm pissed at you too. But then I'm sort of glad she didn't tell me."

"You know, I'm sure this won't make you feel any better, but after a while, it just became the truth. It didn't feel like a lie."

"She didn't drown," I say cautiously, hoping Elsie lied about that part.

"No."

"I feel like a fuckin' idiot. All those swimming lessons." I squeeze the lemon wedge, mushing it hard between my fingers. The waitress arrives and slaps the bill down on the table. Aunt Sharon pulls a twenty out of her wallet and slides it under the salt shaker.

"It's best to focus on the future, Snow. The past is the past."

I slam back against the vinyl booth. "What the fuck does that mean? Why do adults talk like this?" I say, glaring at all the grown-ups in the restaurant. It's these little shot-glass sentences adults use. Like the quickest way to numb their thoughts is through these little clean phrases. "Speak your mind, will ya?" Aunt Sharon waves her hand downward, gesturing for me to lower my voice. "Who cares if someone hears?" I yell. "I don't care!" I pick the lemon wedge out, rip the pulp flesh from its skin, and drop it back in the water. Then I pick at the peel, flicking the pieces onto the floor until nothing is left in my hand. "It was better thinking she died right after I was born," I mumble. How can you live your life knowing you were a mistake? Like given the chance, your mother would have rubbed you out.

"Snow . . ." she says, but that's all she says, because there is nothing left. I cringe hearing her say my name. For the first time ever, I'm embarrassed of it.

"Is that all Elsie told you?" I ask, giving her one last chance to tell me she knows about the pregnancy.

"That's all she could say. We got in a fight. I hung up on her. Why . . ." She pauses. "Was there more?"

I shake my head.

"She was a good person, Snow," Aunt Sharon finally says. "I'm glad you had such a good impression of your mom. She had a lot of potential. She was just really messed up. Had the wrong friends, clashed with Elsie. I think from the day she was born she was trying to get out of that house."

"And you?"

"I was older. I got out earlier." Got out. From what? I'm tired of this "Jeopardy" game. Tired of being given the answers when I need to figure out the questions.

"What the fuck is wrong with us?" I say, shaking my head. Aunt Sharon's lip disappears under her front teeth, like she is clamping down on words she wants to confess to me. The waitress returns, a stupid smile on her face for the first time. "Have a nice day," she says, placing the change on the table. Aunt Sharon leaves her an undeserved toonie tip and passes me a five-dollar bill.

"All families have skeletons in their closets," she says. "We just happen to have a whole graveyard under our basement."

• • •

It feels like a long time since I last saw Eric, even if it was only two weeks. A lifetime, really. A time when I had a boyfriend and a birth mother who wanted me. I don't tell Eric about Mark leaving. Or about my dinner with Aunt Sharon. Instead, I divert him with talk about my anger. I tell him about flipping out on Ms. Dally at school. The ability to distract a counsellor from what's really bothering you takes practice, but after a while it's very easy to do. Just know which bone to give them and they'll chew forever.

"And what do you think you get out of it? Getting angry?" Eric asks.

"I don't know. Probably nothing. It's like I can't help it."

"You probably get something out of it, you just haven't identified it yet."

"Yeah," I say, not telling him what I'm really thinking. "I suppose I'm tired of feeling numb. I just want something to prick me alive." I can tell by his look that he's impressed. "Do I sound like your textbook?" I ask, nodding toward his stacked bookshelf.

"Why, did you steal one?" he jokes and taps on his fishbowl. "What do you think, Fred? Is she a thief?" We both sit there for what seems like forever, staring at Freddy happily swim around in his bowl. Then Eric gets all serious. "You see, Snow . . . It's like a junkie who has to shoot up in his penis because there's no vein left."

"Eric," I say, no idea of what he's trying to say. I lean forward and whisper, "I hate to tell you, but I don't have a penis."

"No, but when you run out of places to feel, you'll eventually get to that point where you'll either stop or go over the edge."

Sometimes Eric says the most bizarre things. I wave my hand over my head, which is my usual indicator that I have no idea what's he's talking about. I look at my watch. We still have ten minutes. I try to think of another topic, maybe the girls at the home, but Eric moves in too quick. "So, what's going on with Mark?"

"Oh, yeah," I say, as if it had already slipped my mind. "He moved to Montreal. Left a couple weeks ago."

"Is that what's making you so angry?"

"No."

"You okay, then?"

"Yup," I say, as if I was surprised he'd be concerned. "I'm fine." He pauses in his non-verbal could-you-explain kind of way. "I'll deal," I add, realizing it's pointless to tell him how I really feel. Eric couldn't possibly understand this kind of love. He'd extinguish the all-consuming flame with a quick and logical pinch of the fingers. I feel myself starting to get upset, my eyes get watery. I bend down like I'm looking for something in my knapsack.

"You know, it's understandable if you're upset. You were together for—what?—five months?"

"Seven," I correct him. I keep looking in my bag, like I'm searching for something really important. "I'm fine. What can I do? I mean, he's an asshole. Everyone says so."

"He must have had some endearing qualities for you to stay with him."

"Yeah, but it's not like I thought we'd be together forever."

"You might want to talk about it sometime. I mean, you were together a few months, right? He did just take off. You have a right to be angry. It's all right if this is what's been making you upset."

I shoot up from my bag, my eyes now dry. Look him straight in the eye. "What makes you think I give a fuck about him?"

"I don't know. I just thought . . ."

"Read my lips: I don't care. Okay? *I . . . don't . . . care.*" I say it slowly and clearly. "It's not a big deal. It's not like I don't have other guys."

"Oh, sorry. I just . . . thought . . . he was your boyfriend."

"Yeah, well, just 'cause he's my boyfriend doesn't mean I don't fuck other guys."

"Okay," he says, holding his hands up as if surrendering. The room becomes uncomfortably silent. I pick up my bag to show him that I'm going. "Did you find it?"

"What?"

"The agenda." He motions to my knapsack, but smiles somewhat so that I know he's on to me.

"Yeah," I say, getting up to go.

"Sorry," Eric says again as I leave.

"Don't worry about it," I say, more out of obligation than anything else. I hate the power of that word. *Sorry*. I hate its insistence on a reply. The way it forces forgiveness out of you, like the obligation to exhale.

•   •   •

"You little bitch!" Tammy is up in my face, her crossed-eyes now abnormally straight. We are in the TV room and I am refusing to stop flicking the channels. Tammy pushes over the bowl of chips from the coffee table where my feet are. I knew this was coming, since I fooled around with Steve, this guy she's liked for months. She must have just found out.

"You're blocking my view," I say calmly, knowing it'll piss her off.

"You fuckin' little slut," she yells, and I feel her spit on my face. She wants me to throw the first punch so that she can claim self-defence and it won't affect her probation.

I peer around her head to get a better glimpse of a TV show I'm not even interested in. "He's not your boyfriend," I explain. "He doesn't even like you. He thinks you're scat." When I say this she flips her lid. Goes all twitchy-like and throws a punch that gets me in the shoulder. I jump up, pushing her back into the TV stand.

By now Jasmyn is off the couch, grabbing Tammy so I can get to her. Only, I don't even want to. For whatever reason, I don't even want to fight. Which ends up not to even matter, because Jasmyn needs no invitation to do damage.

"Let go of me, you fuckin' cunt," Tammy yells at her. "What the fuck does this have to do with you?"

"'Cause I can't stand you," she says. And then Tammy and Jasmyn start going at it. Slapping and pulling hair and kicking around the TV room. It doesn't stress me out too much since I know Jasmyn is just messing around with Tammy. I know, because if Jasmyn were serious, Tammy would be down in a second.

Within a few minutes, Pat and Miranda are already in the room, yelling at me to go upstairs and get some air. They jump between the two interlocked bodies and split them up. Jasmyn immediately backs off, but Tammy starts kicking, her legs going crazy in the air. It's like she's gone completely crazy and we all just shut up and stand still, shocked, because she's absolutely losing it. Even Jasmyn stays back. Tammy starts knocking over chairs and spit flies out of her mouth. "You want a piece of me? You want a piece of me?" she yells in my direction, but Miranda is blocking her way. Finally Pat moves in, puts a hold on Tammy, and brings her down to the ground. But Tammy keeps kicking and yelling that she's fucking going to kill me, so then Miranda pins her other shoulder to the floor and Tammy lies there flat out on her stomach, slowly giving up the struggle. "Let me go, man," she mumbles, her face pressed into the carpet. Pat speaks calmly into her ear, telling her to just relax. And after a while all you can hear is Tammy's breathing, slow and heavy. I start to feel all shaky and strange and I just have to get out of there.

Mute Mary arrives home while I'm standing outside the front door and I explain to her what just happened. "How fucked is that? What a nutcase," says Mary. And I realize I'd never talked with her before, really talked, and she's kind of okay. She's being really friendly to me for a reason; she says she's pissed at Tammy because she keeps borrowing money and smokes off her and doesn't pay back. She bitches about how Tammy keeps on making up stupid lies about giving money to her family or about someone stealing it. And we start laughing about how weird she is. About how she always picks at her crotch and how she stinks up the bathroom, even when she's taking a pee.

Suddenly, out of nowhere, Tammy comes tearing out the front door. Before I know it, her fist is in my face and my hands fling out instinctively, hitting flesh and teeth and bone. With my eyes closed, my other senses sharpen. I taste blood in my mouth. I hear Jasmyn and Miranda and Mary screaming at Tammy to back off. We all become one large, thrashing cluster and somehow move out onto the lawn. I break free from Tammy's grasp and stare in disbelief at the clump of my hair still in her clenched fist. But I don't go after her because, with the sudden release, thoughts of the baby fill my head. My hands move in front of my stomach, Jasmyn jumps in front of me as Mary goes to hold back Tammy. And we're all out there on the front lawn, four girls in bare feet, screaming and shouting at each other. Tammy must finally realize that it's three against one and she takes off down the street, barefoot, her white oversized T-shirt blob fading into the distance. For some reason, I chase after her and behind me I can hear Jasmyn's heavy breathing. Within seconds she passes me, wide stride, her heels kicking up high behind her.

Lucky for Tammy a bus pulls in at the stop on the corner and she clambers up onto it, racing to the back window as it pulls away. I catch up to Jasmyn, who is now standing, surrendering hands up in the air. Breathless, I hold one hand on her shoulder for balance. We watch the bus converge into darkness, Tammy's smiling, crazy face against the back window, her fingertips pressed against glass. Flicking her tongue like a snake and giving us the finger.

"Look at her—she's fuckin' nuts," Jasmyn says.

"Yeah," I say.

"You're a bit of a screwball yourself," Jasmyn turns to me, a smile widening on her face. She playfully pushes my shoulder.

"Certified," I joke, and we share a smoke that Jasmyn finds in her jacket pocket on the way back.

"Look at my nose," Jasmyn says, pulling one nostril to the side. "The earring's sunk in. Fuckin' bitch got me right in the face." I look closely at the almost invisible glint of diamond under the streetlight and start laughing. "Shut up! Hurts like hell," she says, sticking her finger up her nostril.

"You'll live."

I hold my hand up to my jaw and move it around a bit. "Look at your face," Jasmyn says laughing. "You're going to be one ugly bitch tomorrow."

"I know," I say, picking out the drying blood from the edge of my nose. And we recount the whole event, from the TV room to the front lawn, play by play. It's all like one big joke. But our smiles quickly fade when we see Staff on the front porch, arms crossed, staring down our approach.

"You're going to be in shit," Jasmyn warns.

15

The next day the group home calls for a family meeting. I tell Pat I won't go, that I've had enough meetings about every little thing. I tell her I'm sick of talking with everyone and never getting anywhere. "I'm all worded out," I say, poking at my fat lip.

But I don't have a choice. She tells me the house is calling the meeting and it's obligatory. Only it's Aunt Sharon who comes, not Elsie. We sit in the front room of the house, sinking into the worn couches, knees level with our chins, while Pat and Miranda tower over us from straight-back chairs.

I jokingly stick my tongue out at Miranda, but her face remains fixed in a serious gaze. "What!" I blurt out. "Is this *Invasion of the Body Snatchers*? Where's Miranda?" I wave my hand in front of her glare, as if trying to snap her out of it. "Earth to Miranda!"

Pat ignores my comment and starts the meeting. "We called this meeting to review your time here, Snow. But we are also concerned about your behaviour lately." She darts a look to Aunt Sharon. And it starts to bother me that Aunt Sharon is sitting in

this room, as if she had anything to do with my life. I look to
Miranda who is now staring down at her notebook in her lap.
"We'd like to hear from you first, Snow. Do you have anything to
say about your recent conduct?"

All heads turn to me, staring, waiting. The pressure is unbearable. I have no idea what Pat wants me to say. I almost feel like just
blurting out that I'm pregnant. Just to prove how clueless they are.
Instead, I stare at the ground and shrug my shoulders. I try my
hardest to find the words, but all I come up with is, "I don't know,
maybe I'm going through a phase?" I look at Pat, hoping this is the
right answer.

"I think I can fill in the blanks a little bit here," Aunt Sharon
pipes up. "There were some family things that happened last
week. Snow found out some things about her birth mother that
were upsetting. And, well, with Mark gone, I think she's just
having a bit of a rough time."

"What are you talking about?" I challenge. "This has nothing to
do with Mark." And all of a sudden it pisses me off that Aunt
Sharon is talking like she knows me, like she has any idea what I'm
about.

Aunt Sharon looks quickly to Pat and then at me. "I thought
you might be acting out because you're hurt about Mark. I
thought I'd help you make them understand—"

"You don't know me. You think because you take me out for
dinner, you know anything about me?"

"I just wanted to help."

"I don't need your help," I say. "I never needed your help." It
occurs to me how great Aunt Sharon must look to Pat and
Miranda. How supportive she must seem, like she's all concerned
about me. But if she was so concerned, she would have let me live
with her.

Aunt Sharon turns to Pat, a look of embarrassment on her face. "I think she's a little upset at me too."

"I can speak for myself." I cross my arms and face the door, my back entirely to Aunt Sharon.

"Are your family concerns something you can talk about with me, Snow?" Miranda asks me.

"No."

Pat straightens her back and shuffles the papers in front of her. "Well, I guess we're at a bit of a roadblock here. Perhaps you can talk about what's bothering you with Miranda, later on."

Anger surges through me and I feel the need to escape. I stomp my foot on the ground. I can't stand these people on my back. They don't help me when I need help, and then they criticize me when I mess up. I turn to Pat and look her straight in the eyes and then I speak slowly so she can fully understand: "I . . . don't . . . want . . . to . . . fucking . . . talk. Got it?"

Pat's eyes become narrow and her jaw muscles start twitching on the side of her face. "Well, regardless of what's going on in your personal life, we need to have a safe environment here. And that means getting along with everyone, including those you don't like."

"I didn't start that," I snap at her.

Pat holds her hand up to stop me. "We're not getting into it," she says firmly.

"But—"

"Drop it!" she says sharply. "What I'm saying to you, I've said to Tammy as well." She speaks in generalizations, about certain "incidents" both here and at school. And about the dramatic change in me since my arrival. She makes it sound like I've done a thousand things wrong and nothing right. Pat does most of the talking, like she's the heavy, with Miranda jumping in every once in a while to ask me my point of view.

At the end of the meeting, we all stand at the door and Miranda tells Aunt Sharon that I'm a very special girl and I have a lot of potential. She says she would like me to get into a co-op program where I can live with just one adult role model and a few other girls in a house. "I don't think this is a positive environment for Snow," she says. And I storm past all of them and head up to my room.

. . .

Jasmyn asks me to her new boyfriend's party on Saturday night. His name is Hayden, he's twenty-four, and he has a blond goatee and tattoos of snakes and fire all over his arms. He screams in a band, pisses on the audience, and has tons of girls after him. I tell her I'll go, just to get away from Staff.

"They call it the fuck-hut," Jasmyn claims as we enter Hayden's apartment, "but that's just a joke." Looking around, I get the feeling it's not a joke at all. The walls are painted black, the ceilings are red, and there are massive artsy murals of what look like naked girls with nipples the size of melons all over the walls.

There are people everywhere and the music is so loud it vibrates the floor. "Hayden's roommate's an artist. Isn't he amazing?" she yells, as we stand below a mural full of dizzying thick strokes of paint and a glob of steel wool sticking out from where the woman's crotch would be.

"What's that?"

"Her kooch, stupid." Jasmyn laughs and I follow her down the narrow corridor, jammed with people. Some guys nod at Jasmyn as she passes by, but no guys even look at me, and I figure that I must be giving off some pregnant scent because they wouldn't be able to see my stomach under my bulky sweatshirt. In the living room, spliffs are being served like appetizers on a tray. We find

Hayden in the kitchen. He is gorgeous and sexy and his blue eyes penetrate your soul, just like Jasmyn said. She hangs off him, laughing too much at his jokes and agreeing too much with everything he says. He gets us drinks all night, mine with only a little alcohol.

"She's sick," Jasmyn is quick to say, but I know it's not because she's concerned about covering for me. It's more because she's embarrassed her friend doesn't drink.

After a few glasses, I go to the washroom because my head is spinning and I think I'm going to throw up. I lean against the counter, staring at my face as it drips and contorts in the mirror. And I realize it can't be alcohol making me feel so crazy, there had to be something more in the drinks. The music pounds in my head and a person appears in the mirror behind me. At first I can't make it out, but then I focus hard and see that it's Hayden. He's taking my hair and brushing it off my face, his head moves in close, hot breath on my eyelids. Then his lips are on mine, hard and sucking. He jams his tongue down my throat. The door shuts, voices are distant and vague. Hayden pries my mouth open, sucking my protests into his wet mouth. As my limp hands try to push him away, he starts to get all forceful and rough. And then the clinking of his belt buckle shatters in my head like glass.

He pushes me to my knees and tries to stick his dick in my mouth, but my head falls back, my neck muscles weaken. He swears angrily, calls me a cunt and slut, grips both his hands on my head, and forces himself into my mouth, squeezing my head harder and harder, yanking my hair, and I squeal in response, like this little pig, which turns him on even more. And I think he's going to kill me. He will twist my neck. I will die tonight. I taste blood in my mouth as I allow my teeth to rip the inside of my lips because I am terrified of what he might do if I cut him. I focus all my energy on not throwing up. Jasmyn pounds on the door as her boyfriend slams his body into me, coarse pubic hair jamming up my nose.

"Thanks, sweetheart," he says when he's done, releasing my head and zipping up his fly. The warm fluid drains from my numb lips, down my chin. I lean forward, throw up all over his feet, and he kicks me to the floor where I crumble onto my own puke.

I wake up hours later, on the floor by a dresser in one of the rooms. There is a couple sleeping in the bed and another guy on the rug a few feet away. My head pounds. I pull my body off the ground and stumble to the washroom, study my puffy, red mouth in the mirror. My hair is matted with dried vomit. I brush my teeth with someone's toothbrush and gargle with gobs of toothpaste. Without cash for the bus, I have to walk home. I stumble out the front door and down the sidewalk, past perfect little families on their way to church. They are nicely dressed, their proper shoes click-clicking on pavement. I see the parents stare at me from the corners of their eyes, reach protective arms around their innocent children as I pass, drop to my knees and vomit in a bush.

I am relieved to finally reach the group home. My mouth is so dry I think my tongue will crack. Jasmyn comes out the door, just as I walk into the house. As if she were waiting for hours to time this perfectly. "Slut," she says, brushing past me. "Don't talk to me."

"What are you . . . ?" The words seem to evaporate as soon as they hit air.

Jasmyn spins around quickly, her face right up to mine, our noses almost touching. With a clenched jaw she firmly repeats, "I said, don't talk to me." Then she turns and storms away.

I enter the house a slut and boyfriend fucker. If Jasmyn is angry at someone in the house, then everyone is angry at her. Staff may have their house rules, but the residents have a far more effective punishment. I lie down on my bed, clothes still on, hair matted, and wait for my inevitable persecution.

Girls jump on hate here. They fight over scraps of me like vultures to a dead animal. I fuel them. I am ignored, brushed up against. Rooms clear when I enter. If I speak, I am attacked. If I remain silent, I am guilty.

.   .   .

The next morning I sit outside Eric's office door and wait for him to arrive at work. I can tell from the expression on his face when he sees me that I must look like hell.

"What happened?" he asks, staring down at me, his keys clenched in his fist.

I open my mouth to answer but then my eyes cloud and I start crying. I drop my head into my knees, crying so hard I start to gag and then throw up all over the bottom of my pants. Eric bends down beside me, rests his hand on the back of my head, and holds back my hair until I'm done. Then he waits until I can lift myself up and follow him into his office.

I spend the next two hours with Eric. He cancels all his other appointments for the morning. I sit on the couch, a blanket wrapped tightly around my body. In front of me is a box of Kleenex, a glass of water, and a garbage pail to throw up in. My body is shaking. Stomach muscles ache from crying so hard. If it weren't for my skin, I think I'd break apart.

I tell Eric everything. Almost everything. Some words spill out of me and others are forced up through my throat. Sometimes Eric leaves to give me privacy to cry, other times he sits silently across from me, patiently holding out Kleenexes as if he were offering peanuts to a squirrel. I tell him about the pregnancy. I tell him about my birth mother being a fifteen-year-old druggie. I tell him about Mitch in my room that last night at Elsie's. I tell him about Hayden and about smoking and drinking and about sometimes just wanting to die. I tell him I'm scared.

I strip my mind. I don't care what truth he knows. I have nothing to hide except the marks on my body. Those I keep for myself. I couldn't risk him taking those away, because if he did, I'd have nothing.

At first Eric says things he is supposed to say, like, "I encourage you to report this to the police." And then he says other things he shouldn't: "Goddamn punk should be castrated." As he's speaking, his face gets red and his fists are tight and small bits of saliva collect at the corners of his mouth. He catches me staring, intrigued at his response. His anger makes him human. Faulted. Like me.

He quickly shifts in his chair and returns to his responsible, flattened expression. "Sorry."

"It's okay," I say.

At the end of it all, I sit, exhausted, in a tight ball on his couch, stomach pressed hard into my thighs. I clutch clumps of wet tissues in my hands. My head pounds, my mouth is dry and tight. My eyes burn. I feel cleansed and terrified all at once.

Eric puts his hand on my knee and holds tightly. "We will get through this one layer at a time, Snow."

"I just want to be told what to do," I say, completely drained. I have no fight left in me. "I don't want to think anymore."

THREE

· · ·

16

My dreams are about the baby now. No longer overexposed ghostly memories of my mother. Instead, these images are dripping and dark and pungent. I dream of a purplish yellow fetus, floating in liquid in a large jar. It has a bony, prickly spine, bulging head, and tiny curled seahorse body. The jar is on a counter in a lab with test tubes and microscopes, and there are people in long white coats who are staring at crystals through thick goggle-like glasses. My eyes return to the baby, only to find it flailing about, the liquid churning like a stormy ocean. Its hollow mouth gasping up against the glass, drowning. I feel my own lungs fill with fluid. And I yell to the people in the white lab coats to help it, but they ignore me. So I finally lift the heavy sealed bottle and smash it on the floor and the baby splashes out, flipping on the ground like a gasping fish. And I don't know what to do, so I lift up its slimy body and hold it to my chest. And I sing the only lullaby I know, *Hush little baby, don't say a word* . . . as it starts to relax and eventually turns blue and stiff in my hands.

.   .   .

"I guess I'll keep it," I announce casually as if I were talking about a stray dog or a duplicated gift. Three wide-mouthed youth workers circle around me in the office. Miranda rises to shut the door. The books I stole from the library are spread out in front of me. Staff cautiously await my next move. I could get angry, flip the table, or throw a book. I could say it's illegal for them to snoop through my room, but what they don't know is that I left the books where they could find them. Eric gave me the idea. He said it might be easier to break the news that way.

We are quiet for a moment.

"We just can't believe we didn't know," Pat finally says, as if they think I might be lying. As if what's most disturbing is not that someone in the house is pregnant, but that they didn't pick up on the signs. They sigh a lot and talk in whispers, as if I'm dying, avoiding any upsetting words. Tell me I have *options,* or *alternatives,* too afraid to say the real word: *adoption.* They tell me *we'll* take one day at a time, that *we'll* need to find some community supports, that *we'll* have to watch *our* diets and stop smoking.

When I leave the room, Miranda follows me, tugs at my sleeve, and whispers, *You know, I was adopted.* When I ask her why she's whispering, she turns all red and chokes on words.

.   .   .

Staff sends me to a health clinic that same afternoon. I don't understand why I just can't wait a day, but they say that I should go as soon as possible, considering my activities. The waiting room stinks of sickness and mothballs and diapers. It is packed with old people and kids running around sneezing and wiping their snotty hands on the chairs.

The doctor seems angry with me the second I walk in the room. Without even raising his eyes from his file folder, he tells me to close the door and sticks a wavering finger out, directing me to climb up on the table. He is old, with grey hair and pale folds of flesh that hang like saggy elephant skin from his face. It's as if age has drained his body of colour. It gives me shivers. But then he raises his head and I spot two beady blue eyes glimmering through his thick yellowed-glass lenses.

Immediately, he starts to give me quick orders, like hold out your tongue, breathe deep, inhale, exhale. He taps me on the left elbow and tells me to roll up my sleeve so he can check my blood pressure.

I panic. "Can you check my other arm?" I blurt out, knowing that if he says no, I'll run. A doctor would send me straight to the mental hospital if he saw my cuts. He motions that he doesn't care which arm I pick, and so I reposition myself on the examining table and offer him my unscarred right arm.

"Well, you seem healthy enough. What's the problem?" he finally asks.

"I think I'm pregnant."

"Is that why you're here?" He looks up at me. I see that it's not only his glasses, but the whites of his eyes are yellow too.

"Yes."

He looks down to his file folder. "They didn't write it down," he mumbles, irritated. "Why didn't you say?" The man is looking at me as if I were an idiot.

"You didn't ask."

He sighs, puts away his stethoscope, and leans back against the counter. "Any symptoms?"

"No."

"No upset stomach? Breast tenderness? Headaches? Constipation?"

"No," I lie, thinking maybe he'll just send me away.

"When was your last period?" He positions his pencil to write the date down.

"I'm not sure."

"Come on, now, you've got to know. It's important."

"But I don't know."

"Guess."

"I don't know. Probably about six months ago," I say, shrugging my shoulders.

I'm surprised to see colour actually leak into his face. "And you haven't seen a doctor?" I shake my head. "We'll have to get going then. You're young and healthy. Everything should be fine. I'll just check your tummy. You'll need an ultrasound appointment to check dates and make sure there are no anatomical problems." He doesn't ask me the things other people do. Like *how come you waited so long* or *how could you not know you were pregnant,* or *what did you think, it would just go away?* Instead he asks me, "Do you smoke?"

"No."

"Drink?"

"No," I say. "Well, maybe a little."

"A little what?"

"A little smoking, a little drinking," I say weakly.

I'm ready for him to scold me, but instead he just takes a lab form from the desk and starts frantically scribbling and ticking boxes. He passes me the sheet to take down to the lab in the basement. "They're routine checks," he says. "Hemoglobin, syphilis, rubella, hepatitis, HIV, blood type." The medical words swirl in my head. I think of fluids and tubes and pus and open sores. I start to feel dizzy, reach out a hand to brace myself on the table.

"You okay?" He quickly pulls a chair out from against the wall, "Here, sit. Put your head between your knees." I lean forward on the chair, my head buried in my hands, focusing on the white-tiled floor. He continues talking, telling me about fetal alcohol syndrome and the effects of smoking on baby size. "If you are using drugs and not telling me, I need to let you know there are risks with congenital abnormalities and premature delivery." I don't even understand the words. His voice is muffled and distant. I start to sweat, my mouth gets dry, my muscles slip from bone, and I can barely keep myself on the chair. I tell him I'm going to be sick and he whisks a garbage pail in front of me. Instead I faint.

When I wake I'm on the chair, the doctor's hands are holding me upright. "You with us now? You just fainted, but you're all right," he says, helping me up to the examining table. After a few minutes I am left alone to rest, lying on the crinkly paper. I close my eyes and concentrate on breathing. My face tingles as I feel the blood rush back to my skin. The back of my shirt is wet from sweat and I curl up for heat.

When the doctor returns he insists on continuing his checkup, poking and prodding my limp body. He takes my blood pressure again, weight, checks my ankles and hands for swelling. He writes down the names of the vitamins I need to take, recommends exercise, and tells me about a pregnancy book that young people like me seem to prefer. As I slip down from the table, he tells me a list of no's: no smoking, no drinking, no drugs, no hooliganry at night.

"You mean sex?" I ask, concerned.

"No. That's fine. Protected of course. I meant just be safe."

Before I leave he gives me a referral to an obstetrician who deals with young ones like myself, and then writes down the name of a counsellor who can help me with *things*. I stand there, collecting his little slips of paper in my hands. Then he reaches out and gives me a little tweak on the cheek, in an almost loving way, which stuns me. I hate that. Teachers or social workers do it all the time. Lay it all down harsh and then find some way at the end to come across as nice, like they're sweet people. Like they're so afraid they'll be hated. "It'll be a long road," he says and then pushes me out the door.

In a white lab in the basement of the medical building, I wait to get my blood tests done. Middle-aged ladies with blue lab coats sit behind a large counter, mispronouncing names and arguing with people who don't have their health cards. I find a seat in between a wheezing elderly man and a woman with her toddler, who is outstretched on the floor, colouring a flower black despite his mother's offering of the pink crayon. I'm surrounded by kids everywhere I go now, and I'm unsure if it's just that I've never noticed them or that fate is trying to get me used to the idea. Across from me is another woman, who has this perfect little baby in her lap, staring wide-eyed at the little kid on the ground. It makes soft gurgling baby noises and every once in a while the mother leans down to kiss its perfectly round little head.

I hold my knapsack up in front of my stomach to hide my pregnancy. I do this, even though my sweatshirt and baggy pants already cover any curves. I think of the cigarettes and the drinking and the junk food I eat. I consider what kind of one-eyed, hairy-tailed creature might be growing inside of me. I start scraping my sharp fingernail along the back of my hand, scratching a triangle into skin. And when this doesn't feel like enough, I slip my fingers up under my sweatshirt and gouge my nails into my stomach.

Already I am a bad parent. You will not forgive me. You will be born screaming, not at this unforgiving world, but at your own mother.

. . .

I wake up the next day, wishing I hadn't told anyone, wishing that this baby hadn't become the centre of my nothing. All Staff wants to talk about is my pregnancy. I am asked into the office for endless meetings about my health, about where I will live, about giving up smoking and about drinking more milk. Still, the confession is like a huge weight lifted from me. My jaw no longer aches, shoulders and neck relax, and I don't have to worry every second about hiding my pregnancy. I can now wear just a T-shirt when I'm hot and I don't have to force myself to finish what's on my plate. And if my hands end up resting on the curve of my belly, I don't have to pull them away.

Staff wants to organize a house meeting for me to make the announcement about the pregnancy to the other residents. As if anyone is really going to care. But everything has to be processed in this group home. People can't even fart without there being a group meeting about it. I think of an excuse in order to delay the confession a few days, because if I tell the others I'm pregnant, they will say, *That's what sluts deserve.* I need to wait until things die down, which happens sooner than I expect because two days later Nicole tells me that Jasmyn broke up with Hayden after she found out how many girls he's been fucking behind her back. And that night, after dinner, Jasmyn leads me down into the laundry room, which is where all the residents' really private conversations take place.

"I'm sorry I was such a bitch," she says, among the humming and clanking of the dryers.

"That's okay." I smile and we hug, but my uncommitted arms loosely drape over her shoulders. I don't forgive her. And really, deep down, I hate her.

We start to climb the stairs. "You heard what's going on?" she asks, and then Jasmyn tells me all the juicy details of how Nicole caught Mute Mary masturbating with a Barbie doll in the third-floor bathroom last night. And by the time we reach the top stair, she has linked her arm with mine and exits with a dramatic howl of laughter that makes all the other girls' heads turn.

And so four days later the residents gather in the living room at seven, as we normally would, for announcements and house meetings. The others are especially rowdy because today is also the day we plan our monthly group outing and they have hopes of Wonderland.

"I'm gonna have a baby," I announce to a now silenced circle of bodies lazing on couches. I stare down at the ground as they try to read my expression.

"Is that a good thing?" Mute Mary finally asks.

"I don't know. I'm getting used to it."

"Well, congratulations?" Mary says as if it were a question.

"Yeah, congratulations," Nicole adds.

"I had no idea," Tammy says reflectively, as if it explains my behaviour. As if I'm forgiven for everything.

I dart a glance at Tracy, who's staring at the door, a blank expression on her face. I wonder what she's thinking, because she's had two abortions in the past year.

"I've known for weeks," Jasmyn pipes in. "I was dying to say something." And she starts to recount all the close calls. The conversations almost overheard by Staff, the pregnancy test boxes in the torn garbage bags in the backyard, the pregnancy pamphlet Nicole found in our bedroom last week. And of course, Jasmyn takes full credit for redirecting suspicions of my enlarged tits with her quick-thinking explanation of a new padded Wonderbra.

17

I try to keep busy, focus my mind on the baby, but my mother keeps creeping back into my head. She forces her way through my entangled thoughts, dense and prickly, her small hands bloodied and rough from the thorns.

What do you do when you find out your mother was only fifteen when she gave birth? When the arms that have carried you all these years suddenly disintegrate and you're left in the empty grasp of someone who probably feared you more than she loved you? My birth mother's protective whispers at night have become childish tantrums demanding understanding. Her voice is needy and whiny. *I owe you nothing,* I whisper back into the dark, *I am not your mother.*

I choose not to look for her. At least, not in the obvious places. I will not ask Elsie or Aunt Sharon for stories of my mother, stories that may or may not be true. I will not go to her old school and talk to her guidance counsellor. Instead, I will search for my birth mother in safe places. Places like buildings, where I can choose to enter or walk away. And it will be *my* choice, this time, to need my mother.

The truths Elsie gave me are no longer truths. My mother did not grow up in that apartment building five blocks away, like Elsie said. Her feet never touched the lawn I lay on. Her hands never grasped the metal door handle I so often ran my finger along. In truth, real truth, my mother lived in the west end of Toronto, with Elsie and Aunt Sharon, in the stockyard neighbourhood that smells of meat and blood. The area where, on a hot summer's day, the smell of death forces you to breathe through your mouth.

"She left home when she got pregnant," Elsie says over the phone. "After that, she lived at friends' houses and I think some house on—"

"Just give me the address of where you guys lived," I say quickly. "I just want to walk by, that's all."

Elsie stutters and is confused over whether the unit they lived in was unit fifty or fifteen. "I don't know, it had a prickly brown shrub just to the left of the door. The basement window had a crack in it, eh? I always thought they should fix it. You know, it's a housing complex, you know, not very nice, it—"

"That's good," I say, not wanting her story.

"I just want you to be—"

"Enough," I say sharply, slicing off her words.

"But . . ."

"Bye." I hang up the phone.

·   ·   ·

The real place where my birth mother grew up is simple: a small building with cement walls, and a front lobby that smells of urine and cigarettes and curry. A broken elevator and a piss-stained

stairwell. Bed sheets and tin foil line windows. Rusted balconies
are stuffed with bikes and old chesterfields.

Unit five has a paint-chipped door leading out onto the street
and a cracked basement window. The yard in front of the building is unkept, discarded cigarette packages and white plastic bags
line the wire fence. I position myself in front of the apartment,
wishing time could overlap, fold in upon itself for just a brief
moment. My eyes take in everything, every angle, every colour.
The curve of the road stretching down to the corner. The green-
painted bricks of the building next door. The initials scraped into
the cement walkway. The two dents on the silver doorknob, like
dimples on a face. I just stand there, slowly twirling in full circles,
ensuring that something I see must have been witnessed by my
mother's eyes.

Before I leave, I take one last look and I am strangely satisfied.
I deeply inhale the smell of blood and flesh from the few remaining slaughterhouses. I think about my mother and her home and
being fifteen. I think about her wanting to escape from here.
Think about how, in time, maybe, I stopped being a mistake and,
at some point, I became a way out.

.   .   .

Miranda tells Aunt Sharon about my pregnancy over the phone.
Our deal is that she will make the initial phone call but I will have
to follow up and meet Aunt Sharon to talk to her in person. I
agree to anything, as long as I don't have to be the one to hear
Aunt Sharon's voice when she hears the news. I pace the hallway
of the group home, listening carefully to Miranda's tone as she
answers Aunt Sharon's questions.

"Did she sound mad?" I ask Miranda when she hangs up the
receiver.

"No," Miranda says thoughtfully.

"Surprised?"

"No."

"Disappointed?"

"No."

"Then what?"

Miranda thinks a moment. "I don't know. Sad, maybe? She's coming over."

"Now?"

"Yep."

I take a deep breath and go up to my room to fix my face and brush my hair. I put on my baggiest clothes and my hooded sweatshirt so that when I put my hands in the pockets in the front, you can't see my large stomach at all. Aunt Sharon comes over just an hour after Miranda hangs up the phone. I wait for her on the porch of the house, and throw up once in the bushes before she gets here.

"Hey," she says, warmly smiling.

"Hey," I say, embarrassed. I slowly get up and descend the few stairs to meet her on the pathway.

"You want to walk?"

"All right." And we travel about a block before I start to speak. "Elsie knew about this. I told her that day she told me about my mom. I don't know why she didn't tell you."

"God only knows. She probably thought it would bother me to be left out. She'd take pleasure in that."

"But you'd think she'd take pleasure in telling you how I fucked up."

"You'd think," she says, obviously without realizing how cruel it was to agree with me. "So how are you doing?"

"I'm fine," I say. "You know, it was a surprise at first. But what can I do? I'm gonna have it, so I might as well make the best of it, right?" I hear myself saying the words but I can't believe they're actually coming from my mouth. I have no idea why I'm trying to sound like everything is so great.

"How pregnant are you?" I feel like Aunt Sharon can see straight through me, like she can see my top lip nervously twitching.

"About six months."

"Jesus"—Aunt Sharon stops in her tracks—"that's a long way." She looks down and skeptically studies my stomach area under my sweatshirt. "You can't be that big. You sure it's in there?" she jokes.

I lift my shirt and expose my round stomach.

"Look at that!" Aunt Sharon exclaims, her hand immediately pressed against my skin.

I tell her about my doctor's appointment and the pregnancy homes that Staff is looking into. I tell her the baby might be Mark's, but that I'm not really sure. I'd rather sound like a slut than get Mark in trouble.

"I went by your old house off Keele," I say, just before we reach the group home.

"You did?" she asks, surprised.

"Yeah. It's kind of gross."

"Yes, it was."

"You ever been back?" I ask.

"No," Aunt Sharon says, smiling politely at me. "I left that place a long time ago."

. . .

Now that I'm not hiding my pregnancy, I see that pregnant people are treated differently. It's like you have this innocence about you, as if you're a representative of Mother Nature herself. I figure it must be something instinctual, this communal need to protect those with child. Bus drivers wait until I sit down before pulling out from the stop. People open doors for me. The girls offer to do my laundry. Staff allows me to eat in between meals and skip my chores if I don't feel up to working.

My stomach becomes our new household pet. On command, I pull up my sweatshirt to reveal my bulging tummy. The girls place their hands on my tight skin, cold palms cupping my belly in search of movement. They act all excited for me, but I've noticed that there are fewer condoms in the jar by the bathroom door.

"It's so hard!" Mary says, pulling her hand back fast, her face half-disgusted, half-amazed.

"Feels like a lot of gas. I fart all the time," I say. "I look like I've got a bowling ball in my stomach."

"Yeah, but look at your tits," Nicole says. "What I'd give for tits like that."

They suggest names like Destiny, Electra, and Rain. They become instant experts on diet and suddenly recall their mothers' secret recipes, like cucumbers on your swollen feet. Suddenly, they think they have the right to boss me around, ripping cookies and cigarettes right out of my hand. And of course, we have discussions about labour. Nicole tells me that after delivering the baby, her cousin shot out a chunk of flesh full of teeth and hair and little toenails. Tammy says her sister shit all over the delivery room. And Jasmyn's friend's friend almost died giving birth to a baby that nearly ripped her body in half. There is laughter about all this, mostly due to Tammy's gruesome accompanying sound effects. I pretend to laugh along, but really my stomach churns and acid rises to my throat as I imagine my body snapping like a wishbone.

"Don't worry," Pat, who has two children of her own, says. "By the time you're full-term, you'll volunteer to get hit by a bus to get that baby out. Mother Nature takes care of everything, even fear."

On weekend nights I watch thin bodies float carefree past me while my fat stomach anchors me to the couch. Jasmyn and Tracy suddenly become best friends and laugh at stupid inside jokes about guys they know. It seems like they intentionally have more fun when in my presence, but I know Jasmyn doesn't really like Tracy. She couldn't possibly, after all the bad stuff she has said about her.

My social life has become the Staff, because no one else wants to hang out with a pregnant girl who can't party or smoke. To make me feel better, Staff buys me chocolate milk and cheddar cheese. My community time is reduced to playing Scrabble on Friday nights. I am strangely content doing this, staying in my pyjamas, as if life for me is now one continuous lazy Sunday after-noon after a very rough Saturday night.

.   .   .

The house sends me to take a tour of a pregnancy home right away. Beverley, it's called. Apparently, my group home isn't allowed to have me there after my seven-month date. "We're not equipped," says Pat, as if she were talking about electrical capacity.

"That's okay," I say. "I don't really fit in anymore anyway." Which is true. The more I'm forced to witness what I can't do, the more I resent it.

The visitors' room of Beverley House is lined with practical couches, probably donated by the guilty consciences of wealthy women who as teenagers disappeared to Nova Scotia with chubby stomachs and returned in time for summer vacation.

There are four of us in the visitors' room, each slouched on our own couch, cross-armed, and refusing to acknowledge each other's presence. Only one of the other girls looks pregnant, the rest just look angry. The girl with teased black hair listens to her

Discman and taps her lighter loudly on the wooden arm of the couch. It's meant to annoy us, but I say nothing because I know that would be exactly what she wants. Instead I focus on the voices of the bubbly staff speaking baby talk and cheerleader chatter down the hall. Without even seeing their faces, I know what they're like. Occasionally, one skips past the door, confirming my suspicions, dressed in overalls and a pink T-shirt. Their happiness seems inappropriate to me, like laughter at a funeral.

Finally a youth worker walks into the room, her flabby body bulging out from under her T-shirt and jeans. You can't even tell the difference between her rolls of fat and her tits. It's disgusting. And I can't stand the thought that I'm starting to look like that.

"Hello. Well, I guess that's everyone," she says, smiling around the room, a clipboard jammed into one of the folds in her folds. She has short hair, no makeup, and an earring only in one ear.

"We'll just get started. Welcome to Beverley. My name's Meg and I'm one of the youth workers here." She sits in the chair off to the side. "We'll start the tour here. This is our visiting room where the residents can receive guests, only two at a time and no shared visits. It can also be a nice quiet spot if you want to be on your own. I'll tell you a bit about the house and then I'll take you around the facilities." She starts to tell us about the house and its history and how the home was started sixty years ago in Toronto, "but things were very different then." Only I look in her direction, the rest of the girls continue staring at the floor. After a couple of minutes, she walks over to the black-haired girl and motions for her to turn off her Discman, which she does reluctantly, kissing her teeth.

The worker goes through her routine, citing off privileges and rules and chores you do to earn money. She points to charts and chore boards and point systems. Speaks of curfews, goal setting, arts and crafts, and mandatory evening programs on health and fitness.

"Mandatory?" the black-haired girl speaks up, her lip curled up to her nose in disgust.

"Yes, mandatory," the worker says firmly in that *don't fuck with me* tone that we have all heard before.

"Screw this," the girl says, picking up her knapsack and storming out. She bumps her shoulder into the door frame when she leaves. Part of me walks out with her. Our eyes focus back on the worker as if nothing happened. We are all used to scenes like this.

"It's a voluntary program but it's not for everyone. If you don't like it, that's okay. We're just trying to offer help to those who want it," and then she goes on, unaffected.

Meg takes us through the old Victorian house, institutionalized with its thick fire doors, mesh wire pressed in glass, red-glowing exit signs, and sealed-up fireplaces. The house is much more impressive than my group home, with bright carpets, gold-framed paintings, wood trim, and huge velvet drapes. It's like a movie set. I visualize women in nineteenth-century skirts and tightly wound hair, drinking tea from china teacups. And ghostly men with suspenders and tiny, round glasses strolling the hallways. I think about how these God-fearing people would shudder at the thought of stray teenage mothers, a hundred years later, living in their home. I think about the wife, who probably hid her underwear under a sheet on the clothesline and thought the word *clitoris* referred to some kind of buzzing insect.

We poke our semi-curious heads into the kitchen, TV room, laundry, and dining room; watch the backs of residents as they leave the room, not wanting to be part of the sideshow. The bedrooms are functional and bare, as if you could spray them down with a hose for a fast clean in between girls.

At the top of the stairs, Meg stands in front of a closed door and explains that the dorms are split into two sections, the pre-baby and post-baby sides. She holds her hand up to the stained wood. "We can't go in here, due to confidentiality reasons and privacy. But this is where the new mothers are located." I stare at her fingers, pressed against the door, just inches away from a world I don't want to know.

During the tour, Meg draws our attention to the furnishings: the new TV or the spacious fridge that holds limitless cheese and yogurt. My eyes follow her pointing finger in the opposite direction, rest on things like the cleaning-duty list beside each entrance and the small orders taped to the sides of things: *Don't waste electricity* and *This window is to be closed at all times* or *No smoking in bedrooms.*

At the end of the tour, Meg gives us each a form where you have to write a paragraph saying why you want to be at Beverley House. "This will help us in evaluating your motivation for being here," she says with a smile and passes out pens. I leave the paragraph section blank, fill out my name and address, and then hand it in before I leave.

When I get home, Staff is waiting for me.

"Well? Did you like it?" Miranda asks enthusiastically.

"No."

"Will you go?"

"Do I have a choice?"

"You could go back to your grandmother's," Pat says.

I raise my arms in surrender, then take my seat in the office while Pat calls to arrange an intake meeting. Beverley House tells them that they'll have a bed for me in a week.

18

Eric is the one who brings up Mitch's name first. For some reason, he has chosen this as his first layer to peel. After he pours me some green tea, he gets right to the point. The tea thing is something he started a few weeks ago and there's something about the hot liquid that makes the words seep effortlessly out of my mouth. We talk about the night I left Elsie's place, about Mitch in my room and how Elsie didn't kick him out.

"I think he kissed me," I say. "I don't remember. I was sleeping, so I was pretty out of it, and all of sudden he was there, in my face." The details are sketchy in my mind, but the feeling sends shivers down my spine. I put the cup to my mouth, burn my top lip, and then pull away. "Hot," I explain, and then blow on the steamy liquid.

"You may not want to remember," Eric says. "And that's okay, for now," he adds.

"It wasn't that big of a deal. I mean, he didn't molest me or anything. But still, it made me feel awful. And dirty. And gross."

I wrap my arms around myself, the thought of Mitch that night making me shudder.

"Coming into your room at night and touching you is a big deal, Snow. It's not always the extent of the action that's damaging, it's the utter violation. You trusted him."

I start slurping my tea cautiously and think a while. "But I don't care so much about him," I say. "He's just a pervert. A total loser. It's Elsie I'm most mad at."

"Elsie is your caregiver. You expected her to protect you from things like that."

"Yeah, that's it," I say, amazed how he can sometimes put my thoughts so clearly. It's as if he's inside my head, collecting my messy ideas and ordering them into nice tidy sentences. "That's exactly it."

Eric leans over and pours me some more tea out of this little Chinese ceramic teapot. "What can hurt most is the betrayal by the people who let it happen, or moreover, turn a blind eye," he says. I wonder if it's the tea that is making him talk in little fortune-cookie sentences.

"I think that's when I stopped caring," I say, slurping my truth serum. "Stopped caring altogether about Elsie. I think that's when something in me broke, for good."

.   .   .

That week I go for my first ultrasound. The hospital is cold and uninviting. White and blue lab coats flutter by me like wings too tired and disinterested to take flight. I sit in what isn't even a waiting room, more like an alcove off the hallway. Cold metal chairs with faded upholstery are set around a table full of boring magazines like *Time* and *Reader's Digest*. There are three women seated, two of them look like they're in their twenties and one appears about Elsie's age. All of them glance at me when I arrive only to quickly look away, disinterested. I cough and try to look sick, so they think I'm there because I have cancer.

A short, Filipino nurse comes around the corner. "Snow Cooke?" she asks, smiling at me, and I rise, catching the glares from the women sighing and shifting positions in their chairs. They were all here before me. "No one else with you?" she asks, looking behind me. I quickly shake my head.

As we walk down the hall, the nurse compliments me on my lovely hair that I explain used to look really good with blonde highlight streaks. She talks about her daughter, about my age, who is playing in a soccer tournament next month. She makes me feel normal, not like a kid, and I surprise myself when I smile and laugh at her small jokes. Instead of taking me to the ultrasound room, she takes me to another waiting area, only this one is like one big shower room with individual curtained cubicles on either side of a narrow corridor.

"How many waiting rooms *are* there?" I whine, my gut starting to hurt from a swelling bladder. It's like Alice in Wonderland and those endless little doors Alice had to face. Only, she had the good fortune to be tripping out on drugs at the time. At least, that's what Jasmyn says. The curtains ripple as I pass the little stalls. I see naked bums and bare feet and the tops of women's heads. The nurse stops at one of the stalls at the end of the row, pulls aside the curtain, and patiently explains how I should tie the blue paper gown. I panic, thinking of my scars, and tell her I want to leave my shirt on. She smiles, says there should be no problem, and pushes me into my pen.

I sit half naked on a tiny bench, clutching my belongings. I feel like I'm in jail. I am told not to go to the washroom just before the ultrasound, but after about half an hour, I think I'm going to piss my pants. I rock back and forth until finally I have to shove my fist at my crotch, pushing hard to keep it all in. I stick my head out, every once in a while, trying to spot a nurse, but they whisk by in the distance, avoiding eye contact. I get so angry, just being left like that, behind these cheap yellow curtains. And I can't say anything because there's something about being barefoot and naked under these stupid paper gowns that makes you feel totally powerless. Just as I'm about to bolt to the washroom, a different nurse whips back my curtain.

I follow her into a dark concrete room that has nothing in it but a stool, a machine, and a bed. I lie on the cold table, waiting for her to adjust the equipment. It's so bare and sterile in there. I figure this is what it must feel like to be in the centre of bone.

The nurse rubs cool gel on my skin, gentle and smooth. Then she draws the cold scope over my slippery stomach. I tell her I'd like to know the sex. "I guess you're done with surprises," she says, gesturing to my stomach, and I'm unsure if she's being sarcastic or cruel because she doesn't smile. I stare closely at her eyes, looking for signs of terror as she reads the monitor. I start to worry when I see her brow crease and her head shake while she moves the scope back over curves of my stomach. I want to ask if everything is okay, but I don't. Because I don't want to know if it's not.

After about fifteen minutes, she finally says, "You thought of a name for your little girl?" A smile cracks her dry face.

"A girl? You sure?"

"Yep." She turns the screen so that it's now facing me. "She was a little shy at first, but there she is." It's not a fixed picture, like in the books. Instead, it's a shadowy, liquid image.

"There's nothing dangling down, caught in some shadow?" I ask, hopeful, staring at the fluid darkness. A boy would be so much easier than a girl.

"Nope. It's a girl all right. See here—that's the spine, see it? Those little lines?" She uses her pencil to point to white, jagged, sharp bones, like the backs of dinosaurs. I see them and an amazed smile sneaks to my mouth. But then the nurse starts outlining a huge alien head, a dark eye socket, a pulsing heart, and kicking legs, and I can't see anything she's describing. All I see is dark and light shadow. She points out its tiny knuckles, one, two, three, four . . .

"Oh, there they are!" I exclaim, pretending they're crystal clear. Not wanting her to know that I can't even see my own baby. Then, I lie back down, resting my head on the pillow, while she prints out a picture for me to take home. My first duty of motherhood and I've already failed.

"So, any names?" she asks, wiping off my belly with a paper towel. But now I wish she'd go back to being a cold miserable bitch because I don't want to talk.

"Something plain," I answer. "Like Beth or Susan. Something that won't make her believe she's more than she is."

I have to sit in the waiting room for a while before the woman behind the counter calls my name.

"Six months, sixteen days," she announces. "Everything looks good."

I smile faintly. "Thanks," I say, turning to leave. It's not like it's a surprise, but hearing someone confirm it makes it sound so calculated. Strange how the only times I ever hear people break time down into weeks is when they're pregnant or dying.

. . .

I find myself standing in doorways a lot lately, or beside solid, weighty furniture like a desk or table, something I could quickly duck under. As if at any second my surroundings will collapse around me. This is where I am when I say goodbye to everyone. In a doorway. My back pressed up against the frame, my hands clenching wood, fingers red and orange from the chips at my little party. I smile one last time to faces that I will soon no longer recall.

The farewell party is a rare occasion, most girls are discharged or just AWOL. The chips in plastic bowls, a glass jar of Smarties, large bottles of Sprite and Coke, and Miranda's homemade squares. There is a present on the table and a card that all the girls signed. Inside the box is a blue baby blanket and an ugly nursing bra with a sticky note that says "For yer leaky tits."

The girls each take turns, lean down and say goodbye to my stomach. I don't know if it's my pregnancy or what, but the girls all cry and wish me luck. It's all very fake and perfect, as if we're performing one of the role-plays from our "relationship" class, simulating the proper way to resolve conflicts or communicate our needs. Staff stands to the side, like proud parents watching their children bond.

Jasmyn is the last to say goodbye. She doesn't lean down to my stomach like the others, but instead gives me a hug. "Call me, okay?"

"I will."

Miranda grabs my bag, hurrying our moment along. "We better go," she says, whisking past Jasmyn. Miranda's never liked us being friends. When she can, she sticks her thorny body between us.

The group-home van clunks across the city to the east end. Miranda's body looks tiny in the large driver's seat. She throws on her oversized square baseball cap that she says just seems to feel right when she's driving this "beast." The radio is broken and so she insists on singing old country tunes that she somehow knows all the words to. She is trying to lighten the mood, encouraging me to sing along, but I stay quiet, leaning my head on my arm, resting out the window. The light posts pass like measured countdowns to another life. It strikes me that soon everything will be different. Tomorrow I will wake up in a new house. And Miranda won't be yanking my tired body out of bed. And Jasmyn won't be playing her annoying loud music. And I won't go down for breakfast to listen to Tammy annoying the hell out of me with her lies about what she did last night. Even the things I hate most, like sick routine and weekly chores, all of a sudden don't seem so bad.

"You know," Miranda says, breaking my sad little nostalgia session, "I shouldn't say this, but in a way I'm glad you're leaving." I turn to her, surprised she can say something so mean. She keeps her eyes fixed on the road. "I mean, I'll miss you tons, but you're not like these girls." She pulls the wheel hard to make a right-hand turn. "You shouldn't be here."

I don't say anything but her words make me smile. It's a Miranda compliment, strange and honest. And I remember how when I first came to the group home, I didn't belong. How I saw all the girls as losers on a fast road to nowhere. I laugh to myself, thinking about the first time I met Jasmyn and how I thought we were so different. But then the smile starts to slip from my lips as I realize that somewhere along the way I stopped feeling like I didn't belong. At some point, I saw them differently and I actually wanted to belong. And until now, I thought I did.

19

When I arrive at Beverley House, home for pregnant girls, Karyn, the youth worker at my intake meeting, shows me to my room. She wears overalls, a tank top, and thick wool socks with Birkenstocks. Tiny seashells and small blue feathers hang from a piece of leather around her neck. I follow her down the hall, fixated on her long brown hair, swaying limply about her waist like a horse's stringy tail. Without looking back at me, she asks me how far along I am.

"Almost seven months," I answer, not interested in conversation. She picks up on my cue and, after showing me how my window opens, leaves me to unpack my things. The room is as I remember from the house tour. A bed, a desk, a dresser, a sink, a yellow rug, and a white-tiled floor. I think of my old room at the group home and wonder who will be sleeping in my bed tonight, resting her head on my pillow. Who will wake in the middle of the night, comforted by Jasmyn's breathing.

I hang some shirts up in the closet, put a few pairs of pants in the dresser, and line my shampoos and body lotions up on the window ledge. On the dresser by the door, I put the photograph of my mother, now in a frame Miranda gave me. On the little table beside my bed, I prop two pictures of Mark up against the alarm clock. One is of him lying on the grass in the park with a panting Spliff lying across his chest. The other is a close-up of just his face, and if you tilt it just slightly, lip prints from my good-night kisses show.

When I'm done unpacking, I stand, hands on hips, and sigh deeply at the huge cork-lined wall hovering before me. The empty space is intimidating. I search through my schoolbag to find something I can post. I tack up my A-plus math test, a portrait of me that Kevin drew, crumpled, and then whipped at my head in class, and a photo of me and Jasmyn, on the house bowling trip last month. Then I remember Mark's drawing, the one of the angel, that I took and kept pressed in the calendar Staff gave me when I first arrived at the group home. I carefully pin this drawing in the centre of the wall, comforted by the angel eyes following me as I move around the room.

Karyn comes back about an hour later to see how I'm doing. I am sitting at my desk, doodling in the journal Eric gave me. She plops herself down at the bottom of my bed and tries to get a feel for me. I don't like her. Her face bothers me. It's homely and ugly. I decide I won't give her a chance.

"So, how do you like the room?" she asks. I point to the *Carmen sucks goat dick* liquid-papered onto my cork wall as my answer. Karyn looks shocked, then embarrassed, and suggests I paint over it.

"So, how did you like Delcare?" she asks.

"Good," I say, shrugging my shoulders.

"I hear you did well in school."

"Sort of."

"What was your favourite subject?"

"Math." I keep staring down at my journal, tracing the letters over and over again on the page.

"Math? Wow. You must be smart, then. I'm awful at math."

"I'm okay."

She gets up from the bed and saunters over to the corkboard. "Wow, you *are* good at math. Look at that! A plus." I curse myself for putting that up. Make a mental note to take it down as soon as she leaves. "Who's this, Snow?"

"Huh?" I turn to see the photo of me and Jasmyn held up close to Karyn's face. "Oh, a friend from my group home."

"Well, she's very pretty. What's her name?"

"Jasmyn." I start to write the words FUCK OFF in big block letters in my book. I press hard with my pen, ripping through to the next page.

"Oh, wow! This drawing. This is unbelievable. This is absolutely amazing. Did you draw it?"

Now I turn my whole body to face her. She is staring at Mark's drawing. I can see that she's not faking it. That she really means what she says. I am remotely interested. "No. A friend did."

"Well, your friend is *very* talented. Look at her eyes."

"Ya, it's my favourite," I say, smiling slightly, which was a mistake because now she thinks we're going to chat. She comes back to the corner of the bed and I drop my eyes back down to my page. There is uncomfortable silence and Karyn decides to fill it talking about herself. She tells me about all the new initiatives she's been doing at the house, trying to set up a partnership with the daycare centre down the road and organize a fundraiser evening for new classroom computers. She tells me about her volunteer work in Africa building houses and the walkathon she did last week for breast cancer.

"Aren't there people in Toronto who need houses?" I ask. She's not like Miranda. Miranda does this job to help others. I can tell already that Karyn does it to help herself.

She smiles weakly and holds out her hands as if surrendering. "I'll leave you alone for a bit. Dinner is downstairs at six, if you like." I lie and tell her I've already eaten. I can't stand the thought of walking into a roomful of hungry pregnant girls stuffing their faces with meat loaf and canned peas. I'd rather sit in my room and stare at the wall.

When she's gone I lie down on the hard bed. The sheets smell of bleach. The plastic-wrapped mattress beneath me crinkles. Karyn explained they had a problem with bedbugs and it's the only solution, but I think the plastic is really there to stop you from getting too comfortable, even in your dreams.

I don't want to be here. I want to go back to the group home. I can't be bothered with new rules, new staff, new residents, new shower pressure. I roll up my sleeve to examine the scars that snake across my skin like sticky tar on city roads. *I will split open again,* I warn the flaking seals.

My body is shaky. My heart races, and even though I haven't had a cigarette in a while, I have this urge to inhale smoke. I shuffle down the hall, walking like a penguin, short little steps, feet slightly pointed outward. I follow the faint cigarette smell to the room at the back of the house where, Karyn says, "smoking is not encouraged." I waddle in quickly, pretending I know exactly what I'm doing. There is only one other girl in the room, sitting on the couch by the window. Her foot is up on the cushion and she is picking at her toenails, her tongue sticking out from between her sliver-thin lips. She is pasty white and sickly thin.

"Hey," I say, walking in and sitting down.

"Hi." She looks up at me for a moment, her eyes travelling my body from head to toe.

"Can I bum a smoke?" I haul my feet up onto the coffee table.

The girl reluctantly leans forward and tosses a package of Benson and Hedges. "Consider it a loan. I'm low." I take a smoke and light it, deeply inhale, and tilt my neck back. "You new?" she asks me.

"Yup."

"When are you having your kid?"

"About two months. You?" I ask, not even noticing a bulge in her stomach.

"Oh, no." She leans over to put out her smoke in the ashtray. "I had mine already. A month ago. It was fine. Until the doctor decided to rip the placenta out of me, instead of waiting. Thought I'd die. You shouldn't be smoking."

I ignore her last comment. "Wha'd ya have?"

"A boy. I adopted him out. This great couple, you know, everything you wished you could have had, but didn't."

"Yeah," I say, pretending I know exactly what she means. She returns to picking at her toenails, her face strained from heavy concentration. Her skin is so thin you can see the purple veins through her cheeks and temples. It gives me the shivers. "That must have been hard," I add.

"Yeah, but, what could I do? Raise it?" She releases her foot and looks back up at me. "Who am I fucking kidding? Can't even take care of myself. It would have been selfish to keep it."

"Yeah," I say again. I inhale once more and let my head float in its rush. To myself, I admit it. Admit the things I've considered. Like leaving my baby on a doorstep, in a basket, at some huge house in Rosedale. Or wrapping it in newspaper and dropping it off at a hospital. Or even just leaving it in a mall washroom or on a bus. But I know I couldn't do it. I couldn't live my life, every day, knowing that she's out there. Every day, walking down the street and not knowing if she's that kid squeegeeing on the corner or bagging my groceries or serving me my Big Mac. I couldn't handle her knowing that I gave her up, just like that, and I was going on with my life. As if I had just dumped a heavy load off my back and wiped my hands of the mess. I know what it's like to have a mother who doesn't want you. And I wouldn't wish that on anyone.

"So, if you already had your baby, then why are you still here?" I ask.

"Where am I going to go? I'm getting kicked out soon. They're worried about me 'cause I'm depressed or bipolar or whatever label they choose this month." She shows me the underside of her arms, exposing hundreds of scars scattered all the way up to her shoulders. I am shocked when I see them, stunned that someone else does this. Seeing a freak like that do it only makes me wonder if I'm as weird as she is.

"Ouch," I say sympathetically, and pull down my sleeves, making sure my own cuts are covered.

"It doesn't hurt. Not even when I'm doing it," she says, as if she's all proud of herself. As if I'd be shocked or impressed to hear it. And I just don't get that. I don't get why anyone would want to announce to the world how crazy they are.

But is it so strange, really? Miranda goes to the gym when she's angry and says she sweats it out. Sometimes, she says, she runs so hard on the treadmill, and her legs burn so bad, she starts crying invisible, sweaty tears. And Mark goes to his friend's house and fights with a punching bag dangling by a chain from the basement ceiling till his knuckles are bloody and swollen. And Aunt Sharon shoves her mouth full of chips and pretzels until she bends over on the couch, gripping her exploding stomach. So, really, even normal people hurt themselves. I suppose how far you go just depends on how bad the monster is that's living inside your skull.

The girl lights up another smoke, gestures to offer me another one, but I hold up my hand and pat my stomach, indicating I shouldn't. She tells me her name is Sky, but her real name is Sara.

"Staff is pretty cool here. Oh, and you need to stock up on maxi-pads because you bleed like hell forever after."

"Thanks for the tip," I say sarcastically, but she thinks I'm being sincere. After a while, I realize she probably doesn't have any friends because she starts making plans with me for the weekend, but I just don't have the energy to be nice to her, even though she gave me the smoke, so I tell her I think I'm busy. And with barely a pause she starts talking about these crazy random things, like the milk seeping out from her tits and her grade two teacher's Hyundai and the time she threw up on the roller coaster at Wonderland. I begin to get the feeling she's sort of slow. Not really retarded, but almost, as if she's got just a slight strain of retard in her blood.

"I gotta go back to my room," I announce, not waiting for a break in her words because by now it's quite obvious there won't be one.

I'm in my room for only a few seconds, just enough time to get into bed, prop up some pillows, and open a book, when Sky appears at the door. I ignore her as she pokes about my dresser, lifting my deodorant and my lotions, inspecting the labels. I am hoping she'll just leave, but after a few moments she moves closer toward me until she's standing right beside my bed. I pretend I'm really into my book, move my lips a little to show I'm reading.

"Coming to dinner?" she asks.

"Not hungry," I say, turning the page.

"That's okay. I'm not eating much either. I'm on cleanup," she says. "I can never eat much when I'm on cleanup."

"Why?"

"'Cause I know I'll be wiping all the plates into the garbage and the look of it, all that half-eaten food, will make me barf. I've done it before," she says. "Who's this?" In her hand is the framed picture of my mother. I rip it from her grasp and put it face down on the bed beside me.

"My mom," I say, figuring there's no point lying to Sky when she doesn't really matter.

"As a kid?"

"No. As a fuckin' midget. What do ya think?" I say, annoyed, and she starts to laugh, misinterpreting my sarcasm as just being funny.

Sky literally pulls me out of my bed to go to dinner, and I almost can't believe it, but I don't have the energy to fend her off. She thinks it's funny, starts giggling hysterically, but I just think it's psychotic and immature. We enter the dining room, located in the basement. It's a bare, pale-pink room with six large round tables. The paper snowflakes on the windows, made by last year's students, curl up at their edges as if cringing from the cold wind outside. Off to the side are a kitchen and serving area with deep metal trays of fish sticks, potatoes, and beans. A bunch of faces look at me for a second and then turn away, unimpressed. I grab a plate and follow Sky to the food.

"Hey, Sam," she says to the middle-aged East Indian man behind the counter. He tips his baseball hat at her.

"He the cook?" I say, more to make conversation than anything else.

"Ya. And the repairman and the van driver and the painter and the plumber. Aren't ya, Sam?" she asks, and I can tell by the way he politely smiles at her that he finds her annoying. "He does every-thing around here," she continues. "Sam, Sam the handyman."

We eat our dinner at a table with three other girls who all look about as pregnant as me. At the table next to us are the new mothers who only come to the school program during the day. Each girl either has a slobbering baby on her lap or a toddler in a high chair. Sky says they are mother snobs who think they are so much wiser than the girls who haven't had their babies yet. They are allowed to be here after the delivery in order to help them get off to a good start. Some of them even have a couple of kids. Sky says the blonde girl is eighteen and pregnant with her third child. "It's like an addiction," Sky whispers to me. "She can't stop popping them out." She raises her finger to her temple and twirls it in the air—"Cuckoo!"

As I eat my dinner, I watch the next table of mothers. In the high chair beside the blonde girl is this perfect little baby and on her lap is a little boy, his face smeared with ketchup. Thing is, the girl looks perfectly happy. And what freaks me out even more is that she looks like she's a really good mom. Thankfully, our table doesn't talk about babies. We talk about movies and smoke brands and guys. No one mentions pregnancy, except for Lynn, the skinny girl with the sunken face who keeps counting her glasses of refilled milk aloud. "I've gotta drink six a day," she says to me, gulps the last one down, and slams it on the table—"Ta-dah!"

"What do you want, applause?" Sky asks, wiping Lynn's proud smile off her face.

"Fuck you," Lynn replies, mildly irritated.

Sky faces Lynn, opens her mouth full of half-chewed food and spills it slowly in chunks out onto the plate.

"Ugh," the girl with long red hair squeals, "the afterbirth," and we all start to laugh.

20

There is no escaping your baby here. My limbs and head withdraw beneath my belly like a turtle disappearing into its shell. I become this walking, talking stomach. Stray thoughts of mother or Elsie or Mark are lassoed back into discussions about nutrition or labour or finances. I hear their struggling whispers in my head, throats tight and bruised from the silencing ropes around their necks. They are not used to this restraint. Like me, they resent this unborn thought elbowing itself into their centre.

The house keeps us busy. In the evenings and on weekends we attend workshops on relationships and parenting. We learn new skills like CPR and balancing chequebooks and mushing carrots in a blender. We write resumés and research careers. Most girls immerse themselves in their projects, happy with this new focus and direction. No longer sluts or dropouts or punks. They welcome this new label: *Mother*. So pure and clean and untouchable. But then there are those like me, who sit on the edges of groups, reality pinning all illusions firmly to the ground.

Our Thursday night parenting group is compulsory. I am sitting in a circle of small metal chairs with twelve other girls, our bellies protruding like membership pins. We're in the big empty room beside the kitchen in the basement, used for birthday parties and agency meetings. All six of the Beverley House girls are here, as well as some others I don't know. Most of them look older than me, maybe seventeen or eighteen, and only one girl looks younger. They stare me down and whisper in each other's ears like little grade school kids.

"So, Snow," Karyn says to me at the beginning of our session, "why don't you tell us why you're here."

"Because I'm pregnant," I say, arousing laughter from the girls, the glares sliding off their faces like melting wax.

"Well, yes. We know that." Karyn smiles and I'm disappointed that she isn't fazed by my response. "But tell us why you chose to be here and not somewhere else. You don't need to divulge anything personal if you don't want to. But you'll probably be surprised at how many of us here are in the same boat."

I think for a moment. There are many reasons to have a baby. If you want to leave home, but you can't afford it. If you want to have your man's first child, so you have baby-mom rights over the other girls he fucks. If you want a baby to make you finally straighten out your screwed-up life. If you want to prove to your mother that you aren't as useless as she says, that she's the one with the problem. If you want your boyfriend to commit. If you want someone to love you.

"I didn't choose to be here. My group home made me come. And I don't live with my mother because she's dead." I shrug my shoulders, indicating I'm done.

"I'm sure we are all sorry to hear that. And thank you for sharing something so personal and obviously painful." Then Karyn turns to the group: "Let's all tell Snow a little bit about ourselves." She makes each girl speak for about a minute, about how they didn't expect this to happen, about how it was a mistake. Despite what they say, in some ways, I know they've all planned this. In some ways, I think they all knew this would happen to them, sooner or later. The way rich kids just know they'll probably have a car and a university degree by the time they're twenty-five. I look around the room, listen to all these hopeless stories, and silently add mine to the list: *If I put it off too long, I have no choice.*

.   .   .

School for us pregnant girls is in the basement of the house. It's a tiny room with a large centre table and lopsided bookcases. On the walls are student projects about parenting and tenant rights. The teacher, Miss Lucy, wears a wool sweater with zoo animals embroidered on it. She has white hair and a warm smile and is the kind of teacher you'd imagine instructing grade three children. "Where are the others?" I ask during my academic meeting, motioning to the empty room.

"Who?" She seems surprised at the question. "Oh, the students." She waves her hand in the air, gesturing for me not to worry. "There are always doctor's appointments, upset stomachs, counselling. Sometimes the room is packed, sometimes there is no one. Today is just one of those days. Three young women just graduated from high school here last week."

She asks me questions about my last school, about past conflicts with teachers, about my courses. She is impressed with my half credit of grade ten advanced math. "I think this might be more relevant to your needs right now," she says, sliding a parenting package across the table. "Most young women really like the course. You'll still continue your other subjects, it's just that this will be important as well. It's worth a full credit." I reach out to accept the bound photocopied pages and she gets up to leave.

"Can I have my math book too?" I ask, annoyed at her assumption that I'm nothing more than a pregnant belly.

"Of course!" she says, obviously impressed with my interest. She goes into her office and returns with some algebra sheets. She tells me she'll need a day to get the rest of my work organized. "So why don't you work on the package for now?"

At first I'm resentful, as if our lives are made to stop now that we are pregnant. I stare back at my photocopied package. I flippantly tick off lists, scratch in fill-in-the-blanks, and invert my true or false. *A woman loses a tooth for every baby she has:* true, of course. When asked about my child's values, I reject the suggested adjectives—*controlled, restrained, self-disciplined*—and create my own: *slutty, bitchy, catty.* I get back the first unit with a big red F on the top-right corner. Miss Lucy tells me that I can make up the mark by completing a supplementary writing assignment and puts it down on the table. "A minimum of three pages," she says.

I'm excited to accept the challenge of failure. My vengeful pen ready, I flip the page.

A good mother is . . .

I am wordless. Feel slapped in the face. No thoughts come to my mind, not even rude ones. I sit for what seems like hours, trying to think of something to say, something funny or stupid— or thoughtful. But I stay wordless, watch the second hand coast around in circles, listen to Miss Lucy in her office on the phone, talking to her dry cleaners, then a teacher, then Rogers Cable. I doodle on the page, flowers and stars, and just when I think I'm about to go nuts, I add one word to her incomplete sentence and it's like a door opens in my head.

A good mother is . . . NOT . . . someone who borrows her daughter's bathrobe and returns it with cum stains. A good mother is not someone who lets her child stay up all night to watch TV or just laughs when an eight-year-old tells the grocery clerk to fuck off. A good mother is not someone who leaves condoms in an unflushed toilet or bad milk in the fridge. A good mother doesn't let her boyfriend smash her head in and then say afterward it's okay because it was her fault.

I have so much more to say, I fill up four pages, both sides. At the end I write, *A good mother is not mine.* I staple it and leave it on Miss Lucy's desk. In class the next day she gives me back the paper, a large purple A with the words "good detail" scribbled beside it. "I thought your piece was very insightful, Snow," she says as she passes by my desk. "I like the twist. Knowing what a good mother is not is as important as knowing what a good mother is." I feel her warm hand rest on my shoulder. "Good job."

I make a point of working on the parenting booklet after that. I continue to tick off lists and match definitions and then, after a while, it's like I can't really even bring myself to do my math or geography. I compare breast- and bottle-feeding, write paragraphs on disciplining, and list ten ways to childproof a home. I create logical consequences, set appropriate limits, copy a list of factors that affect the healthy development of the fetus. I read about Erik Erikson's theory of personalities. I fill out charts on Maslow's hierarchy of needs and learn that I have no self-actualization in my life. I read about a study on rats that somehow proves close contact with the baby once it's born is important. Then I stare out the window and wonder how in the world rats can tell us anything about the behaviour of people.

.   .   .

Every girl gets an individual meeting with the supervisor, Ms. Crawl, during her first few days, but since she's been on vacation I'll meet her my third week at Beverley. Ms. Crawl has been here thirty years and Sky says she runs the place with an iron fist. Sky says that when Ms. Crawl walks into the room, everybody loses her smile, even the youth workers. On the day of my meeting, Sky sits on the end of my bed and preps me for what she calls "the initiation into hell." She explains the best way to handle it is just to remain quiet, and if I think I'm going to lose it on her, I should just start counting the pencils in the jug on her desk. "The others think she's out for blood," she says. "They think it has something to do with abortion guilt. But I think she just needs a good fuck." Then she makes a tight fist and forces her finger into the hole to demonstrate. "You know, she's all tight and rigid."

I sit in Ms. Crawl's spacious office, to the right of the house entrance, and wait for her. The large wooden desk is spotless. Papers are neatly highlighted with yellow and pink stripes. Even the sticky notes are placed with precision.

"Good morning, Miss Snow," Ms. Crawl says as she enters the room. She looks exactly the way I had imagined. Pointy nose and chin, bony knuckles, as if she even considered flesh to be excessive. She begins by asking me questions about my pregnancy and about Elsie. She pretends to listen to my answers, but she's not like Eric who listens to me in a way that makes me believe he cares. Eric lets me have my own opinions and doesn't force his on me. Ms. Crawl, on the other hand, is the kind of woman who has an agenda. I am one-dimensional to her. I am a pregnant teenager.

In the middle of the meeting, she gets up to close the door, her shoes squeaking like sick mice. "You seem like a very smart girl, Snow. I feel as if I can be straight with you." She sits on the edge of her desk, so that I'm staring up into her nostrils. Her pointy tits poke through her camisole and her satiny blouse. I find this deeply disturbing because for some reason she strikes me as a woman who shouldn't have nipples. "We sometimes encourage girls in your circumstance to consider adoption. There are so many kind, loving adults who'd like to offer a baby, like yours, a home."

"Like mine?" I say, confused.

Ms. Crawl clears her throat. She reaches out a scrawny hand and smooths invisible creases on her skirt.

"Do you know what it's like to be given away?" I ask her. "You know what happens to those people? They become fuck-ups, like me. That's what happens."

"You know what happens to babies born to fifteen-year-old girls?" she asks me. "They become fifteen-year-old girls with babies." She holds out her hand, presenting me as her evidence. Resting her case.

I shake my head, disagreeing.

"How old was your mother?" she asks, going for blood. Sky was right.

"So what?" I say, disappointed in myself because that was the best I could come up with. And, really, I don't need to speak. There's comfort in being a statistic. To know there's lots of us out there. At least we have those high-risk factors to defend our actions. I don't even need to explain myself to Ms. Crawl. She knew me the moment she opened my file. I suppose all families have their heirlooms: fine china, portrait paintings, teenage pregnancies.

Ms. Crawl stares straight at me, prepared for this. "I didn't create this society, Snow. And believe me, if I could change it, I would. I devote my life to helping girls like you. But the reality is, teenage mothers just aren't given a lot of breaks. You get money from the government, but it sure isn't much, and there are a lot of wonderful women out there who would provide great opportunities your child will never see. It's a harsh reality, but you need to think of someone other than yourself now." She gestures to my stomach, as if I didn't know what she was talking about.

She gives me pamphlets and makes me sit through a fifteen-minute video on adoption. When she flicks on the light and opens the door to release me, I ask if there are any videos on keeping your baby. "Of course. You'll be participating in many groups on mothering. And ultimately, Snow, it's entirely your choice and we'll support you either way. I promise you that. You just need to be aware of the consequences. Sometimes that can get lost in here."

21

People are afraid I won't know how to love you. They don't say it exactly, but it's in the worried way they look at me. At school they give me books and articles and assignments on how to love my child. As if the way I love is wrong. But I never knew there was a right way. I bet most people don't. I bet there are people all over the place, loving the wrong kind of way, but I don't see any fingers pointing at them, say, in the middle of a crowded subway, to the father in the blue suit with a bruised right fist: *You, yes, you—the way you love is wrong.*

"You already are a mother. You're loving already. Think of what you're creating. That's the best kind of love," says Eric, thinking he's comforting me. But inside my body I love you perfectly only because I have no say in it. Under my silent direction, you will come out flawless. But it's when you are in my hands and you are crying and I don't know what to do that I worry about. How will I love you then?

How do you describe love, good love, to someone who has never known it? It's like describing snow to someone who's never seen it. How can you describe something that's beautiful and ugly all at once? Something you can both appreciate and resent. Something that's cold but can feel so warm. How do you describe that love's all about balance? Too little and it will melt away, too much and it will break you. Now, how do you describe all this if you yourself have never seen snow?

"You don't describe love," says Eric. "You give it."

• • •

Once, about two years ago, Elsie told me she loved me. But she didn't mean it, not really. It was in the afternoon sometime. I had walked in on her in the bathroom. She was naked in the tub, but there was no water in it, only powdery pink grains of bubble bath on the bottom. The radio was plugged in, above the sink. It was on some stupid classical music station.

"What are you doing?" I asked, disgusted at her nakedness.

"Having a bath." She leaned back into the tub and closed her eyes. Made a motion with her hand as if she were swishing the water. I was too shocked to comment on the absurdity of this. Her body looked much older naked, her skin layered and breasts low. I quickly closed the door and she called my name.

"Snow?"

"Yeah?"

"Open the door." I cautiously poked my head in. "I love you," she said, for the first time I could ever remember.

"Me too," I said without thinking. And shut the door.

I remember going to lie down on my bed and staring at the ceiling after that. My mind in a fog, no real thoughts coming through. I was unsure if she was tripping out or just being weird. Then I considered if it made a difference. It bothered me that I said *me too;* another obligatory phrase, like *sorry,* demanding a response. Half an hour later, the door opened and Elsie came out, still naked, her head wrapped in a towel. She walked down the hall, bath crystals on her flabby bum as if she'd sat in pink sand.

"It's all yours," she said happily, and disappeared into the living room.

. . .

It's Barb, Elsie's worker, who calls me at Beverley after the hospital had called her. Elsie has fallen down the front stairs of her building. She has broken her arm, a few ribs, and fractured her skull. "It's not an emergency—she was only in overnight—but I thought you'd want to know," Barb says, but the concern in her voice tells me it was more than this. The thoughts run through my head: Was she wasted? Did she really just fall? Did she do this on purpose to get me to feel sorry for her? Was she pushed?

I ask the first question.

"Well, she wasn't drunk. We know that, but the tests did indicate drugs in the system. Perhaps a mix of codeine and Valium, I'm not certain, I'd have to check her file."

"Don't bother," I say, and then try to think of a way to end the call. "Thanks for letting me know."

"Snow?" she says, trying to catch me before I hang up. "She wants you to call her. She told me to tell you."

"Thanks," I say, and quickly hang up.

. . .

Beverley House doesn't like my decision to go see Elsie. They get all serious about it and call a meeting with Ms. Crawl on a Friday morning. I arrive at her office five minutes late, carrying a piece of toast with peanut butter in my hand. I am surprised to see they have gathered the troops. Barb, Ms. Crawl, and Karyn are all circled around the table, thick yellow pads of paper in front of them. I plop down on the couch at the far end of the room with a heavy sigh.

"I'm just going for a night. What's the big deal?" I say, after they tell me why we're meeting. I look for a place to throw my crusts and resign myself to just resting them on the convenient shelf of my belly.

Staff tell me they're concerned about me going. About the state I'm in now both physically and mentally. They think this might be too much for me.

"She's my grandmother. Of course I'm going to go." I surprise even myself with these words of devotion, but I don't let on. Instead, I just allow my mouth to keep flapping. "I mean, I know she hasn't been the greatest, but she's"—the reluctant word falls from my mouth—"family."

"I don't understand," Karyn says, her face scrunched up, as if she were trying to read between my lines. After all I've said to her about hating Elsie, I can't blame her for not being able to figure me out. But there are some people you just have the right to love. There are some people you just have the right to hate. And sometimes I wonder if it's all just the same emotion existing in a different state, like water and ice.

Barb leans in toward me, placing her clasped hands on the table. "We just don't want you to think this is your obligation."

"I don't."

She leans in farther. "We just don't want to put you, and your baby, at risk." And that's when I realize it's not about me. It's about the fucking baby. They don't care if I go back and screw up my life, they just want to make sure I don't take the baby down with me.

"What do you think's gonna happen?"

"Elsie's not well."

"I could have told you that," I say.

"If she's a danger to herself, she could be a danger to you, and the baby. We could arrange something else."

I sigh deeply, start breathing heavily through my nostrils. My mouth clenched. I am getting tired of this scenario. Tired of total strangers who know nothing about me and Elsie's life, sitting there passing judgement. As if their lives were perfect. As if they had a right to tell me what to do.

"I'm going," I reaffirm. "You can't stop me."

Hours later, as I approach the apartment, I begin to consider turning back. I haven't seen Elsie since the day I sat in her kitchen and she tried to explain about my mother. I stop at the parking lot to have a smoke and calm my shaking hands. Like a strong wind, the I-told-you-so of Staff presses at my back. To turn back now would require too much effort. Too much explanation. It amazes me how many things I do only because I'm told I'm not allowed to.

"Come to poison the invalid?" Elsie yells when she hears me come in the door. "Suffocate me in my sleep?" I know she is only half joking. She is lying on the couch in the living room, a half-eaten bowl of chicken noodle soup on the coffee table in front of her. The bright white cast on her left arm looks too clean for the rest of her body.

The living room reeks of sweat and shit and mint. "What's that stink?" I say as I approach the couch, holding my hand up to my nose.

"Oh, that's the cream they gave me. Got nothing to do with my arm. Sandra, my nurse, just gave me it for rough skin. It's peppermint, eh?" Sometimes I think Elsie actually likes going into the hospital. Like it's a little spa for her, where she's served tea in bed and gets massages for her sore feet. She looks at me out of the corner of her eye, but then quickly raises her body off the couch: "Jesus Christ, you're huge!"

"Thanks a lot."

"My God," she says, staring at me, her jaw hanging open. "I just can't believe it."

"What did you think? It wouldn't show?"

"Jesus," she says, still stunned, "you're enormous."

"Get over it," I snap. "What about you? You look like shit," I say, moving in closer to her face. Her right cheek is puffy and swollen and a yellowish purple colour. Just beside her half-opened eye are four black stitches tied like little sloppy knots of thread. Without thinking, I reach out to touch them but Elsie pulls away.

"Well, I wasn't planning no beauty contests." She licks her dry lips. For a split second I feel bad for her, seeing her all broken like that.

"I'm only staying tonight," I say, snapping myself out of this pitiful moment. I waddle into the kitchen to get to work. I open the cupboards that are mostly empty, except for a few cans of tomatoes, some old packages of chicken broth, and some spaghetti.

"What do you eat?" I yell, not expecting an answer.

"Got no energy to shop!" she yells from the living room. "All these painkillers, eh?"

Everything feels so normal. Like I never left. Like I'm not pregnant. Like that conversation outside the grocery store never happened. It's as if I stepped back in time, drank some magical forget potion, and I'm back to the simple life of cleaning up after Elsie.

I decide to start with the kitchen, then the living room, then the bathroom and bedroom. I pile empties by the kitchen door and use a spoon to scrape brown syrupy sludge from the bottoms of mugs. I mop the kitchen floor three times before it begins to look clean, and if I didn't have a bowling ball for a stomach, I'd get on my hands and knees and scrub each square tile. In the bathroom, black algae surrounds the faucets and gobs of hardened green hork in the sink are almost impossible for me to scrape off, even with Elsie's toothbrush. I almost gag at the collection of black pubic hairs under the toilet seat. I open the medicine cabinet and gasp at the mix of pill bottles, some even with other people's names on them.

"Don't touch any of that, eh!" Elsie yells out, her ears remarkably tuned to the dull chink-chink of pills in a plastic bottle. "I'll know if you do!"

The bedroom is the last room to tackle. I figure it will be the easiest. I open the door and the waft of air clogs my throat. I stop breathing. It's a familiar smell of sweat and booze and cheap cologne. It's the smell of Mitch. I suddenly feel the need to escape. My heart thumps in my ears. I listen for voices, but only hear Elsie moving around in the kitchen, her feet shuffling on the linoleum. I tiptoe out and poke my head around the doorway.

"Is Mitch here?" I whisper.

Elsie jumps, startled by my voice. "No, he's not."

"Was he?"

"Ya, he was. So what?"

I stand up close behind her, my feet firmly planted on the floor. I will not back down this time. I stare a hole in her back. "Are you fucking crazy? You been seeing him all this time?"

"Not now, Snow," she says quietly, extinguishing my fire.

Surprised, I change my tone. "Is he coming back tonight?"

"No."

"When, then?"

"Never."

"Never coming back?" I say, doubtful.

"No." Elsie keeps her back to me and turns on the tap. I see her shoulders drop, loose and deflated. And this makes me even more mad, like she wants me to feel sorry for her. Like she's thinks she's some martyr not letting him back into her life. I give her nothing.

"Whatever," I say, not believing her. "His underwear is on the floor by the bed. Is he coming back for that?"

"No."

"What do you want me to do with it then? It's disgusting."

"I don't care." Her voice is tired and annoyingly passive. She reaches out her good arm and plugs in the kettle. I want to shake her. Stir some fury out of her. I don't know what to do with this stillness. I storm back into the bedroom and kick the underwear under the bed. I start to pick up other clothes from the floor but the anger rises in me as I see pieces of Mitch scattered around the room. His cheap watch on the bedside table. His worn shoes by the closet. His Playboy lighter on the dresser. I think of Mitch that night I left. And me in that very bed.

"What the fuck am I doing?" I say aloud to myself, Elsie's bra dangling in my hand. "What the fuck am I doing?" I say again slowly, as if the words needed time to sink into a very dense brain. I whip the ratty beige bra across the room and dump the pile of clothes back onto the floor.

"I'm not staying," I announce to Elsie, who is back on the couch, watching TV.

"Fine," Elsie says, uncaring, reaching out for the TV converter and turning the volume up louder.

"I know why she left," I say, waiting for a response, but Elsie doesn't even acknowledge I have spoken. Her eyes remain fixed on the TV. "I know why she got pregnant," I continue. "To get the fuck away from you. You're pathetic. You can't even take care of yourself. You make everything around you . . ." As I speak she presses the volume button on the remote control, louder and louder and louder, till the TV is vibrating. Till I can't even hear my own voice. I move in closer, stand in front of her, yelling as loud as I can, but she just stares through me, through my belly, as if I don't even exist. Her face is like stone. I pick up the closest object to me, a stupid clay ashtray, and make like I'm going to throw it at her, just to get some kind of response. But she doesn't flinch. And I'm so mad, I do it. I throw it at her, just above her head. It hits the wall and smashes soundlessly into pieces, ash settling in Elsie's hair like black confetti.

22

Our Thursday night pregnancy group is tight now, with only the occasional new girl joining. We have our unofficial designated chairs, our preferred break time, and an understanding of who prefers the fudge cookies to the apple slices. Karyn hands out photocopies of pre-hospital checklists and hygiene tips. We learn about veins in our bums that can bulge to the size of grapes and discuss our fears of foot-long needles jabbed into our spines.

Every few weeks a chair will be empty, and for those of us who don't already know, Karyn will announce the length of labour, the weight and sex of the new baby, accompanied by a collective gasp and a reflexive closing of legs when she announces anything above eight pounds. We are all convinced we'll do it the natural way, despite revisiting mother Kris's comment last week: "I didn't know the human body could go through that much pain and survive."

Tonight we have a special speaker, Cindy, for those hoping to keep their babies. Cindy is a mother of five. She wears a pearl necklace outside of her pink cardigan sweater. Her tits are pointy, right out of the fifties, and she looks like she should be offering us all home-baked apple pie. There are four of us from the house, the others are from the community, still living with their parents. Cindy has chosen to open the floor to discussing the role of mother.

"What kind of mother do you think you'll be?" Cindy goes around the room, asking for volunteers. They all say the same thing. They say they are not going to give their kid the childhood they were given. They say they will be different mothers, that they are going to spend all their money on their kids and give them so much love. I sit and roll my eyes at Rachel who punched out Crystal just last night for not giving back her Discman and Carmen who got so high she had to sneak in through the fire exit at one in the morning. I imagine the truth. I imagine them in their bachelor apartments, TV blaring, a whining toddler being just a little too needy, a broken dish, an unexpected tongue lashing out harsh words, an instinctive slapping of soft skin.

"Don't you think your mothers thought this?" I blurt out, my mind trailing like a leash behind my bolting words. "Do you think they planned to treat you like shit?"

Everyone looks stunned. "You're saying that you repeat what you learn at home?" Cindy asks, continuing her already annoying habit of paraphrasing every comment.

My mind quickly regains control and attempts to explain. "I'm saying it's impossible not to. It's like trying to stop breathing. You just can't do it, no matter how bad you try." The room is silent, all eyes glaring at me. And for a split second I feel bad for ruining this little feel-good party. I consider taking back what I said, or maybe adding an encouraging "of course, there are exceptions," but Jackie speaks up before I have a chance.

"Don't you think we fucking know that?" she says, staring me straight in the eye, not an angry stare but a watery one. She is huge, probably about to give birth any second now. I look back at her, unsure what to say, so I look away.

· · ·

"A watched pot never boils," Aunt Sharon says over the phone when I complain about how slowly my last two months are passing. It's amazing how much I used to be able to squish into my life before I lived here. Now, even one planned event, like a doctor's appointment or meeting with Eric, manages to consume my entire day. I eat, sleep, pee, and lie on my side, staring off into space.

The other girls in the house seem to have more energy than me. They make crafts such as quilted photo albums and bibs with already chosen names stitched on them. In school, they write poetry and personal creeds of motherhood. I attend the fitness classes and participate in the optional weekend trips to the movies and the Ontario Science Centre, but only because I have to. If one were to overlook the bulging bellies for a second, a visitor might mistake this for camp.

Besides Jasmyn calling every once in a while, I have no interest in the outside world. I think about Carla occasionally, think about tracking down her number and calling her. Just to hear her voice again. But then, when I actually go to pick up the phone, I change my mind.

The more I live in this house, the more I fear living outside of it. In here, adults smile at you and it seems like no big deal that your belly protrudes farther than your tits, even though you've only had your period twenty times in your entire life. In here, the young mothers on posters are all white and clear-skinned; and

returning residents are goggled over, while pink and toast-brown
infants hang casually off their hips like basketballs. And I can't
figure out if Staff's endless kindness is genuine or if they are
intentionally stocking us up, filling us to the brim, before a long
drought.

We change shape inside these walls. In the weeks before our
labour, sharp angles erode until we become soft round silhou-
ettes. Jagged bangs are pulled back to expose the gentle bend of a
forehead. Harsh lipliner that once made our mouths look like
knives is replaced by pink-tinted lip gloss. The curve of our bellies
makes angular bone forgotten. We wear soft pastels, pale pinks
and blues. Suddenly we care about feelings and values because we
now have a purpose, a reason for being. We same girls who just
last year were fucking guys up against brick walls and ripping
nose rings out of girls who didn't watch our backs.

·   ·   ·

The moment I walk into Eric's office I can sense something is up.
Things are too clean. Papers aren't scattered on his desk and the
rubber galoshes that have been lying forever by the coat rack are
gone.

"So, what did you have to eat today?" he asks, and I let out a big
sigh of boredom. He is speaking to me differently now that my
growing stomach has wedged itself between us. We talk less and
less about Mitch and Elsie and more about whether I'm getting
enough food and sleep. Or we talk about my fears of having this
baby and how I plan to deal with the emotions of being a mother.
It's all so dull and overwhelming all at once. I ignore his questions
and continue scanning the room, trying to place just exactly what
is different. Then I notice Freddy isn't on the table where he
usually is.

"Where's Freddy?" I ask.

"Oops"—Eric's hand whips up to his mouth—"I forgot to tell you. I found him floating dead this afternoon. Poor thing."

"Ooh, poor Freddy," I pout. "I'm sorry for your loss," I say, making fun of the situation.

"I think I overfed him," he says, thinking I'm being serious. I can tell Eric is really sad about it. About a stupid fish.

We spend the next half-hour talking about his childhood dog and about how there truly is a difference between cat and dog people. At first I like it, just chatting, but then I begin to get suspicious of this easy talk, it seems too effortless. I figure Eric must have something heavy up his sleeve, something he's afraid to drop.

"Listen, I need to talk to you," he finally says when our time is almost up. "I want you to hear this directly from me, so I'm going to tell you before they announce it officially." I wait for Eric's words but I already know what he's going to say. I already know that he'll say he's leaving. I know that tone. I've heard it many times before. "I'm going into private practice," he says, "and I just can't pass it up. It'll be family counselling, better financially and closer to home. I've thought a lot about it and it just seems to be the best thing for me now."

"When do you go?"

"Well, officially, three weeks. Barry's taking over my clients." I take a deep breath and feel my eyes start to well up. "But I did ask for special permission to keep seeing you till after the baby is born. They said that was fine, if you'd like. I know I'd really like to."

I sit there staring at the edge of the table, jab my pen into the wooden rim. The stupid tears start coming down my cheeks and Eric passes me a Kleenex. I am so sick of crying.

"I'm sorry, Snow."

"It's okay," I say, grabbing tissue and wiping my face. "I'm not that upset, really, it's just these frigging hormones. I cry at commercials now. Can you believe that?"

He laughs and relaxes in his chair. "I'd like to stay in touch with you after the baby. Maybe meet for lunch once a month? How does that sound?"

"Cool," I say, forcing a smile. We're both quiet for a few minutes. Eric shuffles some papers as I pull my pathetic self together. It was stupid of me to have trusted him. I'm an idiot for letting him force his words into my small cracks, slowly prying me open. I should have known that there was just a paycheque moving his mouth. That the caring was coming through him, not from him. And really, he wasn't helping me much anymore, anyway.

He talks about his new job and what he'll be doing and how he'll miss working specifically with young people like me. It's as if he's trying to convince himself that he made the right decision. I pretend I'm interested, pretend I care about where he'll be in a month, but I don't. I don't care if I ever see him again.

"I have to piss," I say, interrupting him in mid-sentence. I jump up without waiting for a response. As I approach the bathroom down the hall I quicken my pace until, finally, I'm running. I feel like I'm going to burst. It's that total urgency you get when you're standing in front of a toilet and it's as if all of a sudden you can't get your fly down fast enough. Only now, it's not piss I'm holding back, it's tears.

As I yank open the door to the single washroom, my face collapses and I start bawling. I move to the corner and slide down to the cold concrete floor, crying so hard I'm soundless. My jaw starts to sting and my head starts to pound and I'm pulling at my hair. And then I get angry, slap my fist against the wall, again and again, pretending it's Eric's face. Only it doesn't help because the pain is all bony and flat. I scan the room for something sharp. Something that is capable of precision. I take out the backing of my earring and rip my skin. And this time I don't care if the drops of blood stain the floor.

There is a knock at the door and, startled, I am out of my trance.

"Just a minute!" I yell, and pull my heavy body up. I inspect my face in the mirror. It's blotchy and swollen, my eyes are bloodshot, and the snot is running from my nose. I quickly splash cold water on my face, but it makes no difference.

When I flip up the toilet lid to pee, I almost scream. Freddy's stiff and arched body floats in the slow circular current of the toilet bowl. It's a horrific sight. His eyes are bulging from the sockets. His once bright-orange body is now pale yellow. I knew the water pressure was bad in this building, especially with all the crap kids stuff into it. I even saw a sandwich in a plastic Baggie wedged down the toilet once. Still, I take Freddy's resurfaced body as an omen.

There is another knock at the door, heavier this time. I flush the toilet twice but Freddy keeps reappearing back out from the hole in the bottom of the bowl. So I reach in, scoop his slimy body out, wrap him in toilet paper, and throw him in the garbage.

·   ·   ·

After Eric's appointment I call Karyn. I lie and tell her that I want to stop off at the library to do some schoolwork. She is so impressed that I'm actually showing interest in something and she tells me to not worry about being home in time for dinner.

It takes me forty minutes to reach Mark's old apartment building. I figure he won't be there, but I just want to feel close to him again. For a little while. Some guy with long greasy hair, wearing Adidas track pants, answers the door. His eyes are bloodshot and his teeth are crooked. I don't recognize him, but he looks like the kind of guy Mark would know. I figure he's Josh's new roommate.

"Is Mark here?"

The guy speaks slowly, with a surfer drawl, "No, man." He scratches his head. "Saw him a few weeks ago. Crashed here one night but then the dude took off." Then he looks all interested and leans forward to ask, "Do you know him?"

"Ya."

"Know him pretty good?"

"Ya, really well."

"Like, you're an old girlfriend or something?"

"Ya," I say, excited. "I'm Snow." I wait for his recognition, thinking he must have a message to pass on, or that Mark mentioned he was looking for me.

"Cool," he says, opening the door. The sweet waft of marijuana drifts up my nose like the smell of home cooking. "Ya wanna chill?"

"Sure," I say, walking into the living room, wanting more to just see the place than actually talk to the guy.

We sit on the couch, the same couch that was in the apartment when Mark was here. Actually, everything is the same. The stolen street signs, the flashing construction light in the corner, the cases of empties stacked up to the ceiling in the kitchen. The guy kicks his feet up on the coffee table and turns on the TV. I watch him as he lights a spliff. He's probably about twenty. He's okay looking, under all the hair. No zits or anything. But I couldn't care less about him. I just want to be in the apartment. I want to pretend that Mark is going to come through the door any second. He passes me the joint and I take only two tokes, because of the baby.

"I'm pregnant," I explain, pointing to my belly.

"Oh, yeah," he says, as if he's just noticed. "That's okay." He takes a few more deep drags and then butts it out. Then he reaches out to brush the hair away from my face and chills run down my spine to my crotch. He leans in and kisses me, and I kiss him back because even though I'm not into him, I like him needing me. The way I am. All ugly and fat. It feels good to just be wanted.

"Let's go to your room," I whisper, once I am able to get his tongue out of my mouth for just a second.

We can't have sex the normal way because of my stomach, which is just fine with me because I don't want to see his face. At first I keep my eyes open, trying to transport myself back in time. And for a while, I'm there, with Mark and the Sunshine Girls and Spliff's black dog hair embedded in the rug. But then the guy starts ramming harder and jarring me forward, and I can't ignore him any longer, so I close my eyes, imagining Mark's face, and hold on tight to the corner of the mattress.

Standing in the doorway of the apartment, only minutes later, the guy gives me a dry little peck on the cheek goodbye. "Listen," he says. "Mark took twenty bucks from me before he left."

I immediately back up into the corridor, understanding the deal. "So, what the fuck does that have to do with me?"

"Well, you're his ex, right?"

"Fuck you!" I yell, storming down the hall.

I pace the bus stop just outside Mark's old apartment. It was dumb to come here, to wish Mark even cared. Especially since I know the ways he is. I know that if he could handle it, he'd be with me. I know that he's worried about hurting me and the baby, that he thinks he'd be bad for us. I know because late at night, after he drank a lot, he used to lay his head on my chest, and I'd stroke his hair like he was this little boy. And he'd talk about how much he hated his father and that if he ever saw him again, he'd fuckin' kill him. And I know that when he said, "I'll never do this to my own kid," he meant it. And even though he hasn't contacted me, I know he's upset about not being with me and the baby. In his own way. In a way that makes him punch out a guy who bumps into him at a bar.

I catch the older ladies at the bus stop glaring at me, disgusted, as if I'm an open wound, oozing with sin. They try their hardest to make me lower my head in shame but instead I grab my pack of smokes and light one, sucking deep and hard until I get a buzzing head rush. Then I blow smoke directly at their loose-jawed faces and they mutter something about Jesus or God. I know they think I'm easy. Easy to pass judgement upon. And I wonder how many mistakes they've made in their lives. I wonder how big would their bellies be if they were forced to wear their sins on the outside of them.

On the bus, the boys my age look away from me, like they're embarrassed, as if I had my period smeared all over white pants. I brush closely by them as I walk down the aisle, rub my poisoned stomach against their backs, and watch their shoulders tighten. I take a seat at the back, across from this older man who immediately looks me over like I'm a slut. Like I would screw anything in a second, given the chance. His eyes penetrate me, loose lips mumbling porn-talk. I smile, spread my legs a little, trace my tongue along my upper lip like I can't wait to suck him off. I stroke my stomach, twirl my belly button like it's a nipple, and he squirms in his seat, all hot and horny. Then I whisper to him and he leans in closer. "You disgust me," I say real loud.

23

You used to dip and turn and swim in my stomach but now your kicks are purposeful underneath my ribs, as if you are trying to break out of me. As if you are done with what my body has to offer. I reach down and feel the outline of what I think is your foot, hard and buried, like under a thick blanket. You respond to my touch with more kicks, and I quickly pull my hand away, terrified of this conversation. Terrified that you will be disappointed with empty words and the resentful stroke of my finger.

· · ·

I am given my final assignment for my parenting class in school. I have to make up a children's book for my baby to read in the future. Some of the girls working on the project really like the idea and start planning their stories about girls who fight dragons or little boys who build spaceships. They spread the markers out on their desks and consider complex colour patterns to stimulate their children's brains, like we read in the magazine article Miss Lucy gave us.

I move to the back of the room and stare out the window, my paper blank. I can't think of a thing to write. Fairy tales are dumb lies about talking bears and skies falling and poison apples. Little boys can't build spaceships and little girls can't fight dragons that don't even exist, so why make them believe they can? It's like showing them this fantasy world and then snatching it away. False hope is the cruellest thing I can think of to give a kid.

Miss Lucy comes by my desk when there's ten minutes left in class and tells me that I have to have a plot outline before I leave the room. I roll my eyes and reluctantly pick up my pen. I write about a little girl who receives a puppy for Christmas, but the landlord of the apartment her family lives in doesn't allow dogs. So they hide it for about a month, until one day the puppy runs out the door when the little girl comes home from school. The puppy runs right into the landlord's feet. At first, the little girl and her mother, who is now standing in the doorway, think the land-lord is going to yell and kick the dog. But then he reaches down, picks up the pup, and starts patting it. And at the end, the puppy bites the man's toupee off of his head, and they all start laughing and the landlord makes the little girl promise to not tell anyone about his hair and he'll let her keep the dog. I add the toupee part because I know Miss Lucy's husband has a toupee and she might think it's funny. All in all, I know the story sucks, but I hand in the paper and head off for lunch.

In the afternoon our class of six young women are forced to sit through Ms. Crawl's boring pictures of her vacation in Scotland because Miss Lucy has a dentist appointment. Ms. Crawl says it's important for us to broaden our horizons and see other parts of the world so that our children don't grow up to be naive and ignorant. We sit around the centre table in the classroom as she flips the pages of her photo album and gives us boring details on stone circles and castles. She tries to sound smart, dropping names and dates all over the place, but really, what's most interesting about the photos is seeing Ms. Crawl wearing jeans and posing in front of mountains and lakes. It's strange because she seems out of place in nature.

"What's this?" I ask, speaking for the first time. I am pointing to a picture of a gravestone with a bouquet of purple and yellow flowers in front of it.

"Oh, that's nothing important," she says dismissively, lifting the corner to turn.

"It's a grave," I say, holding my hand down on the page.

"Right," she says, releasing the corner and surrendering to my persistence. "That's Betty Corrigal," Ms. Crawl explains. "Well, that's not Betty, it's her gravestone, obviously. It's in Orkney. Right here." She uses her sharp pencil tip to point to the place on the opened atlas. "On a tiny island called Hoy."

I lean in closer to look at the photo. "Who was she?" The girls on either side of me, who at first showed no interest, now move in closer to the photo album.

Ms. Crawl pulls her chair up to the table. You can tell she's excited to have our full attention, for once. "Well, this local man told me about it and then I looked it up at the library when I returned home. I was biking along the road, in the middle of nowhere, among rolling hills of peat, it was just charming. And I saw this man just off to the side of the road at this gravestone. He was placing these lovely flowers down, so I stopped and we chatted. He had this wonderful Scottish accent and he told me about Betty."

"Was she his daughter?" Tawnya asks.

"No. Betty died a long time ago, in the nineteenth century. But he puts flowers on her grave every month. A few locals do."

"Why would they, if they didn't know her?" I ask.

"She fell in love with a sailor, and after he left for sea, she found out she was pregnant . . ." Miss Crawl hesitates for a moment, as if she's unsure she should continue.

"Go on," I say, now intrigued even more.

"And she was so devastated, because illegitimate children were a sin back then, not like now. The poor girl hung herself."

"That's awful."

"Yes. Terrible. Remember, it was quite unacceptable then to have a baby out of wedlock," she says, trying to make the story into some history lesson.

"What else?" Lynn, the girl sitting beside me, asks.

"The people had to bury her, but because she killed herself, they couldn't bury her in consecrated—that means 'holy'— ground, so they buried her on the boundary between the two parishes."

"That's so sad," Tawnya sighs.

"Yes, it's very sad. Her body was buried in peat and so it remained preserved. But peat isn't like dirt, and her body kept rising up through it, to the surface. The man on the side of the road said that soldiers from the Second World War, during trench-digging training, would get drunk at night and go in search of Betty's body. Apparently, the rope was still around her neck."

A couple of us hold our hands up to our necks, feeling our own vulnerable throats. A door down the hall slams shut and we all jump in our seats and then burst out laughing due to our own edginess.

Ms. Crawl continues with her ghostly tale. "The problem was, she kept rising up. And they tried different things to keep her down, but nothing worked because of the peat. So finally they rigged something up to keep her in the ground, and this local guy, who had made himself some false fibreglass teeth, offered to make her a headstone." Her hand points to the photo: "This headstone."

"That's perfect," I say, leaning back in my chair and clapping my hands together.

"What's perfect?" Ms. Crawl asks, confused.

"The story. It's a perfect story," I answer.

All through dinner that night I compose my children's book in my head. I stay up late writing it, even sketching some pencil drawings of Betty in the grave. At the beginning of the book she has flesh, but then as the story goes on she changes to bone. Some of the pictures look a little too scary for a kid, so I put in some flowers and bunny rabbits around the edges, and some yellow stars in the sky at night. The next day I hand in my book, pictures and all.

When I get it back, Miss Lucy tells me that it's a highly inappropriate topic for a child and gives me an F or the opportunity to redo the assignment. I tell her I like it the way it is and that I won't change it, thank you very much, which makes her just shake her head and return to her pencil sharpening.

•   •   •

Aunt Sharon comes to visit about one month before my due date. She meets me in the visitors' room. When I walk in, Ms. Crawl and Aunt Sharon are whispering.

"Oh, hi, Snow," Ms. Crawl says, not realizing I had walked into the room. "I was just telling Sharon about the hospital plans." She smiles and puts her bony, crow-like fingers on my shoulder, as if she were this loving person. I cringe and make a face to Aunt Sharon.

When Ms. Crawl leaves the room I explain to Aunt Sharon that she's really a bitch. "She just acts nice in front of you," I say.

"I can tell," she smiles. "Annoyed the hell out of me in just five minutes." She lifts up a large brown paper bag that was resting on the ground beside her. "I brought just a few things, things I heard are useful for the hospital. Of course, I wouldn't know." She pulls out a yellow nightie wrapped in clear plastic, some slippers, a toothbrush, and a housecoat with rabbits on it.

"Thanks," I say, picking up the nightie package and studying it. "Can I?" She reaches out to touch my belly.

"Sure."

She pokes her finger in a little and then flattens her hands against my shirt. "So tight," she says. "Does she kick?"

"Sometimes," I say, watching her mesmerized eyes. "Her foot is here—" I lead her hand just below my belly button and hold it firmly to the slight bulge. Her eyes widen. I never understood why Aunt Sharon didn't have kids. She'd make a good mother, with her pie-making and everything.

"That's incredible!" she says, her eyes tearing up. "Isn't that amazing."

"Yeah, it's cool," I say, just to make her feel good.

We both sit down and she starts talking, nervous talk, all fast and breathless. She tells me about how busy she is at work, how she's hardly ever home anymore. I mention Elsie's broken arm, but she quickly changes the subject and talks about this party she's having at her apartment, where women come to her house and buy Tupperware.

"You hate Elsie?" I ask her, interrupting.

Aunt Sharon opens her mouth to answer but then stops herself. "Jesus, the questions you ask." She takes out a cigarette and starts to light it. I'm in shock. I can't believe she smokes. Aunt Sharon never smoked. I can't believe she even has cigarettes on her.

"What are you doing?" I yell.

"What?" She looks at me and then looks down at her body, taking a quick survey to see what the panic is about.

"You're smoking!"

"Oh," she laughs, and continues to light her cigarette. "Sometimes I do. Every now and then."

"I can't believe it," I say, astonished.

"It's not so strange, is it?" she asks, taking a deep drag. She looks so natural, like she's been doing it for years. But it seems so wrong for her to be smoking.

"You can't smoke in here," I say. "Ms. Crawl will kill you."

"Ms. Crawl can kiss my ass," she says, and I'm happy with this new side of Aunt Sharon.

"I asked you if you hated Elsie," I remind her.

"I know."

I wait for her to tell me about all the bad things Elsie has done to her. And then I could tell her all the bad things. And we could share in this whole I-hate-Elsie session.

"It doesn't help you to know what I think. You're not me." A responsible adult answer. She disappoints me. I thought she'd have more bite.

"But do you love her?"

She laughs a little, her shoulders bobbing up and down. Only it's not a happy laugh. She looks off, beyond me. "I don't know. Does it matter?"

"Well, if you had to say something you hate about her, what would it be?"

"You've been watching too many talk shows," she jokes, taking another drag. She turns her head to look out the window, like she's deep in thought. I lick my lips, anticipating her juicy answer. I imagine her hateful answers gooing out of her mouth like venom. A mix of cursing and tragedy. And then she finally replies,

"She gave me a life I can't crawl out of, I guess." I wait for a few minutes, but that's all she says. And I'm left in confusion as Aunt Sharon finishes her cigarette in silence. Because it always seemed to me that Aunt Sharon was doing just fine in her life.

24

I read that babies can sometimes sense when you're dreaming. This thought terrifies me. Blood rushes to my face as if I have just been caught in a lie. Having access to my body is one thing, but my mind? *How much do you know?*

Do you know about the bloody babies that look like dead puppies? Have you seen my pale hands reach down to push you back inside while the faceless doctor sews me tight with what looks like yellow wool? Do you remember me giving birth in a subway washroom stall and then just watching you crawl away, leaving a slimy trail of goo and blood behind?

And now I wonder, When you kick my stomach, are you really kicking *at* me? And are you clutching that umbilical cord not because you're playing with it, but because you feel the need to hang onto something? Like if you let go, you'd be thought to extinction?

. . .

It's four in the morning. I am startled awake by my own thoughts. I sneak downstairs and carefully make my way down the back hallway. I tiptoe, hop, and zigzag a complex trail of quiet footing along the old hardwood floors. Step in the wrong spot and even the slightest creak will alert Staff on the night shift to my presence. Within a few weeks of living here, all residents have figured out how to avoid these landmines of sound.

I lean up against the wall and rest the phone on my belly. Music from a cheap radio mixed with the tap-tapping of a computer keyboard filter out from underneath the office door down the hall. I dial Elsie's number. The phone rings forever before she finally rips it off the hook.

"What the hell?" Elsie yells groggily into the phone. "Someone better be dead and bloody to call this late!"

My voice is small. "Who's my father?"

"Snow?"

I take a deep breath so she can't hear me shaking. "Who's my father?"

"Jesus Christ," she snaps. "I'm not getting into that now. It's too late."

"I want to know. I need to know. Now," I command.

"I told you. He was some guy your mom hooked up with. I don't know who. She didn't tell me. Now, I'm going to sleep." And she hangs up.

My heart pounds in my chest. I immediately call back, letting it ring and ring and ring until I'm sure Elsie has pulled the plug from the wall. I stand there for what seems like hours before I leave the receiver on the table, its distant ghostly ring resonating down the hallway behind me.

●   ●   ●

When I wake in the morning, I call Aunt Sharon at work. I tell her I need to speak to her: "Today. Now."

She doesn't ask me what's wrong. She simply says we can meet at eleven, outside Licks in the Beaches, down the road from her office. "We'll have a morning ice-cream," she says cheerily.

I arrive at the restaurant where Aunt Sharon and I are to meet an hour early. I pace up and down the street, staring into store windows and moving out of rich people's way. At the corner a man with worn plaid trousers and a stained shirt passes me a flyer, our pinkies touch, and I pull my hand away. The shock of soft, warm skin under the dull-green paper sends tingly shivers down into my stomach. Suddenly, I'm embarrassed. I continue walking, staring down at the paper claiming "Canada's Best Mattress Sale" and think about all the hands I touched today: the woman who gave me change when I bought my gum; the man who held the door open for me; the bus driver who passed me my transfer. I think of how it's even possible I can feel so alone, when I'm surrounded by so many people.

When I get sick of being bumped and jarred, I find a doorway and slump my bloated body slowly down to the ground. Some older guy with dreadlocks and a Marley T-shirt passes by and asks me if I'm selling. I figure he means selling my body, so I tell him to fuck off, but then a few minutes later I realize he may have only been talking about weed and I feel bad for being so harsh. I slip off my shoes and study the imprints that run deep and red into my skin and someone tosses a loonie at my feet.

At eleven o' clock, I head over to Licks. Aunt Sharon is waiting on the bench outside the door. She buys me a mint-chocolate-chip ice-cream cone and orders herself a double-scoop rocky-road waffle cone. "So good to get out of the office," she says, oblivious to my face of stone. "We should do this more often." She leads me down through the park and onto the boardwalk. I walk slowly, breathing heavy, my lungs squished inside my own body. I am quiet and unresponsive, trying my best to get her to ask me what's wrong, but she doesn't. Instead, she's annoyingly upbeat. I'd swear she was being happy on purpose.

While Aunt Sharon points out seagulls, cute dogs, and interesting cloud formations, I rehearse my words about a thousand times in my head. My heart races, my lips are dry. It's as if I'm standing at the edge of a cold pool, psyching myself up to jump into something I know will take my breath away. But it isn't until we are at the entrance to Aunt Sharon's office, her hand on the door, that I finally spit it out.

"I need to know who my father is," I say.

"Jesus Christ." She brings her hand up to her forehead and squeezes tight, as if she's suddenly sprung a migraine. And it starts to make me angry that she thinks this is such a big hassle to her. Like I'm this annoyance in her day. She exhales deeply and shakes her head. "You need to talk to Elsie."

"She won't tell me anything. I asked her last night."

"What did she say?"

"He was a fling. Some guy she didn't know."

"I don't like this, Snow." Aunt Sharon fiddles with the ring on her finger, nervously twisting it around and around. "I don't think this makes things better."

"It's not going to make anything worse. It can't get much worse. If I know the truth, I can go from there. I mean, was he in jail? A murderer or something? A priest? Her teacher? A perverted school janitor? A—"

"It was Mitch," she says, cutting me off. She stares at me intensely, waiting to see what I'll do.

I feel like life just whipped out its hand and slapped me hard in the face. "What?" I say, even though I've heard her.

"This isn't good, Snow. I told you." Aunt Sharon's eyes dart around her, as if the helicopters are going to appear on the horizon and she'll be gunned down by secret agents. She's said too much.

I start to feel sick to my stomach. A rush of memories speed through me. I think of all the times Mitch has been in the apartment. I see him on the couch, I see him at the kitchen table drinking a beer, I see him standing at the bathroom counter shaving. I see him hovering over my face, that night he was in my room. "Did he rape her?" I ask, preparing myself for the worst.

She turns to me with a disgusted look on her face. "Rape her? God, no. I think she loved him." My jaw drops as the whole world slips out from underneath me and I'm left alone, feet dangling in the air. I have no idea what's real anymore.

Aunt Sharon silently motions for me to follow her. We go into the building and through to the stairwell. I lean up against the metal railing while Aunt Sharon sits on the concrete steps. Her voice is dry and bare in the hollow stairwell. I collect her words like bread crumbs marking a trail back to my beginning.

She tells me that a couple of years after their father left Elsie, Mitch moved in. Mitch was younger than Elsie, about thirty at the time. My mom was fourteen. She and Aunt Sharon liked him because he partied with them and didn't pull the man-of-the-house crap that Elsie's other boyfriends did. But since Aunt Sharon moved out a few months before Mitch arrived, it was really only my mother who got to spend much time with him. She says Mitch and my mom got along really well, like friends, and that used to make Elsie mad. Everyone had a feeling they were sleeping together but no one knew for sure. And then, one day, my mother announced at a Christmas family gathering that she was pregnant with Mitch's kid. She said it in front of everyone and

Elsie flipped her lid, almost killing her. Some great-uncle I've never even heard of had to split up the fight. My mom was sent to the hospital with a fractured skull, two missing teeth, and a broken nose. She never went home again.

"And after that?" I ask.

"Mitch disappeared. I don't know if he saw your mom during the pregnancy. He's the one who brought you to Elsie a few months after you were born. I saw him at your mom's funeral and never again after that, until Jed left. You were about six then."

"Why would Elsie let him come back?"

"You think Elsie could ever survive on her own? Who do you think paid your rent?"

"Fuck off," I say in disbelief.

"What did you think? Jesus, Snow. For someone so eager to know the truth, you certainly have your head in a cloud. Elsie can't afford that place, never could. She spends all her cash on booze. Besides that, she's so pathetic, she still loves him."

"If my boyfriend fucked my daughter, I'd kill him." I start to think more about this, the anger growing. "I'd fuckin' kill him. I'd shoot his balls right off."

"Well . . . your mom wasn't exactly a victim."

"What?" I glare at Aunt Sharon.

"She wasn't exactly an angel in all this."

"What are you saying?

"Forget it."

"No, what? You think my mom was a little slut, don't you?"

"No, I don't," she denies, but I can tell she's just backing down. I can tell she's lying but she continues on, anyway. "Elsie did want to kill Mitch. At the beginning. But then your mom died, and Jed left her about three years later, and she totally lost it because there's no way she could handle things on her own. She

258 LESLEY ANNE COWAN

was drinking more and taking pills, and then Children's Aid got involved. I don't know exactly when Mitch started coming back around, but all of a sudden Elsie started to blame your mom for all her problems. Saying that your mom seduced Mitch. That she asked for it."

"Asked for it?" I shrivel my face in disgust.

"Came on to him. Like Mitch was some victim."

"You think that?"

"No," she says. "But I think Elsie convinced herself of that because she felt guilty. I told her so."

"And what'd she say?"

"Uh, let's see. What did she say? I believe it was, 'Get the fuck out.' Yes, that's probably it. She stopped talking to me. Wouldn't let me come around for years."

We sit a few moments in silence. I don't even feel upset about it all. I don't have the energy. There comes a point when you just feel nothing. When the shit is piled so high, whatever's dumped after that just slips down the outside of you.

Aunt Sharon clears her throat. "You okay?"

"I wish it wasn't him," I say, my eyes locked in a bug-eyed trance. "Anyone but him." I hear a sniffle and quickly glance at Aunt Sharon. For the first time I realize that maybe it was as hard for Aunt Sharon to say all this as it was for me to hear it. "Thanks for telling me," I say.

"I'm sorry you're a part of all this." She stretches her legs out in front of her, knees cracking.

"All what?"

"This family."

We stay a little while longer in silence. I feel the baby squirming and kicking, as if it were reading my mind, getting ready to flee this moment. Finally, Aunt Sharon extends an arm and grabs the handrail to haul herself up. "You know, I look at you and see her," she says.

"You do?" I ask, deflated. I can tell she means this in the best way. And there was a time when I would have taken those words and carefully preserved them between my thoughts like dried flowers between the pages of a book. But hearing it now only makes my heart sink, as if I've been told I'm a carrier of some defective gene. And it's like all of a sudden I realize that all this was bound to happen. Like an indoor plant that only blooms in the spring, I am guided by a memory that precedes me.

25

When you are born I will lay you down, flat against my chest, or I'll stand above your crib, and I will tell you about the women in your family. I will tell you about your life, so that there are no surprises, so that you don't waste your time believing that you will be any different. I will tell you that you will be born smart, that you will be good at school, but that teachers won't like you because you miss too many classes and you have the occasional outburst. You will do things without thinking, like put crayon shavings in the kindergarten guinea pig cage or bite the hand of the fat boy who won't let go of the blue ball. You'll have what people call a temper and that some days you won't feel like getting out of bed because just the thought of breathing will feel like a chore. I will tell you that you will have these awful tendencies: you will crave things on your lips, like cigarettes, joints, or the burning of vodka. That boys will like you because you're pretty and you will like the power this gives you over them. I will tell you that you will become pregnant too soon, and that this will be the best and worst thing that ever happened to you.

I will tell you that you are now a woman in this family. And even though you know all these things, even though I warn you, you will do them anyway.

You'll see.

.   .   .

The visions come to me more and more now. Only, now they linger a little longer, so that I can actually see my face all tight and twisted during my free fall from the bridge. Or I can actually see the tiny bloated wrinkles on my fingertips as my lifeless hand floats like a white lily-pad in a bloodied bathtub.

I am no longer my body. I am a capsule for you. I eat only to feed and water you, as if you were a plant on my windowsill. I start to sympathize with discarded banana peels and empty milk jugs. All things with skins and shells. I take boiled eggs from Sam's kitchen up to my room and spend hours carefully peeling away the shells. The small white pieces overflow out of a glass beside my bed, but I insist Karyn not throw them out.

I pretend I'm listening and laughing and thinking, but really, I am so far, far away. I force my body through the day just so I can sneak under my covers at night and cut myself, feel the warm blood trickle down skin like watery confirmations of my existence. Then I cut again, because even blood doesn't convince me anymore.

I long for sleep, so my mind can be still. Only the second I close my eyes, it's like my thoughts are wildly spinning in a blender and the only thing that surfaces clearly out of this messy whirlwind is Mark's face. I breathe in the faint smell of sweat from his old T-shirt that I keep under my pillow. I press my nose into the armpit and breathe deep. I imagine Mark in soap-opera scenes, picture him at the hospital, the day of the delivery, our eyes locking through the small square window of the birthing room. In another scene, I see him lying on a bed with red satin sheets, rose petals scattered everywhere. He's holding the baby on his bare chest, tenderly stroking her face the way he lovingly caresses Spliff.

During the day it's different. My head is vacant. A sludge of half-digested thought settles at the bottom of me each morning. Chunks, like my mother's truth, are whole while other thoughts, like my hate for Elsie, are thoroughly minced into tiny pieces.

Staff keeps coming into my room and trying to force me to talk. They tell me that if I don't start communicating with them, they'll have no choice but to send me to the hospital.

"Can you at least *try* to tell me what's on your mind?" Karyn asks when she brings her offering of chocolate milk.

I try to answer, I open my mouth, but my tongue is heavy and confused. "I can't put it into words. It's like I need another language." I say, frustrated, and she returns fifteen minutes later with a sketchbook and a box of pencil crayons.

I call Delcare to talk to Jasmyn, but Miranda tells me that she left the house a few days ago and hasn't been back since. "She was really going through a rough time," Miranda says carefully, and I roll my eyes at her so-called *confidential* vagueness. "We're hoping she comes back." She quickly changes the topic. "And how are you doing? It's so good to hear from you! You're due soon, aren't you?"

"Ya, a couple weeks."

"Well, I'm not the best substitute for Jasmyn, but I'd love to meet you. Are you up to it?"

.   .   .

We meet on the corner the next day at Coffee Time. I am nervous to see her. Even though it hasn't been that long, I feel like the person she knew is gone. As if each new house makes me a new person. I'm afraid Miranda will be disappointed in what she finds.

"This place is sort of raunchy, isn't it?" she says, shivering her shoulders and looking around.

"I think it's okay," I say, taking a second look around me. It's like any other coffee shop. People drinking from cardboard cups, a couple of men smoking by the window, playing backgammon. An old lady sitting by the door, shopping bags at her feet.

I start to think that this is a bad idea. I can just imagine Miranda going back to Delcare, telling Staff how badly I'm doing. I can hear the satisfaction in their we-knew-it response: *We knew she'd screw up at some point.* I try to fake that I'm happy and fine, but I know Miranda can tell something's wrong. She buys me a rainbow doughnut and I put all my focus into picking off the yellow sprinkles.

"You don't like the yellow ones?" Miranda asks, poking fun at me.

"I just don't feel like yellow today," I say seriously, continuing on my mission. I want to leave. It feels different. Awkward. Like we have nothing to talk about anymore. Luckily Miranda is in a chatty mood. She tells me about Delcare. She tells me that one of the youth workers is taking pregnancy leave and that Pat is looking into buying a new van for the house. She says that most of the remaining residents are doing all right. Nicole is finally going to school every day and Mary will soon be applying for independent living. As I continue picking at my doughnut, she begins to go into detail about the road construction out in front of the house and the zoning proposal for the building across the street.

"I'm not sure I can do this," I say, piling the sprinkles into a pyramid on my napkin.

"What?"

"Have a baby."

Miranda laughs, like I knew she would. "Well, hate to tell you, kiddo, but you can't reverse it now." She is trying to make light of this. But when I don't laugh back, she gets serious, her eyes darting back and forth as if she were searching for the right words.

"How am I supposed to do this?" I don't look at her. I lean my face down to the napkin and blow at the pile of yellow sprinkles, scattering them across the table. "How am I supposed to raise a baby if I can't even stay in school? If I can't even keep a boyfriend?"

Miranda sighs deeply. "I don't know, Snow. I'd be lying if I said it wouldn't be hard. You're too smart to hear that. But you have supports. You have people who can help you. You're not alone."

Alone. How can she possibly understand its meaning when her partner's small black initials are tattooed on the back of her hand, just at the base of her thumb.

"What if I can't do it?" I ask, my voice small. So small that if she chose, she might not hear it.

"You can," she insists, but the words hang like stones in the air, unclaimed by either one of us. "Snow, do you want this baby?"

No one had ever asked me that. Straight out. With no bushes to hide behind. Do I want the baby? If I say no, I'm selfish because I am putting my needs first and I don't want the burden. If I say yes, I'm selfish because I won't give my baby the best chance in life with a good family. It's an impossible question, with only one right answer that will let you sleep at night.

"Yes," I say, "sort of."

"Well, 'sort of' ain't going to cut it, Snow." She starts ferociously stirring her coffee with the stir stick. I watch her lips tighten and her nostrils flare as she stares into the cup. Finally she slams her opened hand down to the table. "'Sort of' isn't going to get you through a night of crying and wailing and stinky diapers. This is a huge commitment. You'll have this kid forever. You have to think about this."

I start to get upset and angry all at once. I don't hide it, not anymore. I just let tears pour out of me, down my chin. I don't care who sees.

"I'm sorry if this is upsetting you, but frankly, I don't care. You better start making some choices."

"I want it, I want it—okay?" I say, wanting her to just shut up. "There's my answer. You happy?"

"Am I happy? Listen to yourself. It doesn't matter if I'm happy. It's you that matters. Are you happy?"

"No." The tears tickle as they slowly drip down my face. I reach up to rub them off. "No, okay. I'm obviously not fuckin' happy. What do you want, blood?" I wipe my face on my sleeve and Miranda passes me a rough napkin. She won't say sorry. I know her. She won't fold to my tears like most people do. She used to say crying just makes her more angry. That most of the time crying is just manipulation. And whether it's deliberate or not, it's a very clever way of getting people to back off.

"I'm not supposed to do this," Miranda says. She reaches into her bag and pulls out a piece of paper. She writes down her home number and gives it to me, telling me I can call any time I want.

"You mean a lot to me, Snow," she says before I go. "I want you to know I'm here for you." She reaches out her arms to hug me. But it's not the kind of hug Miss Lucy or Aunt Sharon gives me. When they hug their bodies fold, delicately absorbing my round stomach, fingers lightly touching my back. But Miranda presses me tight into her, her hipbone jabbing my belly. And it's like she's the first person who's ever tried to stretch around this baby to reach me.

. . .

Now, when I sit in the TV room and stare at the screen, my mind isn't always blank. I think about things. Like about Betty Corrigal, and how people still put flowers on her grave. And about all the other unwed girls of the past whose secrets grew in their bodies like death warrants. I wonder what happened to the ones we don't hear about. The girls who were washed up on distant shores, their swollen bellies at the feet of puzzled fishermen. Or the ones who collected poison berries in skirt pockets and then hid behind woodpiles, dropping the sour red balls into their mouths.

I think about what Ms. Crawl didn't say. What's left out of Betty's story. The dull parts of her life. The details that are either too insignificant or too dirty to be considered. About fetching water at a well or mending the hole in her father's sock. Or about her lying spread-legged in the barn, leading her lover's fingers to a place she and her mother don't discuss.

And then I think of worse things. Things no one likes to talk about. Like, what happened before she strung that rope around her neck? What if it wasn't her seafaring lover's baby, anyway? What if it was her uncle's or the priest's or the married man's down the road? What if that noose was something she longed for since she was young and the baby just gave her a legitimate reason to make it so?

26

My water breaks and I'm convinced I've pissed my pants. I had expected it would be like in the movies, fluid exploding out of me as if from a sudden broken pipe.

"It's not gushing," I explain to Karyn who is on the other side of the cubicle. We are on the main floor of the house, in the ladies' washroom. It's just before dinner. "It's more like pee," I explain.

"Let me in," Karyn says, rattling the door. "Let me see."

"No way!" I yell. I start to panic. The pee is sort of red, not clear. My head starts to wooze, the back of my neck gets hot and sweaty. I have this dull aching pain in my back. It's two weeks before my due date. I'm not ready for this.

. . .

When I arrive at the hospital with Ms. Crawl and Karyn, I have to sit in the waiting area until a room is ready. I had pictured it differently, doctors running around, crowds parting to let the pregnant girl through. Instead, no one seems to care that I'm about to explode.

"What's taking so long!" I yell, standing up from the uncomfortable plastic chair. I'm in total agony but I won't admit it. I told myself I wouldn't wimp out, that I'm above the pain. But I can't imagine it getting any worse. I don't think my body can take it.

"It won't be long," Ms. Crawl says calmly. "Just . . ." The contraction waves through my body, so painful I can't hear the rest of Ms. Crawl's useless sentence. She holds the stopwatch in her hand up to her face, squinting her eyes to read the small numbers. "That's five minutes, eight seconds," she says and records the number down on her pad of paper.

"Just try to relax," Karyn consoles. "Do you want your crossword puzzle?" She's about to reach into my bag before I grab her wrist and twist it away.

"I don't want a fucking crossword! Jesus Christ!" I just want the pain to stop. I start to panic. My eyes scan the room for someone wearing a name tag who could possibly understand what I'm going through. "Where's my room?"

"I'll go call your aunt." Karyn heads toward the payphone. Meanwhile, Ms. Crawl marches up to the lady holding the clipboard and I'm relieved someone is finally taking charge. But they start chatting and laughing, like they're old friends, and I don't think Ms. Crawl is even talking about me. After a few minutes she comes back to our seats.

"The nurse will come soon to assess you, Snow. Don't worry. It'll still be a while now. Your contractions are just about right." She smiles and rubs my back, her bony fingers poking into my shoulder blade. For a split second, I'm glad she's here. I'm glad someone knows what's going on. Because although I hate the bitch, I know Ms. Crawl wouldn't let anyone cut any corners with me.

When I finally get moved to my room, I can't sit still. I get up and walk around, lean over on the chairs and then squat down. Each new position seems to release the pressure in my back, but then I have a contraction and the middle of my body is squeezed like an accordion. This goes on for what seems like hours. Every once in a while, a useless nurse comes in to check me and then leaves.

"Open a window," I command as I pace the room.

"I can't," Karyn answers. She is sitting on the side of the bed, watching me. "They're sealed."

I walk over to the window and angrily slam my open hand against the glass. "I can't breathe!"

"Take off your sweatshirt," Ms. Crawl suggests from her chair by the bed. She puts down her paperback novel and stares at me. Then she lifts her juice and takes a sip. It's as if she's at the beach. "You must be roasting," she says.

"No, it stays on," I warn.

"It'll have to come off sooner or later," she persists.

"I'm leaving it on," I say, thinking about my scars. "I don't want any perverted doctor getting a free peep show."

"Don't be ridiculous," Ms. Crawl laughs.

"I'm leaving it on," I say, resolute. And Ms. Crawl just shrugs her shoulders.

I kick Karyn off my bed and prop some pillows up behind my back. A few minutes later, the nurse comes in the room and tells me she needs to take my blood pressure. "You'll need to take this off," she says, tugging at my sweatshirt. I dart a look at Ms. Crawl. It's as if they had planned this.

Another contraction tears through me. The pain is so unbearable, I don't care anymore. I rip the sweatshirt up over my head and reach to the table for the nightgown Aunt Sharon gave me.

"Oh my God," the nurse exclaims. Her eyes dart between my body and Karyn.

"Jesus," Ms. Crawl exhales.

"Snow—what happened?" Karyn raises her hand up over her mouth as if she's about to throw up. Her face is pale with red splotches.

At first I'm embarrassed, but then I just get angry. "What?" I snarl. I give up on trying to cover myself with the gown wrapped around my waist. "You wanted my shirt off. There!" I throw it on the chair in the corner and lie back down. "It's off. Satisfied?" I rise from the pillows, inhale deeply, and thrust my bare chest out. "Take a better look, why don't ya," I challenge.

The letters on my skin are rough and messy. I follow Karyn's eyes as she reads my body's Braille. Her head slightly tilted and brow creased, I watch her decipher M-O-T-H-E-R etched on my left forearm. And then S-L-U-T, faint and red, arching along my bicep to my shoulder like a sagging rainbow. I see her eyes widen as she pulls back her horrified face and I turn to face the wall as I sense her tracing the thin messy lines across my chest. The U that runs along the side of my body, up to just under my armpit and back down again. Then the letters G and L, sharp and jagged across my breasts. And finally Y, on the right side of my torso, disappearing along the curve toward my back.

Everyone in the room remains silent as if time is frozen. Finally, a contraction clenches me, I fold and scream and people start moving again. Karyn helps me with my nightgown. Ms. Crawl leaves the room quickly and the nurse is suddenly exceptionally accommodating. And nothing more is said about my marks.

When Aunt Sharon arrives, Ms. Crawl talks to her outside my door for what seems like forever. Through the window, I see Aunt Sharon's head nodding and shaking and her hand goes up to her forehead, as if she has another one of her migraines. I can't stand thinking about what Ms. Crawl must be saying about me. About how crazy I am.

"I know you're talking about me!" I yell angrily from my bed. "Stop talking about me!"

They finally enter my room, intense looks on their faces. Aunt Sharon greets me with a confused and concerned expression. "You okay?" she asks.

"Hurts like hell," I mumble, pouting a little bit. I am just relieved that Aunt Sharon is in the room now and Ms. Crawl isn't filling her head with her theories on me.

"No, I mean, are *you* okay?"

"Oh, yeah." I respond, embarrassed that she now knows about my cuts.

Ms. Crawl and Karyn leave the room to go buy coffees and I realize that it's already one o'clock in the morning. After they leave a nurse slathers my belly with slimy jelly and then straps a belt around me. The red numbers start blinking, numbers rising and falling like video game scores. She explains that one number is the baby's heartbeat and the other is my contractions. A roll of paper starts coming out of the machine and curling onto the floor.

Just when I thought the pain couldn't get any worse, it does. Aunt Sharon keeps pulling down my nightgown over my legs and then shutting the drapes after the nurses leave my bedside, the metal rings scraping like fingernails on a chalkboard.

"Jesus Christ! Just fucking leave it! I don't give a shit if someone sees," I snarl. Without saying a word, she dramatically yanks the curtains open wide, drops down on a chair in the corner, and pulls out my crossword book. I feel guilty almost immediately. "You have know idea what the pain's like," I explain, without thinking how offended she might be by this comment. Her eyes rise from the page, she glares at me a moment. "I mean—"

"Just shut up," she says flatly.

Finally, the doctor comes back in the room. "Busy night!" he says cheerily. "Everybody having babies." He glances at the machine and then looks at me. "I'm Doctor Freeman, Snow. I'll be delivering your baby. How are you feeling?"

"The contractions kill," I complain.

He smiles, as if this were amusing him. "Hang in there. Let me see how far you've progressed." He moves to the bottom of the bed and tells me to bring my ankles up together. "It'll just take a second," he says and then he shoves his fingers up inside me. "Three centimetres dilated. Looks just fine. Did you already discuss an epidural?" He looks to me and Aunt Sharon and we both nod our heads. "We'll have the anesthetist come in a few minutes. You'll feel better after that." He gives me a supportive squeeze on the knee and then heads back out of the room.

Shortly, the anesthetist walks in and I like him because he's wearing jeans under his white coat and he talks like a regular guy. "I'm every pregnant lady's genie without a bottle," he says. "Make a wish." I lean forward like he tells me, roll my spine, and feel a prick as the needle slides between my bones.

"Make sure there's enough," I remind him because I've heard about the doctors who don't give teen moms enough painkillers, so they aren't tempted to make this mistake again any time soon.

Ms. Crawl and Karyn return from a very long coffee and we all sit and wait. Soon, my legs become heavy, then the pain is gone. Every few minutes the nurse enters the room, holds out the paper scrolls, and checks the flashing numbers on the monitor. But this time, I notice her forehead is creased as she is frantically recording things on her chart. She murmurs something I can't quite make out and then she quickly darts out of the room.

"What'd she say?" I ask, leaning up on my arms. I turn to Ms. Crawl's chair. "What's she doing?" But Ms. Crawl is already following the nurse out of the room.

I turn to Aunt Sharon, who has a worried look on her face. "What the fuck's going on?" I demand.

"She said something about the baby being in stress. I think they're a little worried about the heart rate. It's all right. They know what they're doing. You're in good hands."

Right away the doctor and nurse come rushing in. They look at all the flashing numbers and printed scrolls, talking about contractions and heart rates and numbers as if we weren't even there.

Then the doctor turns to me. "The cord is around the baby's neck. Each time you have a contraction, the baby doesn't get any oxygen. We'll have to do a C-section. Now." I can hear the urgency in his voice, and before I know it, I'm being wheeled quickly down the hall, Aunt Sharon and Karyn and Ms. Crawl following behind.

The operating room is all steel and tile surfaces and bright lights. It's freezing, but I don't even care because all I'm thinking about is the baby and the cord around her neck. And it's like I know what she's doing. Strangling herself. My baby would rather die than be born to me. And she's killing herself and I'm killing her, and it's all the same thing.

Everything happens so fast. A bunch of people start moving about the room and I can't tell who they are because they're all wearing the same green scrubs and masks and caps. One nurse sticks an IV in my arm, and another starts shaving my stomach and some of my crotch. When the buzzing stops she looks up at me and asks, "You doing okay?"

"Just get her out!" I shout, panicking, because I don't want the baby dying inside of me.

Then the IV nurse starts slathering my belly with yellowish brown liquid. Someone hoists a white sheet up in front of me so I can no longer see below my chest. "Tell me when you can feel a pinprick," I am surprised to hear the anesthetist say from the bottom of my bed because I didn't even see him enter the room.

"Just get her out!" I yell. "You're taking too long."

The doctor arrives with a mask and gloves on, and I start to get really scared. "Hi, Snow. How are you feeling?" He stands beside me, all relaxed, as if we're chatting in a garden somewhere.

I'm shaking now and my head feels woozy. "Not so good," I say as he moves down to the bottom of the table.

"You're going to be just fine, Snow. Just take nice deep breaths. Everything looks good. We're going to make an incision just above the pubic bone. You won't even have to worry about a scar on the beach," he says jokingly. "We're going to get the baby out as fast as we can."

"Hang in there, sweetie." I feel Sharon's hand on my forehead. I turn my head to see she's all covered up as well. I had never noticed her eyes before. They're almost the same colour as mine.

A nurse pops her face into my vision. "You'll hear a sucking-vacuum noise and that will tell you we're close," she says, before disappearing once more.

"I'm gonna barf," I murmur so quietly I don't think anyone can hear me, but before I know it, Aunt Sharon is holding a bowl beside my head and I'm puking my guts out.

I can't feel a thing below my belly button. No pain, but I feel an unbearable pressure at my ribs. The doctor has a hold on one side of me, pulling, and the nurse has a hold on the other side of me, pulling. My body wiggles on the table. I look up to see a reflection in the metal lights above me, but all I can see is bright red. I get this vision of a horror movie and I think of a monster flying out of my body.

"Congratulations! A lovely baby girl!" the doctor announces a few minutes later. And I see this bloody, goopy blur being carried over to the warming table.

"Is she all right?" I ask, and then I hear her cry, crackly and rough.

"She's just fine. Just fine," a nurse says. "What's her name?"

I lie there, motionless, speechless. All my panic about the baby being alive and normal leaves me and I'm left with this blank and cold head. It's like I'm just realizing, really realizing, that I have a baby. Only it feels like nothing's changed. I don't feel like an instant mother. I don't feel anything.

"What's her name?" Aunt Sharon repeats excitedly, and I see that she's been crying.

"Betty," I say.

"Betty?" the nurse repeats, looking up to Aunt Sharon's nodding head for confirmation. "Well, that's a beautiful name. Betty."

Aunt Sharon follows the baby and the nurse down to another room while they take out my placenta and then sew me up. I can barely keep my eyes open, but I force myself to stay awake because I can hear the nurses taking inventory of their tools and I don't want something to be left inside. When it's all over, they wheel me down to the recovery room.

The nurse keeps appearing at my bedside, reminding me that as soon as I can wiggle my toes I can go and see my baby. So I lie there, hoping that my legs will remain numb. I concentrate on keeping them still. My eyes get heavier and heavier. And when the big toe on my right foot jiggles, the nurse gets all excited, but I pretend it was a muscle twitch. And she looks confused and stares at me in the strangest way.

"I just want to sleep. I'm so tired. Can I sleep now?" I ask and close my eyes, not waiting for an answer.

. . .

When I wake I'm in my room. I see a different nurse in front of me, holding my baby in a white blanket. I am still hooked up to IVs and my head is groggy. She tilts the bundle so I can see her face. "Your little girl!" she says, excited. "All six pounds and nineteen inches of her," she announces, but I don't even know how long that is. She extends out her arms to pass the baby to me and I panic, looking around the room for Aunt Sharon. "Your aunt told me to tell you she had to go to work," the nurse says. "She'll be by tonight." She pushes the baby toward me and I have no choice but to reach out to take her tiny body into my hands.

"You'll need to be careful of lifting," the nurse warns. "It takes a while for the incision to heal." She moves in closer and puts the weightless bundle into my arms.

"She's so small," I say, touching the baby's tiny cheek with my pinkie. Her light hair is still damp, and she has Mark's perfect little nose and his perfect little lips. There is a yellow plastic clamp on her belly button, all bloody and gross, which I cover up with the blanket. I pull out one of her hands, so tiny, with little pink-shell fingernails. I can't believe such perfection came out of me.

Then she starts crying, this dry wailing, and her hands start flapping in the air. I quickly reach out to pass her back to the nurse, who simply smiles at me and retracts her hands. "You'll need to calm her," she says, and stands over me, watching. "It's important to start the bonding right away." She stays by my bedside, occasionally giving me directions: "Hold her close to your chest and try to relax a little. She's not so fragile. You won't break her."

After about five minutes, my door opens and someone calls the nurse away. "I'll come back in a while to start you breast-feeding," she says, rushing out of the room.

"Wait!" I scream, not wanting her to leave.

"I'll be back," she assures me, halfway out the door.

I don't know what to do. What if the baby stops breathing or chokes or turns blue in my hands? "Fuck!" I yell out in frustration. The nurse stops in her tracks and glares back at me. Her face is controlled, her mouth tight as if she's literally biting her tongue.

"You're not a little girl anymore," she says, barely moving her jaw or lips. And then she leaves.

I hate the bitch for going. For leaving me with this baby I know nothing about. I am terrified. I want to throw Betty into someone else's arms, anyone else's arms. I jiggle her up and down a little until she stops crying and opens her eyes. I wait for that feeling of motherhood to come over me, wait for my face to nuzzle down onto her tiny head. I wait to feel something, anything other than this blankness inside. I wait for what must be at least ten minutes, then look away from her piercing eyes and whisper, "I'm sorry," into her soft skin.

27

After three days in the hospital I'm back at Beverley. I lie in bed all day, wearing the nightgown Staff gave me, with a buttoned slit at the chest for breast-feeding. I can barely move. My insides feel as if they've been taken out of my body, jumbled up, and just shoved back in. I stare at the baby's crib in the corner of my room, watching for the quick rise of her chest. Karyn's words repeating over and over in my head: *Careful, because even a mere blanket over her face could suffocate her.*

Staff is watching me closely now, concerned after the discovery of my scarred arms and chest. They tell me that I'll need to talk to someone, immediately. They tell me they want me to be honest with the social worker, say how I feel, and not to worry about a thing because they'll help me with the baby. They won't let me shut my bedroom door, even at night. And I laugh at this, like it's the most hilarious thing in the world. That after all this time, a few scratches in skin was what it took for anyone to notice me. That it all comes down to broken skin.

But there's another cut on my body now. An uninvited one. The pain is not the same as when I cut my arms. The pain is not mine. It taunts me with each movement and breath. It won't even let me laugh without stabbing me. When Karyn comes to change the bandages, I can't bear to look at it. I am jealous of the privileged blade that sliced through my layers of muscle and flesh, layers I didn't even know I had. I am mad that someone found a way inside and then sealed the entrance behind him.

*   *   *

Karyn finds reasons to pop her head in my doorway. "Your grandmother keeps calling. What do you want me to tell her?" she asks.

"Tell her about Betty. Say I'll call her soon."

"Would you like her to come by?"

"No," I say quickly. "I don't want to see anyone."

Every few hours, Staff comes into my room, grabs my tit, and forces it into the baby's greedy mouth. Even though they are more patient than the nurses at the hospital, they still ignore my squeals of pain and order me to relax. I reluctantly give in, kicking myself for never having realized that a tiny creature chewing on your nipple might not just hurt a bit.

"She doesn't seem to be getting any milk," Ms. Crawl says as she and Karyn move in on my dysfunctional boobs, tweaking and prodding. They try not to stare too long at my chest, and I'm unsure if this is because they're being considerate or because they don't want to see my scars.

"I'm not good for her," I mumble, staring up at the ceiling. "Just let her use a bottle."

"Don't be so silly," Karyn persists, "you're her mother."

Underneath my skin, milk prickles and buzzes like freshly poured Coke. I stare down at my stomach, saggy and lifeless, and then turn my eyes to the baby's sucking mouth, allowing her to consume me. I think to myself, if it weren't for this milky evidence, I'd almost believe my body was dead.

. . .

Sky comes into my room and sits on the edge of my bed, updating me on her life as if she were filling me in on a TV show. She doesn't look at Betty lying in the cradle beside my bed. She doesn't even comment on her. Instead, she rambles on, her words so fast I only catch the end of her sentences. I try hard to focus on what she's saying, but it requires such an effort. It's like that time at the group home when I didn't get out of bed for so long. When things were muffled and voices seemed so far away.

She says something about leaving the house, something about a psychiatrist, something about school. My eyes fixate on her thin fingers, twirling a strand of her newly dyed purple hair. Staff told her they can't offer her the help she needs anymore and her refusal to receive any outside care is just unworkable. They said her needs have changed since she first came here, and because she's seventeen, she'll need to make room for younger residents. They are giving her a week to find a place to stay or she'll be discharged regardless. If, on the other hand, she wants to go to Smithwood Health Residence, they'd be open to arranging a meeting.

"What's that?" I ask.

"A place for wackos. They don't tie you down or anything, but they have shrinks and shit."

"So, are you going to go?"

"I don't know. Probably," she says, laughing. "What else am I going to do?"

I shrug my shoulders. I thought she'd be gone a long time ago, and to be honest, I couldn't care less. Even though she's my only friend in this shithole, she's been getting really freaky and last week she started to pull out her hair. At first, it was just a few strands on her head, but now it's everything, including her eyebrows and eyelashes. She's tried to cover it up by drawing on a face, as if she's intentionally trying to be some high-class model, but I tell her she just looks stupid. For one small moment, I consider telling her about me—about my thoughts, about my cutting—but I don't. I wouldn't want her to think that I was copying her.

"They knew you'd say yes," I say, watching her fingers search her brow for stubble.

"I know," she says.

. . .

The day after I arrive back at Beverley, a Children's Aid Society social worker comes to the house and meets me in the visitors' room. Apparently the hospital called her. Ms. Crawl pushes me through the door, and without even looking at the woman standing by the chair, I stumble into the room. I head straight over to the couch, slowly lower my sore body down, and sprawl out on my back. Then I roll up my sleeve and extend my scarred arm, as if she were going to take blood. I keep staring at the ceiling because I don't want to look at her face.

"I'd rather talk to my own counsellor, Eric," I announce. The woman tells me she's not here to counsel me, but to have a better understanding of my needs. She says Children's Aid is very concerned about me and my baby and that seeking medication and counselling would be in my best interest.

"Humph," I scoff. "Counselling."

"I need to tell you that if you're unco-operative, then we could impose a condition that in order for you to keep your baby, you need to seek medical attention and counselling. It's not a punishment, Snow. We're trying to help. We are very concerned about depression. We want you to feel better."

"Just give me the pills," I say. "I'll take 'em. But no counselling. It's a waste of time."

She asks me questions about my cuts. When I do it. Where I do it. How I feel when I do it. And then she asks, "Do you know why you do it?"

"Because I'm crazy?"

"No, you're not crazy. In fact, it's not as uncommon as you might think. People do this for different reasons, when regular coping doesn't work anymore. Most often, they cut lines in arms, legs, anywhere really. Sometimes it's where people will see it, like a call for help. I guess it's a way of communicating, though instead of using paper, they use skin."

I turn my eyes toward her for the first time and I stare her up and down. My body is none of her business. I own it and can do what I like. Just because I'm a teenager doesn't mean I'm public property. I'd like to see her shed her clothes, stand naked in this room, and explain the scar across her breast, and the bruise on her thigh, the rose tattoo on her bikini line, and the reason why she bought such ugly earrings. "It's not for you," I finally say. "It's for me. The words are meant for me to read."

"Yes, you did them."

"No," I correct her. "I uncovered them. They were always there." They have always been in my body, waiting to surface. The way a sculptor claims his hands only release the shape from stone.

As the thick glasses slide down her sharp nose, she tells me she's going to talk to Ms. Crawl about a counselling referral to an adolescent mental-health clinic.

"They won't understand it," I say before I leave. She thinks because I carve letters, people can read me. But it is my own language of blood and skin.

.   .   .

Aunt Sharon comes to visit me at Beverley five days after the birth. She saw me once in the hospital but I was too out of it to really care about visitors. She brings me flowers and body lotion and a few bags of diapers, even though I get them for free. She doesn't comment on my greasy hair or my puffy eyes. Instead, she sits on the chair in between me and the baby's crib, and asks if she can hold Betty. I motion that it's okay, and she gently lifts Betty's tiny body out and takes her into her fleshy arms. She smiles lovingly down at her and runs two fingers over Betty's small head.

"She's so beautiful," Aunt Sharon says, "so very beautiful." She looks over to me and then back to the baby. "And so tiny. Hello, Betty."

"She pees all the time," I say.

Aunt Sharon laughs. "I bet she does. Don't ya, sweetheart? Don't ya, sweetheart. Don't ya sweetheart," she keeps repeating, tweaking the baby's little chest until she starts squiggling.

"Why didn't you have kids?" I ask her.

She stops rubbing the baby's stomach, but doesn't look up at me. Instead she gently places the baby back into the crib. "I don't know. It wasn't in my cards I suppose," she says with a weak smile. "That doesn't mean I never wanted one, though," she adds.

"I think you'd make a good mom."

"And so will you," she says, heading toward the door.

I watch her walking away but I don't want her to leave. I want to tell her to stay, but I can't. "Thanks for the flowers," I blurt out, just as she's about to exit.

"You're very welcome," she answers and waves goodbye.

When she's gone, I slowly heave my sore body out of bed and pick up the baby, the way Aunt Sharon did. I lie back down, placing her on my chest, her warm skin against mine. Then I reach for the children's book I wrote in class and read the story of Betty Corrigal aloud to my daughter.

28

New dreams haunt me at night. I am unsure if they are good dreams or nightmares, or something in between.

· · ·

Betty Corrigal's body is rising through the peat. Her face is peaceful and loving and sorry. She's not a skeleton. She's a young woman with blonde hair and a blue dress and red lips. Sometimes, she has my mother's face, what I imagine it to be. Her lifeless body surfaces up to the salty Scotland air as fishermen and farmers wearing black rubber boots pass along a distant road. In my dreams, I am standing over Betty's grave. Her lips are moving, and I hear a whispery, windy voice, but I can't make out what she's saying. So I drop to my knees and lean my head down, into her cold, open grave, closer to her fluttering lips. Then suddenly her grey eyes open and she stares straight into the depths of me. Her pleading voice echoes clearly in the darkness. "Bury me, bury me . . ."

I understand what to do. It's so clear. I reach out my hand, hold it firm against her pale skin, pressing my fingers over her gasping mouth, and push her under the thick peat. I keep reaching out, transferring all my weight, and push her under.

. . .

Three weeks after Betty is born, Eric invites me to his going-away party for work. One of the other counsellors is having it at her house and he says a few of his other young clients will be there. He tells me to bring Betty so he can meet her. Ms. Crawl and Karyn try to convince me to go because they say it will be good "closure" for me, and I finally give in just so I don't have to hear their nagging voices anymore. So they pack up my baby bag, strap Betty into her car seat, and whisk me off to a big house in Oakville with a circular driveway.

I stumble up to the front door, Betty's car seat hooked onto one arm and Eric's present in the other. Karyn had bought a mug for me to give to Eric, wrapping it up nice. We fought for about ten minutes about me having to bring it.

I knock on the door but no one answers, so I push it open and enter the house. I have no idea what to expect. I have never been to a rich person's party. In fact, I've never been to an adult party. When I enter through the front door I am surprised to see balloons and streamers and a big silver flashy banner hung across the living-room wall that says *Goodbye*. There are about thirty people standing around, wineglasses and beer bottles in their hands. No one notices me. I spot Eric circulating around the room, his Adam's apple bobbing up and down with laughter. When he sees me, he shouts my name and walks toward me, stopping along the way to pick up a huge basket full of things for the baby, like pacifiers and diapers and baby talc.

"You look great," he says to me, his hand squeezing my shoulder. He places the basket on the table. "I'm sure you'll be needing some of this stuff."

"Thanks," I say, but it's unclear whether I'm thanking him for the gift or the compliment.

"I think motherhood has made you even prettier," he adds to my unconvinced smile. He bends to his knees to get a close look at Betty on the ground beside me. "And this one's for Betty," he says, pulling a pink stuffed bear out from around his back and holding it up close to her face. She opens her mouth to suck on its glossy black nose.

"This is for you," I say, passing him my present. I know I should sound more enthusiastic, but I can't get my voice to jump out of its sleepy tone. He unwraps it, wildly tossing the paper on the floor.

"Ah," he exclaims. "That's wonderful! I'll drink my coffee from it every day. Thank you, my dear!" he says, bowing like he's from Japan or something. I can smell the beer on his breath.

I want to leave after that, because there's nothing more to say to him, but he pulls me around the room, introducing me and Betty to a few fat frumpy ladies. They ooh and ahh at the baby and ask me questions about labour and how I'm sleeping at night. I mumble one-word responses until Eric finally dumps me on the couch in the far corner, obviously reserved for dysfunctional teenagers. Across from me is a dumpy-looking girl who eats a chunk of cheese and then stabs at her zits with the toothpick. Beside her is an equally ugly guy, face hidden under a baseball cap. When the girl looks like she's about to talk to me, I dart my foot out to rock the car seat and she reclines back into the couch. It hasn't taken me long to learn that Betty's presence either stops conversations with people my age or starts ones with adults. The guy ignores me for a while until he insists I take a sip of his Coke, even though I tell him no three times. An understanding smile breaks my mouth as I finally hold the pink frosted glass up to my mouth. The powerful stench of rum burns the inside of my nose and I lower my eager lips into the stinging liquid. I finish the entire glass, smack my lips, and pass it back to him.

Finally, a fat woman in a yellow skirt starts clanging her spoon against her glass to gather people together for a few toasts. Eric is called up through the crowd and stands to the side, beaming as if he were a child about to be given a ribbon. The fat woman starts by saying how she's known Eric for ten years and how he's been as much a part of her life as coffee and parking tickets. Everyone laughs at this, and then the next person pipes up how the first time she met Eric, he had tripped down the office stairs and landed at her feet. After hearing a few of the same comments, I feel the need to get out of that room. I pick up Betty's car seat and head to the kitchen.

The kitchen is huge and white and has a silver fridge with an ice-cube maker on the door. At first I just pour a glass of orange juice for myself, but then I notice all the liquor bottles over by the stove, and making sure that no one is around, I grab the half-empty vodka. Without thinking too much about it, I slip the bottle under my sweatshirt, pick up the baby, and head out the side door. Pain sears through my side as I squat down, my back pressed against the brick wall, my feet stretched out in front of me. I lift the bottle to my lips and take large, hungry gulps. At first, the harsh liquid makes me gag, but then a warm burn travels down my throat and through my veins. My body becomes numb and nothing matters anymore. I finish the whole thing, stashing the empty bottle in Betty's car seat, under the blanket.

After a while I pick up Betty and hold her close to me as I stumble along the side path toward the backyard, the interlocked brick below my feet like a dizzy, moving puzzle. When I turn the corner, I spot the pool, the water shimmering silver under the moonlight, just like in a movie. It's one of the most beautiful views I've ever seen. I open the black iron gate and carefully lay Betty down on the ground, up close to the fence. Then I trip up to the side of the pool and plop down on the edge. I take off my shoes and immerse my legs, the water like cool pudding on my swollen feet.

I sit there for a long time, relieved to be away from the music and bright lights. Fingertips skim the rough concrete around me, sweeping stones into my hand. I start tossing the pebbles into the water, contentedly watching them disappear into the calming darkness. Then I throw in a leaf but it refuses to sink, taunting me with its hesitation. Angry, I get up, twist off a long branch from a bush, and return to my position. Leaning out over the water, I fiercely stab the leaf until its pierced body drops just slightly under the surface, away from the thoughts that scream in my head.

Then I hear you crying, your piercing wail rising above the clanging of glasses and the laughter. And I know that you're crying to be fed, or because you need your diaper changed, or just because. I know you're crying for me, and I hold my hands up to my ears to block you out because I know those pleas will turn to resentment one day. I know you'll wish you were never born to me. "Shut up! Shut up! Shut up!" I yell, pressing my hands over my ears, squeezing out your cries. And I just want it to stop. I just want silence.

I fiercely poke my stick into the half-submerged leaf, shaking and ripping, until it's completely shredded and the fragments begin to sink. The words in my head repeating over and over again: *If I rise, bury me. If I rise up in you, bury me.*

ACKNOWLEDGEMENTS

Special thanks to my agent, Jackie Kaiser, my editor, Barbara Berson, and everyone at Penguin Books for their support and belief in me. Thanks to friends and readers of the manuscript: Julie Zwillich, Kristina Steponaitis, Mary Bell, Johna Janelle and Marcia Beck. Thanks to Melanie Nicholl for sharing those well-earned Friday lunches.

I'm appreciative of the many creative writing instructors for their astute feedback and encouragement. Thanks especially to Barbara Greenwood for planting the seed, Antanas Sileika for reminding me that it's still there, and to Ann Decter for finally helping it grow.

Thanks to my best friends, Andrea and Sabine, for a lifetime of support. And an extra special appreciation to John for thinking everything I write sounds so wonderful.

I am grateful to my incredible family: my brother, Grant, for being someone for me to look up to; my sister, Erin, for having shoes too big for me to fill; my father, for reciting poetry on long road trips; and my mother, for not buying me that silver metallic jacket.

And finally, heartfelt gratitude to the young people whose lives have touched me in ways they will never know. Learning is both given and received. You have blessed my life with lessons I can never teach.